Three Lives in Three Seconds

Michael Girik

ISBN Paperback: 978-84-09-61269-7

ISBN Hardcover 978-84-09-61591-9

Cover designed by the author with Adobe Cloud

Visit **www.michaelgirik.com** for additional information about this book and the author.

For my daughters: three lives of love in my eternity.

Chapter 1

The Mysterious Encounter

South of Spain – thirty-four hours after the accident

I was lying on the muddy ground, with two men holding me down. Around me, only a forest with pale and skeletal trees. However, I knew this was the typical landscape of where I was. From the ground, I only saw the sky filled with dark clouds.

Did I scream? Yes, I shouted. We shout for help when in trouble but are only sometimes heard. In this case, the thunder's roar obscured my cry of despair.

"Take her energy out through the jugular," one of the bosses instructed from a distance.

A third man approached, carrying a cylindrical metal object with a needle on the end. Like the other two, he was wearing old and torn clothes. He placed one of his grimy hands on my head, the only part of my body that I could still move. He wanted to make my neck more accessible. His face, white, pale, and disfigured, was so close to mine that I could see the details of his sickly expression.

The cruel smile on his face showed off his crooked and decayed teeth. His odour was no different from the murky river nearby. At that moment, I realised that my fear was decreasing. It was transforming into a powerful and uncontrollable hatred…

Suddenly, I heard a woman's voice: "Señorita, ¿necesita un médico? ¡Voy a llamar una ambulancia!"

I woke up and looked at my watch. It read 6.49 a.m. There was only one minute left before the alarm I had set to wake me up sounded.

Was it a nightmare? My rational mind tried to question me, but unfortunately, it was not. I had recently had several strange experiences, and this was a detailed recollection of one of them. They were real memories! There was a hidden reality that needed to be revealed to the world.

An elderly couple were looking at me with concern. I imagined what they must have been thinking. They had spotted an English woman lying on a bench near the beach, elegantly dressed in a dark blue blazer, wearing big silver hoop earrings, and using a beautiful handbag as a pillow. Indeed, it was a strange scene for a sunrise landscape. It was the first day of summer in Malaga, Spain.

My attention turned to the woman. What was she saying? Shame on me; at thirty years old, I was dedicated exclusively to studying science, had a PhD in physics, and couldn't speak Spanish. At least I understood the word 'ambulance'.

"No, no, I'm fine, thank you. Gracias, gracias," I replied, getting up quickly. They understood and continued their morning walk. I straightened my long black hair and put on the shoes I had left under the bench.

I had left London the day before without any luggage. I managed to arrive in Malaga in the early morning. Unfortunately, I was forced to sleep on a bench, on the pavement, facing a beach.

It would be dangerous to go to a hotel. I didn't have any money and couldn't use my credit cards. Nowadays, we are all connected. They could quickly locate me. I had borrowed a phone from a friend but was afraid to turn it on. She was also involved in the accident. It was on this beach that my intense mission would end. It was called experiment Lambda 3 (λ3). But for this, I would still have to meet an unknown man; I didn't even know his name.

My watch sounded: 6.50 a.m. The sun had not yet risen over the horizon, but the sky was already clearing, warning me that it would be a scorching day. I looked at the calm sea, hearing its small waves while seagulls flew over the horizon.

I sighed deeply to help relieve the tension. My unusual date was just around the corner.

There was a public toilet nearby, where I washed my face, combed my hair, and redid my make-up. I attempted to cover up my tiredness and stress from the last intense hours. Unfortunately, I had no way to change clothes. My travel bag was ready; however, it had stayed in my flat in London. I couldn't go back for it. I left the country like a fugitive.

Around 7 a.m., I admired the orange sun rising over the Mediterranean Sea. It was a true spectacle of nature, and with it, I felt that a new woman was being reborn within me. My friend Adhya had assured me that a man would meditate on that beach at sunrise on the summer solstice. She had not told me his name, appearance, or age for security reasons. I only knew the latitude and longitude where he was supposed to be. I couldn't confirm the exact coordinates, but the place was close. I had used the phone of a taxi driver, who had driven me to that beach last night.

I held my shoes in my hands and walked barefoot across the sand towards the sea. A few people were walking, but no one was sitting or meditating nearby. I went closer to the shore, touching the tips of my toes to the water, which was freezing.

To my right, I saw a man standing about twenty metres away, utterly immobile like a rock, looking at the sea. I approached him. He took his phone out of his pocket, snapped some pics of the sun's first rays hitting the ocean, and then proceeded to walk in the opposite direction.

I felt a sense of relief only when I turned around completely. In the middle of the beach, I spotted a man sitting on the sand in a meditation position. I walked quickly towards him. But when I got closer, his eyes were already closed. The man was wearing a white shirt with black lettering. He had shaved hair and a long grey beard.

His face had a calm countenance and he remained motionless, like a statue of Buddha.

I sat down next to him, keeping about three metres away to avoid disturbing his ritual. I was exhausted and apprehensive. *How long does this meditation last? Why not poke him?* It was a test of my patience.

After more than twenty minutes, which seemed to have lasted hours, he finally opened his eyes. The sun was already shining brightly. He made a gesture of thanks towards the sea with his palms pressed together, bowing. He stood up, still concentrating without noticing my presence, staring at the ocean. I coughed purposefully a few times. He was so focused that he couldn't hear me. I coughed harder, and he finally turned his head and looked at me. I got up and took the opportunity to approach him, smiling and gesturing with one hand.

"Hello, good morning! I'm Sandra," I introduced myself in English with the smile of someone who wanted to start a conversation. He frowned sceptically, and returned my good morning in English without saying anything else. Then, he turned his face, held his slippers in his hands, and started to stroll towards the sea.

I walked beside him. In a voice like someone begging for something, I said, "Listen, I need to talk to you about something important."

He hurried his steps and replied without looking at me. "I'm not interested. Please leave me alone."

I walked faster beside him, thanking God that at least the man spoke English. "Listen, please! I've come from London to find you. It's a long story…"

He continued walking without stopping, looking at me from the side, visibly annoyed. "London? You're confusing me with someone else. Sorry, it's certainly not me."

I started to get very nervous. I jumped in front of him, and he stopped walking. He looked at me with a strange expression, having a closer look at my not-very-beachy clothes and the shoes in my hand.

Then, he gazed directly into my eyes and said, with the calm voice of a psychiatrist treating a patient, "You don't look well at all. I'm going to call for help. They will find the person you are looking for. Stay calm, and don't worry."

He took his phone out of his pocket.

I looked at him more closely and said, "Wow! I saw you on the beach a few hours ago."

He froze and looked at me.

I continued, "It was dark. I'm sure I saw you with many other people wearing white clothes. My friend Adhya was with me but didn't tell me you were with the group."

"Who are you?"

"Narquiamides asked me to look for you, to get your help."

"Who did you say? Narquiamides?" he asked, widening his eyes. He probably could never have imagined that name coming from a stranger, in this situation.

"Yes, Narquiamides asked me to deliver some material for you to help me with an experiment," I replied with less anxiety.

His expression changed completely. He was now looking at me with a mixture of astonishment and curiosity. "Narquiamides!" he exclaimed. "I lost contact with him many years ago. Sorry... Sandra? Is that your name?"

"Yes, Sandra Wonlecty," I replied, relieved, and held out my hand to greet him.

"I'm Dennis Duthones. Tell me what I can do to help you and Narquiamides."

"I'm a physicist working for a renowned laboratory in London. Two days ago, I witnessed a car accident. People died. Then, I experienced advanced atomic experiments that our science has not explored yet."

"That's amazing. Finally, a scientist discovered the astral plane."

"You are right... Narquiamides asked me to give you all the information you need to write a book for me. This experiment was called λ3."

When I mentioned a book, his expression changed. He listened attentively, showing increasing interest in my story.

After a short pause, I continued, "Yesterday in London, it took me hours to record audio files with as much detail as possible of everything I experienced. Luckily, a friend helped me edit them. We divided the audio into subjects and converted them into text. I wanted to keep the important details of each moment exactly as they happened. All media and files are safe in a cloud directory. I need a computer with secure internet access to download them."

"So, this is the book at last," he exclaimed with a mix of amazement and happiness. "I've talked to Master Narquiamides only once, exactly seven years ago. I met him in a temple where I was holding a retreat. It was also the summer solstice, one of the most powerful days of vital energy. He told me that I would probably help to write a significant book to reveal truths to the world in the future, but he was not authorised to give further details."

"That's impressive. That's Narquiamides," I observed.

"I finally understand what he predicted: I will write a book for you about your experiences. But I don't understand why you don't write it yourself."

"My friend Adhya told me you are a spiritualist, and I am a scientist. The book represents this union. The world's different religions have been walking apart from science for a long time. For this reason, science has moved away from researching what truly happens when we die."

"That's true." He nodded. "I studied philosophy and religion in France. I've lived in a few countries with different cultures, and I've always said that death should be studied by science. Each religion has ancient dogmas and interpretations of the afterlife. The time has come for everyone to know the astral plane."

"The strategy is quite clever: give the material to an unknown person living in another country to keep it safe. It would not be easy to write it on my own. The scientific community would demoralise and harshly criticise me. But it's not just that. There is an ancient and powerful brotherhood called the Golden Circle. They incite hatred and disunity—"

"I know this brotherhood very well." He looked into my eyes and said, "I'm a member."

"What?"

"Don't worry." He smiled. "I don't go to their meetings any more. It's just that once you're a member, you can never stop being one until you die. They call me an IBM: inactive brother member."

"Wow! That's why Narquiamides chose you..."

"Certainly! After I published a book on healing magic that I had learned on one of my trips to Africa and East Asia, I received an invitation from a professor at the university where I was teaching to join the Golden Circle. He told me it was a secret group for advanced studies in ancient magic. The meetings were in an old house near Paris. Only men are allowed to participate, and they have connections with powerful people worldwide. After a few months, I discovered they wanted to use my knowledge of black magic, which I also know very well. They called me the Great French Wizard. Then, they offered me money and a high position in the Brotherhood and pressured me to accept. I refused, and that's when I decided to leave. A few months later, I went to a meditation retreat, where I met Narquiamides."

"During the λ3 experiment, I realised the strong connections between the Earth and the astral world. Living and dead people co-exist. With this, the Golden Circle influences governments, businesspeople, scientists, and religious leaders worldwide."

"Yes. Unfortunately, they are mighty connected to the depths of darkness. After leaving them, my professional and private image was mysteriously destroyed by fake news. I lost my job as a professor, my wife asked for a divorce, and all my friends moved away from me. I knew the Brotherhood was behind it, but I didn't have the power to beat them. I moved to Spain to find peace and continue my studies alone. But as you saw me a few hours ago, we are never alone."

"Yes, that's a hidden truth... My late father went through something similar. He was a physicist humiliated when he began promoting afterlife ideas that went against established scientific paradigms."

"Noble knowledge is the only way to fight with the Golden Circle. Their power comes from the spiritual ignorance of humanity."

"Exactly. That's why nobody can know about our meeting until I give you the green light for publication."

"Sure, you're right. But you know you will be exposed as a scientist, like your father, for revealing such truths."

"Yes, of course, but I don't care. The truth is the only thing that matters now. I will provide you with all the necessary information and depart without leaving a trace of our meeting."

"How much time do we have?"

"A few hours. I'd better get back to London today. The police are looking for me."

"Then let's start analysing the material for the book immediately," he suggested excitedly.

We walked a few blocks to his flat. When I went inside, I was surprised. There were shelves filled with dozens of old mystic books. On the tables were many crystals, stones, metal pyramids, pendulums, and candles. There were also mystical statues all over the flat and different symbols and mandalas on the wall.

After downloading the files to his notebook, I also used his phone to send a brief message to a friend in London: "*Project Lambda 3 in progress. Book a flight for tonight.*"

A few minutes later, we received an e-ticket in my name. It was a direct flight from Malaga to London at 9 p.m.

Amid incense sticks, we worked without stopping, while drinking coffee and eating snacks. I went through all the files and described my experience in detail. He meticulously made notes. His knowledge of magic was impressive. He was not surprised by my fantastic stories of the astral cities, strange beings, wizards, and witches. I felt I was telling him about a holiday to a different country.

We finished at 7 p.m. After all the effort, I was happy to have accomplished my mission.

"Well, all the material for the book is ready," I proudly stated. "We'll keep the project confidential. Until the final manuscript is finished, it's safer not to talk to each other. I will get in touch with you securely. I must wait for the right moment because the book will expose many people... Besides, I would like to investigate a few points about my father first. Some pieces of this puzzle have not yet fallen into place. And now you know that's just the beginning," I observed thoughtfully.

"I know."

"The important thing is that everything is safe with you."

"I'll wait for your signal. It won't take long to finish it. It's all extremely detailed."

He paused momentarily and looked at me with a brotherly expression. "After knowing who you are, it's an honour to have met you. Now I understand why Narquiamides doesn't want you to write about your experiences. You're the chosen one, Miss Wonlecty. In addition to your safety, it would be a waste of your precious time."

"I'm still processing all this... Everything happened so fast. Tomorrow, in London, I will have to present myself to the police, and I'm still trying to figure out what I will tell them... I'm determined to follow in my father's footsteps, now more than ever."

"Narquiamides will help you… The Golden Circle must already suspect who you are. You know they'll try to kill you, as they did with the others."

"I know… If this happens, publish it immediately."

"Don't trust anyone. You are our last hope. Good luck!"

He paid for a taxi to take me to the airport because I had no money.

Just before I got into the car, he approached me, distressed. "Miss Wonlecty, wait! We forgot one essential detail. The title of the book. Tell me a title to put on your book, please."

"Let's use the title *Three Lives in Three Seconds*. This was one of the last words I heard from Narquiamides."

Chapter 2

The Accident

London – seven minutes before the accident

"Run faster, Sandra, we can't be late," the strange girl I had just met shouted.

"I'm running, Adhya. Where are we going anyway?" I asked her, worried.

It was just before 9 p.m. I was utterly baffled, and a whirlwind of thoughts was swirling in my head as I ran along the pavements of London.

My strong rational side thought: how could this young woman, whom I had never met before, convince me to go with her to some unknown place in only a few minutes? I only knew her first name. Since my childhood, my father had advised me not to speak to or follow strangers. She appeared in my flat and demonstrated unimaginable quantum physical phenomena. All that went far beyond the limits of my PhD knowledge in physics. That may have been her way of persuading me. Indeed, she knew that I, like my father, had always been a curious scientist. Now, more than ever, I was looking for explanations… many explanations…

"I don't have time to explain anything to you now," she replied with the smile of one who was having fun, like we were two little girls running in a park.

Adhya looked like she was about twenty-five years old. She had beautiful brown skin and long black hair, which contrasted with her typical Indian dress: a white saree embroidered with blue and gold tones, which covered from one of her shoulders to her feet. She had a small diamond-shaped crystal stuck between her eyebrows, matching the pendant of her golden necklace. Her striking make-up emphasised the delicateness of her face.

The temperature was pleasant, and the start of summer was only two days away. Many people were walking on the pavements, some looking at us curiously, while most seemed to ignore us. Although I was taller, it took work to keep up with her. Her light steps seemed to float. I passed by Carl, a colleague from the lab I was working in, but he didn't see me, even more entertained than usual by his phone.

Adhya sometimes grabbed my arm tightly to cross streets between moving cars. In front of the Japanese restaurant Seikatsu, which I often frequented, was a man with white hair, probably over eighty years old, wearing an elegant suit and tie. As I passed by his side, I accidentally bumped into him, and his cane fell. I apologised as I kept running.

"More respect for elders! Today's youth is crazy," he shouted as he picked up his cane.

We finally reached a corner where Adhya signalled me to stop. It was a large junction, connecting two important roads. On one of the corners, an advertising light marked 8.59 p.m.

"What are we doing here?" I asked with a mixture of nervousness and anxiety.

"Questions later, please," she replied in a firm voice. "I need you to observe everything that happens, carefully and with the utmost attention. Don't speak, and don't ask anything else for now."

The intensity of her voice and gaze hypnotised me, making me follow every command with complete devotion. Somehow, she knew one of my best qualities: observation. I learned to be a great observer from my late father. With this, I could develop my studies and career in physics.

I spotted a man watching us across the street, at the other corner. He nodded to Adhya, and she reciprocated with a smile. He had long white hair and a beard. His clothes caught my attention the most: a white tunic resembling that of a religious man.

At 9 p.m., as indicated by the advertising light on the corner, there was a violent collision. Two cars were going along the same road, in opposite directions. A truck was coming at high speed on the other road of the junction, followed very closely by a third car. Something must have happened with the traffic lights, because none of the vehicles stopped. The truck crashed into and dragged along the two cars coming through the junction, hitting other vehicles. The third car, following the truck, crashed into it, having its front wholly destroyed. Several other vehicles in different directions also collided, but more lightly, causing an extensive traffic jam. Their occupants got out to help the injured, mainly in the three most badly damaged cars and the truck, and called for help on their phones.

Immediately after the accident, that strange older man looked at us and smiled like someone who had just won a victory. Adhya reciprocated with a girlish smile.

I'd never seen anything like it before. Indeed, people were probably dead and seriously injured. I was in a state of shock. How could this woman be so insensitive? She kept that annoyingly calm expression as if she were gazing at a gorgeous landscape.

Noticing my expression of despair, she said, with the soft voice of a psychologist, "Don't worry, Sandra, nobody died."

Then I heard a man's voice from the centre of the crowd that had formed near the vehicles: "There's a dead man in this car, my God!"

Another man shouted in the background. "The truck driver is wounded, but he is alive."

I could already hear sirens. Ambulances and the police were trying to dodge the enormous traffic jams that had formed.

"People died!" I screamed.

We were interrupted by the presence of that man who had been standing across the street in his white tunic and brown sandals. He didn't resemble the girl. He looked like an English man, tall, with white skin and piercing blue eyes.

He looked at the two of us and commented calmly, "Ah! London. I love this city. It's been a while since I've been here. What a lovely end to spring." He smiled, looking at me. "Miss Sandra Wonlecty, you must be confused, but everything will be explained soon."

"Me, confused?" I replied with total sarcasm. "No, I'm not. It's the beginning of a beautiful night like any other: people dead, fatal accidents, the usual… I want—"

"My name is Narquiamides," he said, looking into my eyes. "Pay attention! You were the person chosen to continue your late father's studies. That is the only reason you are here with us experiencing all this. Understanding death, or the non-existence of it, is only the beginning of your mission."

"Mission? This is insane," I protested. "When Adhya convinced me to follow her, she didn't mention dead bodies and car crashes."

"Would you have come all this way if she had mentioned it?" he asked, in the same voice as one who says checkmate.

"Maybe not…" I was defeated. I remained silent for a moment. "In any case, I've many questions, beginning—"

I was interrupted again. A young man approached us, showing much nervousness. He looked no older than twenty-one and wore white clothes like a nurse.

"Narquiamides..." he stammered. "Three people died as expected, but we had another unexpected death: the driver of Dino's car. He had a heart attack. Unfortunately, the ambulance didn't arrive in time to save him."

Narquiamides and Adhya looked at each other, now reflecting an expression of seriousness on their faces.

"Julian, who was responsible for making a detailed analysis of this driver's life and health before the accident?" Narquiamides asked, with the stern voice of a general to a subordinate.

"It was me..." His eyes turned to the ground. "I failed, and I'm sorry."

"You know Narquiamides will be responsible for this unscheduled death, Julian," Adhya complained.

Julian remained with his head down.

Narquiamides paused thoughtfully and then broke the silence. "Adhya, take Miss Wonlecty to the portal immediately. Its access will close in a few minutes. I will meet you both soon." He went with the boy towards the crash, where there was already a large crowd.

In a quick gesture, Adhya tugged me by the arm. "Come on, Sandra." She looked at me, showing determination. "Trust us! Everything will be cleared up. Hurry, we must run."

"Run again? Where? Did he say 'portal'?"

"You will learn more about quantum physics in the next few hours than you have ever learned in your career."

We ran on the pavement opposite the accident, entering a narrow, dead-end alley. The buildings at its sides provided dim light from their windows. We followed it until we reached the end, which was a big brick wall. Adhya placed the palm of her right hand on it. She uttered some words I could not understand, and a sky-blue hexagon about three metres high appeared. It was a portal that would transport us to some other place. I considered myself a great authority on quantum physics; however, what I was experiencing was far beyond my comprehension. I continued admiring that portal, trying to search in my mind for theoretical explanations for that complex phenomenon.

Adhya pulled me again. "Let's go inside; it will close in a few seconds."

We crossed into the unknown. At that moment, I had no idea that the following events would entirely change how I understood life and death.

Chapter 3

The Death of My Father

Five hours before the accident

It was almost 4 p.m. I was in the physics laboratory of BA Physical Labs in London. I had been working there for nearly a year on quantum physics projects. Previously, I held the position of professor at a prestigious university.

Our organisation provided services for companies and some governments around the world. Due to strict confidentiality agreements, we could not identify their sponsors. Only a select group of directors had access to the specifics and objectives of the global project. I was part of a team working on a quantum computer.

I was putting everything away because I finally had a few days' rest. The next day, I would travel to Italy to visit my mother and younger sister, who live there together.

Alex, my best friend and co-worker, interrupted me. "Sandra, Mr Jordan's secretary asked you to go to his office before you leave."

He made a mischievous expression. "No mortal here goes to the president's office. Is it a pay rise?" he asked jokingly.

"I'm sure it is a workload increase." I laughed.

Alex was an excellent physicist. He was my age but looked younger. His colleagues called him a nerd boy, maybe because of his stereotypical looks: medium height, thin, white skin, black hair, and dark glasses that highlighted his blue eyes. Behind his shyness, he was the kindest and most intelligent person I've ever met. I loved to go out with him for food or drinks after work. He was also a great listener. He was the wall of lament for my frustrated romantic relationships.

Since my teenage years, I've been an outstanding student but terrible at relationships. The most recent one was Peter, a handsome and elegant man from a wealthy and traditional family who ran his father's companies with his brothers. Unfortunately, I broke up with him after eight months together. 'Why did you do that? Are you crazy?' These were my friends' questions, and my younger sister's too. My answer was the same as for all my other relationships: I realised I did not love him. What does it mean to love a man for a woman forged by the exact sciences like me? I questioned myself internally without getting any answers…

I went to Mr Jordan's office on the top floor of BA Physical Labs.

"Good afternoon, Sandra. You can come in. Mr Jordan is waiting for you," the secretary said, pointing to the big door that led to the president's office.

I walked into the impressive modern office; it had pale floors and a carefully decorated ceiling that added to two large windows with stunning views. A sizeable contemporary painting with geometric symbols caught my eye. It provided a sense of modernity and wealth with elegance.

Mr Jordan had been a classmate of my father's at university as a physics undergraduate. Due to his commercial skills, he became an influential businessman, negotiating projects with private companies and governments worldwide.

He was sitting at his desk reading some papers. As he saw me, he removed his glasses and, like a good gentleman, got up in his elegant £2,000 suit to welcome me.

"Miss Sandra Wonlecty! Please have a seat. It's a long time since I've seen you. I've been travelling a lot lately." He pointed to one of the sofas as he asked his secretary for two cups of tea.

"I hear you are doing an impressive job," he said. "Congratulations! I was sure of your talent when you came to work with us."

"Thanks, Mr Jordan."

"I called you because today is a sombre day for your family and me."

He was right. It was precisely a year since my father passed away. He had been alone in his house in Birmingham. My mother had gone out with some friends, and when she returned, their home was in flames… Mr Jordan thought highly of him, so a few days after his death, I received a call from HR at BA Physical Labs. They offered me a job with compensation that I couldn't refuse. That's how I started working for the company. As the president, he was a very busy man. He was always travelling or attending meetings. He rarely went to the labs; he met only the board of directors. It was the first time I talked to him alone.

"You know I was a classmate of your father's at university. I always admired his clever brain and determination. He enjoyed spending hours in the library. His knowledge was above average… I invited him several times to come and work here, but he always preferred to be with his university classes and research."

"It's true; he loved teaching and was obsessed with quantum physics. Since I was a little girl, my father talked to me about atoms, molecules, waves, and vibrations. I remember that my stuffed kitten used to become a Schrödinger game. He put it inside a box, and before opening it, he asked me if I liked that kitten. Then he asked me to pick it up from the box. With it in my arms, he said that the vibration and feeling I felt for the kitten was love. It is up to the will of the one who opens the box to keep this feeling alive and never let it die."

I paused, my eyes filling with tears of beautiful memories. "This is why I followed in his footsteps…"

"Your father was a kind person. He was a teacher whom everyone loved. Unlike him, I ended up going into business. Unfortunately, where money is involved, we must leave all emotions aside. A few months before he passed away, I heard from friends that he had travelled to some regions of India and China to visit exotic places and temples."

I nodded.

He sighed and continued, "Well, when he returned, he was excited to embark on unconventional scientific investigations. They were revolutionary ideas to try to explain issues such as astral travel during sleep, life in subatomic worlds after death, and several other crazy topics that were not accepted by the scientific community. He tried to convince some academics to follow him. Nobody listened, and they started to avoid him. Behind the scenes, they called him a quantum wizard, esoteric physicist, among other things."

"Yes, I know," I said with sadness. "I tried to talk to him many times to understand these strange studies better. However, because of the controversy they generated, he asked me not to get involved. He wanted to protect me."

"He did very well to protect you!" he exclaimed. "Religion and science can never mix. Scientists are not paid to investigate dogmas or people's beliefs. Imagine that one day, representatives of the

Pope appear here in our office, and the Vatican decides to sponsor some scientific study about Jesus. If we prove, through science, that some crucial points in the Bible are wrong, what would be the repercussions of this information in the hands of the media? It could cause chaos in the world. Our image would be devastated by the protests of fanatics, and it would be the end of our company."

"You are right. I had never thought of it this way." I nodded.

"The world is not ready for certain truths. Do you know what people worry about?"

He paused, and then said, "About themselves! Everyone wants enough money to live well with their families, friends, and lovers. Money, and only money, moves the world, makes everyone happy, and helps people achieve their dreams... We scientists are paid to give material solutions to make people's lives easier through new technologies. We work for the evolution of the world! Let everyone have their own religious beliefs that best suit their culture and dreams. It is not our role."

"I agree. My mother and sister have always been very religious. On the other hand, my father and I've always been atheists. We never gave any importance to these matters because they don't have any logical sense. The problem is that something mysterious made him change his mind radically. My mother commented that in the last days before his death, he remained reclusive in our house in Birmingham. He spent several nights there alone and avoided contact with people. Unfortunately, I could not find any notes or books on these mysterious studies, after the fire. His computer was destroyed."

For a moment, I remained thoughtful, analysing how to express what I thought about all that.

"I will confidentially tell you my opinion," I whispered. "I concluded that my dad was hallucinating. He talked to himself, had sleepless nights, and lit many candles inside the house. We should have sought psychiatric help, but it is now too late."

"Your mother knew about our old friendship and called me to help him. I tried to convince that stubborn brain to forget those crazy ideas and come to London, but he didn't listen."

He looked at me and continued, "You have your father's determination, and you will have a bright future. If you keep it up, you will gain fame and wealth, which means power. Remember: power opens the doors of this world."

I left the room grateful and thoughtful. Strong memories of my father now surfaced endlessly. What had happened during his trip to the East to make him start having these psychotic episodes? How was it possible not to find any notes or photos of the places where he had been? *I will never know the answers...*

Back in the laboratory, I said goodbye to Alex, my super-friend, and headed home.

On the way, I received a voice message from my sister.

"*Hi, Sandra, Mummy and I expect you and Luke here tomorrow in Rome. It will be a fantastic week! We're going to convince you to quit your boring job and live here. You are working too hard. Look what happened to Dad. My kids want to see their auntie and play with Luke. I still can't get over how you broke up with Peter. It's like tearing up a winning lottery ticket. Giovanni has a friend to introduce you to. I don't know him, but don't worry because Italians are the best! We will be waiting for you tomorrow at the airport. We love you. Kisses."*

I wanted to have just ten per cent of my younger sister's attitude. She was always cheerful and transmitted positive energy. She was partly right about my work; sometimes, I left my personal life to one side. Since childhood, I'd always been excessively exact, constantly questioning everything. Maybe those endless questions about life, without logical answers, made me colder and less dreamy.

I passed by a church and decided to go inside before it closed. I never believed in the existence of God; however, I thought my mother would be happy to know that I entered a church on the anniversary of my father's death. When I was young, she gave up taking me to church meetings because, unlike my sister, I was very questioning and embarrassed her in front of her friends. I loved to give my opinion about passages in the Bible that I found absurd and illogical. Recently, I only remember entering churches at my friends' weddings.

There were few people, some sitting in the pews and others enjoying the beautiful building and its decoration. In the side aisle, there was a place to light candles. I thought of lighting one and taking a quick selfie to show my mother! It was a simple and silly gesture that would mean a lot to her that day. As I dropped the coin and lit the candle, a man's voice rang out beside me.

"The energy of a candle is potent!"

Standing next to me was a priest wearing an old dark brown Franciscan tunic tied with a cord around his waist and sandals of the same colour. His head was uncovered, revealing his grey hair. He was of medium height with brown eyes and light skin.

With a slight smile and in a calm voice, he continued, "Did you know that lit candles contain the four elements of nature? The fire from their flames, the earth from their constitution, the water from their wax, and the air that feeds their flames. They are a potent symbol of the energetic interaction of these elements. Offer your candle energy to someone."

"Offering the energy?" I asked sceptically. "No, nonsense, sorry, I'm a scientist, this is absurd. It's not logical… I just wanted to take a selfie as a souvenir for my mother. She is highly religious and believes in these silly things. Today is a year since my father passed away. He can't receive anything—"

"Excellent!" He continued in his sleepy voice. "Then it will be a great gift for your mother. Follow my instructions. Look at the lit candle while breathing deeply three times. Then close your eyes, remember your father in happy moments, and finally, use willpower through your love and see the candle's light enveloping you. A fifth element is the transmission of energy."

"Fifth element?" I asked. *This priest now wants to teach me quantum physics, and I have a PhD in the subject.*

"Names don't matter now, young lady. Do what I'm teaching you. Your mother will be happy, and it will be good for you, too."

"OK, thank you…" I said.

"I'm Father José Archiolano, at your service. I will stay here by your side, watching you do it." He smiled slightly and looked at me like a father looks at a disobedient daughter.

What an annoying priest! Since I couldn't get rid of him, I followed his silly instructions. Besides, my mum would love to know about that historic moment. The only candles I remember lighting were birthday candles or scented ones in my flat.

When I concentrated on my father, I had several memories of my childhood with him, such as him teaching me to ride a bicycle, going for walks in beautiful parks, watching films, and telling stories before going to bed…

Suddenly, I saw the image of him smiling and showing me the stars, as he did many times when I was a little girl. A vibration ran through my body like a shock but with a pleasant sensation lasting for a few seconds. *What emotion is that?* There were many memories and intense feelings of peace and love. Something I hadn't felt for a long time. I didn't want to open my eyes because I was dripping tears of longing. I completely forgot about the priest and just kept experiencing that feeling of happiness that I didn't want to end.

A distant voice echoed and broke the utter silence of the church. "Lady! Sorry to interrupt your prayer, but we are closing, and you need to leave now."

I opened my eyes. I saw a man a few metres away with several keys. All the other people had already left. I remembered to take a quick selfie for my mother.

Before leaving, I asked the man, "Please thank Father José Archiolano for me. Tell him what an interesting experience I had. And certainly, my mother will be pleased."

"Father Archiolano? Excuse me, but I've been working here for twenty years, and no one in the church has that name. He was probably a tourist. We get a lot of them daily, and some are weird. See you later, and be with God."

I left the church lighter, with peace in my heart. What an exciting experience that priest had given me. Perhaps for the first time, I understood my father's obsession with studying religion as a science.

Now, a whirlwind of thoughts and ideas was coming into my mind. After all, according to quantum physics, all bodies are natural waves. Studying and explaining these phenomena would be fascinating. How did my brain generate such an intense vibrational state of happiness in a few minutes? Was there a release of endorphins and other hormones? Were the secrets of the mind behind a prayer or a meditation? How could I measure them in a laboratory?

At that moment, I did not imagine that the experiences I was about to have would be far beyond these questions…

Chapter 4

The Big Dream

I lived in a flat with my little dog Luke, a papillon breed, who was very intelligent and friendly. Mrs Evans, my next-door neighbour, was usually with him most of the day. She lived alone and had few friends. Her husband was deceased, and she had no children. So, she always pampered me like a daughter, with delicious homemade food or a tempting cake. I paid her a monthly fee for staying with Luke, which helped with her expenses. She enjoyed telling stories about what England was like in the past and her previous European travels.

I picked Luke up from her and made some tea in my flat.

I sat on the couch, feeling warmly connected to my father's memories. With the laptop, I searched for the name of the priest, Archiolano. I was surprised to find an old painting of men killed in the Inquisition for heresy. One looked just like him, including his clothes. It would be impossible for them to be the same…

Then, I started researching articles about our brain's reaction during prayer or meditation. Soon, I could not keep my eyes open any more. A strange and intense sleep overcame me. I was drained and unable to get up.

Seconds later, I started to hear a humming sound, and at the same time, I couldn't move my body or even open my eyes. *What is it?* I was initially terrified, imagining that I needed to call for medical help.

I saw myself sitting at the top of the Big Ben clock tower watching the River Thames, the constant rhythm of cars and people everywhere. As I looked up at the sky, I realised I was being projected towards it, distancing myself from the Earth's surface at an exponential speed. In a few seconds, I could see London, then the United Kingdom, and then Europe, but I couldn't distinguish the borders between the countries because they only existed on maps made by humans. Faster and faster, the Earth was already a tiny insignificant point, quickly disappearing in the vastness of giant stars and planets everywhere.

Unable to control my body, I felt sucked into a spiral motion. The speed became so great that my brain could no longer process images. I felt my body collapse and I woke up.

Instead of my comfortable sofa, I found myself lying on the floor in a wide corridor. Both parallel walls were over ten metres high and covered with white marble. On one side, windows opened and curved at its upper end, from which came a powerful white light. They were so high that it was impossible to see through them. I stood up slowly. A few metres from me was a double golden door, about five metres high, with strange symbols and inscriptions. I looked back; the corridor was huge, and I could not see its end.

I was in an altered state of drowsiness, as if I had spent an entire night without sleep. My mind started begging me to lie back down right there on the floor of that corridor. Before I could think whether that was a good idea, the golden door began to open. I heard beautiful piano music coming from inside the room. The music echoed louder and louder as the door opened.

A beautiful woman appeared when the door finally opened completely. She had light skin and greenish-brown eyes. Her face was perfect, as if it were a painting. She wore an elegant dark blue dress with silver and gold details. Jewellery, such as earrings, bracelets, and necklaces, embellished the woman.

Around her head, she wore a silver chain. It connected to a diamond-shaped crystal pendant in the middle of her forehead.

"Come in, Sandra! We were waiting for you," she said, encouraging me to enter that room. "I'm Maya."

I was confused and sleepy. When I entered the room, I was impressed by its size: it was round and immense, well over two hundred metres in diameter. Its floor was made of white marble, decorated with gold and black geometric symbols. Its height was colossal. Like old European cathedrals, the ceiling was supported by many arches ending in a giant spiral dome. There were no images, pictures, or paintings. In the centre of the hall was a white grand piano, from which the beautiful music came, and there was a large blue armchair in front of it. The woman gently intertwined one of her arms with mine, leading me towards the centre.

"You are welcome! Come in and sit down," she exclaimed, pointing to the armchair. That was precisely what my sleepy body was begging for.

The music was calm, relaxing, and beautiful. The acoustics of that gigantic place somehow made the sound vibrate everywhere.

As I approached the centre of the room, I looked up, and through the dome, I could see stars and planets. The pianist stopped playing and came closer. He was a young black man with a shaved head, wearing an elegant white suit with a bow tie.

"Welcome. I'm Bhav," he said with a kind smile.

I couldn't even react. My sleepiness was so intense that I let my body collapse into the comfortable armchair, like a tree that had just been felled. It was precisely in the middle of the room, facing the piano, but with its back to the golden door I had entered through.

As if anaesthetised, I just stared at them both. The young pianist brought his face close to mine, looking at me like a doctor examining a patient. Suddenly, a holographic image with various numbers and graphs appeared on my left side, close to my head. I tried to observe the pictures, but I no longer had the strength to move. He carefully analysed the data. In a loud voice, he said nonsense sentences in the direction of someone who had just entered the room and remained distant.

"The silver cord vibration is at 99.7 per cent with almost no density, stable astral body, REM neurotransmitters at their maximum charge, good prana level at 92.9 per cent, slow breathing at deep-sleep level, physical heart less than forty beats per minute and falling."

Falling? With those beats, I must be dying! I realised why I was without strength, not even to speak.

He continued, "Her conscience, within expected normality, partially awakened at precisely fifty-one degrees. The mental body is prepared for the increased vibrational charge. It is almost ready for induction and will easily take off from the astral body. The gold cord will be at maximum vibration. She will be able to reach the Akashic field in a few seconds."

As the armchair was high, I could not see to whom he was addressing his strange words.

The young pianist looked me in the eye again and said gently, "I know you are sleepy and drained. I also know it isn't easy to express yourself. I'm going to ask you just two questions. Try to answer slowly and in a low voice, OK?"

I nodded as much as possible, a tiny movement of my head.

"Who are you?" he asked, with his ear close to my mouth.

"Sandra… Sandra Wonlecty," I replied, whispering with much effort.

"What day is it today, Miss Wonlecty?"

"Today... It is the anniversary of my father's death."

After my answers, he smiled and looked again at the door, where he seemed to have obtained some consent.

"Excellent! You are ready! I will play the piano for you. Enjoy relaxing and travelling with the music and its colours!"

Relax? Is he kidding? I can barely move.

Maya, who was by my side the whole time, removed the chain that adorned her head and placed it on me. The diamond-shaped crystal pendant adhered like a suction cup to my forehead. I felt a burning sensation. My body went rigid, like the most solid rock. My eyes were the only part of my body that had any movement. I struggled to keep them open. She tilted the armchair so my gaze turned to the planets and stars, which could be seen through the dome.

The pianist began to play a beautiful piece of music. The last image I could remember was of luminous beams in the air of various shades of colour coming out of the piano in circular movements. They rose upwards in the shape of a snake towards the stars and planets, which now seemed to move closer and closer to me. At that instant, my eyes won the battle: closing. I could no longer hear the music. I felt sucked in at high speed, as if a hole had been opened in the air, swallowing me in spiral movements...

Finally, I felt myself lying down somewhere motionless. I didn't know where I was. All around me was total darkness with absolute silence…

Chapter 5

Awakening with Adhya

London – fifteen minutes before the accident

Finally, I could open my eyes.

I woke up on the sofa in the living room of my flat, scared at first, a bit disoriented. However, when I realised everything was a dream, I laughed. What kind of crazy dream was that? That colossal building, Maya and Bhav, the pianist…

The wall clock read 8.45 p.m. I still needed to pack everything for my trip to Italy the next day. My mum and sister were missing me.

I got up and approached the living room mirror to see my face. I was sure that I looked awful, but I couldn't catch my image. As I looked to the side, I saw a young woman wearing a white saree with blue and gold tones. She was holding my little dog, Luke, who seemed to like her very much.

"Hi, Sandra, I'm Adhya." She smiled with unbelievable naturalness.

Someone had broken into my flat. I tried to locate my phone to call the police. I turned around and looked at the couch: I was there! My body and Luke's were in a deep, peaceful sleep.

"I'm still dreaming. It's a hallucination!" I exclaimed. "I've died! And Luke's dead, too... No, this can only be one big nightmare."

I closed my eyes and repeated a few times: "I want to wake up. I want to wake up. I want to wake up."

Adhya approached me and said in a quiet psychologist's voice, "You're not dead, Sandra. No one dies as you think."

She placed one hand on my chin, turning my face towards her, while the other held Luke. "Turn around; you can't stare at your physical body sleeping. Otherwise, you'll wake up and think it was a dream. There is no time for this nonsense."

Nonsense? What is she saying?

I remained looking away from my sleeping body, and she continued.

"I know you are confused. I won't be able to explain the details to you now, but I promise to explain later. We don't have much time. You are in an out-of-body experience."

"Out of what? What are you doing here in my dream?" I asked, almost beside myself.

She slapped my face.

"Sandra, you're not dreaming," she said firmly. "Don't let me down. You are a physicist. Please think from now on as a scientist, calm down, and put your emotions aside. You know all the physical theories about the matter of the universe. We are beyond quarks, Higgs bosons, or all the other subatomic particles. We are in another plane, a quantum level well known on Earth as the astral plane or astral world."

I took a deep breath. The rational side of my brain immediately went to work. I squeezed my arms and could feel them. I already knew, of course, from quantum physics, that not even the most complex rock or metal on Earth is solid. Our senses deceive us. They only have low molecular vibrations. However, when I saw my new body and Luke's exact replica of the one lying there, composed of atoms and molecules unknown to humanity... It was like literally living on a subatomic level.

She continued, reading my thoughts, "These bodies have much more intense vibration levels; they are invisible to human eyes. We can visualise these two dimensions at this level on the astral plane. Both the physical and the astral occur at precisely the same time. Look at this little light behind Luke's head; you also have it on your nape. But you cannot see it now because your image is not reflected in the physical mirror."

When I was about to put my hands on my nape to feel the light somehow, she shouted, gesturing with her hands. "Don't touch! Because you will wake up immediately. It was a hard job to make you very sleepy and energise your pineal gland. On Earth, it's called the silver cord, and it's mentioned in the Bible in Ecclesiastes 12.6. It is energetic filaments that connect your astral body to your physical body, but it has an even higher vibrational level. You can see it in the astral plane only when they are very close to each other."

"If it breaks, what will happen?"

"For God's sake!" she exclaimed with a laugh that made me feel stupid. "It's impossible to break it. It is a wave, a quantum entanglement. You know the property. Your two bodies have the same connection, even when separated by vast distances. The astral body can be in Australia or on Mars, while the physical one sleeps here in London. However, this connection ceases to exist when physical death occurs. Observe that I no longer have this light." She turned her head, showing me her nape.

"So, you died; I mean, you no longer have a body like mine?"

"Yes, but it's been thousands of years. You will understand better after the experiment."

"Thousands of years? Experiment? But—"

"Listen," she interrupted my dozens of questions. "You are participating in an experiment called λ3. I understand your doubts. You're a curious scientist keen to dig into everything and figure out exactly what's happening. Unfortunately, our time has run out, and you need to come with me."

She was right about my scientific curiosity. I needed to discover the mathematical equations to explain this strange phenomenon. It went beyond everything I knew about quantum physics. She left Luke, or astral Luke, on the floor, while the material one slept with me on the couch. Then she looked into his eyes, passing her fingers between them, and he fell asleep. His astral body floated away and positioned itself just above the physical one. There, I could visualise the silver energy cord she referred to, a tiny filament of light that connected them behind their heads.

"Luke and I are old friends. I've been following you both for quite some time. Even awake, he can see me; dogs have clairvoyance. By the way, Archiolano opened your astral vision for a few moments in the church, and you could see him…"

When she said this, I realised I had been talking to a dead priest. For a scientist, there were too many situations without logical explanations.

She glanced at my wall clock and shouted, "We must go now!"

I looked at her and complained, "I'm not going anywhere without first knowing what this is all about." I put one hand near my nape, threatening to wake myself up. In truth, I was bluffing. I wanted to see how far it would go.

"OK… We met your father when he was still alive around here. He was a great researcher of hidden secrets from various religions and powerful groups over the centuries. We need someone living who will continue his studies and share his knowledge with the world. You were the chosen one. But if you want, go back to your body and your mediocre little life. I cannot stop you. We will call another more qualified person. We always have a plan B, to employ a term known to you. But if we walk out that door together, we want a scientist as determined as your father."

I confess I did not like the provocative comment about my mediocre little life. After all, I was a scientist with several published works. At the same time, I felt terrible for believing my father's research was pure hallucinations. This was the chance to finally understand him.

"My father was my inspiration in life. I'm in. Let's go."

Adhya gave a mischievous smile and looked at me without surprise, as if she'd already known my decision.

"My phone must be in my handbag," I commented, trying to locate it on the furniture in the living room.

"In the astral plane, we don't need a phone or a handbag."

She grabbed my arm, and we passed through the door without opening it. It may seem strange initially, but it is physically explainable since we were on a different frequency from the physical plane we know. It's like neutrinos, radio, or internet waves that go through glass and walls.

As we walked through the door, I was startled and I screamed. There was an immense man, indeed more than two metres tall, light-skinned, with black eyes, wearing a white tunic. His face was severe and completely motionless, like a statue. With his right hand, he held a white wooden stick upright.

"Don't worry. This is Lucius, an astral protector. He will stay here protecting your physical body, just in case..."

"Why do I need such protection?"

Suddenly, my next-door neighbour, Mrs Evans, opened the door of her flat and came to mine with a plate in her hand. I smelled her delicious apple pie, one of my favourite sweets. As we were on another vibratory frequency, she couldn't see us. When she was about to ring the doorbell of my flat, the protector Lucius, who had remained motionless like a Welsh Guard, looking forwards, put one of his big hands near her forehead without touching it. I could see a bluish light coming from his palm for a few seconds, hitting my neighbour, who gave up and returned to her flat.

Adhya made a happy face; my question had just been answered.

She grabbed my arm and shouted, "Now we're going to have to run fast."

We ran through the streets of London together. At that moment, I had no idea we were running towards an accident that was about to happen, and four people would die.

Chapter 6

The Astral City of Yudh

Just after the accident, when I went through the portal with Adhya, we entered a square room made of stone, with walls about ten metres high. There were no windows, and it was lit only by fire torches held by iron bars on each wall. In front of us was an enormous U-shaped rustic wooden door with black iron bolts.

Adhya opened the door, and to my surprise, we stepped out onto a narrow street made of stone.

"Welcome to Yudh!" she exclaimed, raising her arms. "An astral city focused on knowledge."

A crowd of people of different races, ages, and dress styles walked on the street. Some wore ancient clothes from other times, but most were close to the fashion of the last few decades.

Yudh was in a valley of gigantic mountains, resembling some secular cities of Europe. The narrow streets, carefully lined with trees, were made of stone with high walls surrounding them. I felt like I was in a protected medieval town. However, instead of a castle at its centre, one could see an enormous pyramid at the highest level of the city. It was constructed of metal that reflected the brightness of that beautiful day with an intense blue sky without any clouds.

Along the narrow cobblestone streets, the houses had an ancient building style. Their walls were joined on both sides, two or three levels high. However, above their rustic wooden doors were three-dimensional images of musical instruments in motion, providing a striking visual contrast between the old style of the houses and the ultra-modern images. Each set of places seemed to specialise in a specific instrument. There were images of pianos, violins, and other instruments moving in front of them.

We walked towards the pyramid on the narrow street with a crowd moving in both directions.

I was impressed. "It's amazing, Adhya. I never imagined there could be any life and cities on an unknown subatomic level."

"There are thousands of astral cities around Earth. Unfortunately, most of them mainly have hospitals as their primary activity. Yudh is different; it is exclusively designed for knowledge in many areas of science and culture." She pointed behind us. "We entered through the city's southern gateway. These streets belong to the arts sector. Besides music, we have dance, paintings, and drawings. Here, various ancient techniques are mixed with future ones with artificial intelligence. Our specialists will gradually introduce new technologies, including those arriving on Earth in the future. You can see that some people here are physically dead. Others have a small light on the nape, like you. They visit the city through astral travel. That's how many people learn while they're sleeping."

Seeing my face as I admired those unimaginable scenes, she added, "I know exactly how you feel. You were an atheistic scientist who didn't believe in the continuity of life after death."

"You're right," I admitted. "Everything we've been through so far is so much information for me to process. I don't even know where to start."

"I'm going to help you! Let's start with the basics." She stopped walking and positioned herself before me, looking into my eyes. Then she said, "Answer me: who are you?"

"Are you kidding? I'm the one who must know who you are. I know very well who I am!"

"No, you don't. *Know thyself* is the Delphic maxim written on the Temple of Apollo. The ancient Greeks sought this answer centuries before Christ. Let's try again. Who are you?"

"This is ridiculous. I'm Sandra Wonlecty, and I was born in Birmingham. I'm a scientist living in London—"

"Wrong answer," she said. "This is a temporary physical Sandra sleeping in London. When she dies, her body will be devoured by worms in some graveyard. Who might still be walking down this street with me?"

"The astral Sandra?" I asked, confused.

"Still the wrong answer. She is not yet the one who thinks and learns."

"Who am I, exactly?" I pleaded.

"The question could be this: who are we? I'm not different from you. The only difference is that I no longer have a physical body, like most people around here. Some people call it a soul, spirit, ghost, or other. We prefer to use the word conscience because it is unrelated to any religion invented by man. We are tiny individual consciences connected to an infinite and powerful Cosmic Conscience of Love known on Earth as God."

"Are we consciences, then?"

"Yes. Temporarily, we can name yours as Sandra. Around here, we almost always have the exact shape of the physical body from our last life on Earth. However, this name is ephemeral. Your conscience is inside you now. It's in a quantum plane far beyond here. The astral Sandra will also die one day. She can be reborn on Earth or another planet around the universe."

"And who determines where we are reborn?"

"For most of the Earth's population today, it's still an automatic process. It's a quantum physical phenomenon. It attracts places where each conscience has a vibration in common. Only an old or highly experienced conscience can choose where to be born. Some are assigned to a specific mission. There is a powerful exchange of attraction between planets. Some people who die on Earth go to other planets, and many others arrive. This is the incredible beauty of evolution. We are within the most various multiverses in manifestation."

I couldn't follow everything she said.

"Wow. This is all too complex for me to understand," I admitted.

She laughed. "That is precisely why we have brought you here. See how far science on Earth is from studying physical death, a simple quantum phenomenon. There's nothing ghostly about it. It is just an out-of-body journey like you are having. But with no return."

She continued walking and pointed out a group of five out-of-body children entering one of the houses together.

"Look how these projected children are magnetically drawn here. They will learn music. Most will rarely remember the details when they wake up. However, their consciences are learning while they sleep. The purity of childhood is one of the most important aspects of learning. At this phase, they are nurturing their most beautiful expressions. Some of them will undoubtedly have the potential to be future music exponents."

"So, for these kids, the learning journey begins here?"

"Yes, but they are not children in a literal meaning. Within them, there are old consciences. They are just like you now, projected from their bodies while sleeping. Rational scientists cannot explain, for example, how a young child can compose or play instruments without ever having had contact with them.

According to their dharma or life mission, some children recall what they learned here. It's simple, with no mysteries."

A group of musicians carrying some instruments passed by. They were led by a young black man wearing a dark suit. The man was identical to Bhav, the pianist from my recent dream. I stopped momentarily, looking back as he disappeared into the crowd. We were interrupted by an older black man with a white beard who came to meet us. He was wearing a white African dashiki with coloured symbols, which I later discovered were drawings of the seven chakras.

"Adhya!" he exclaimed with a kind smile.

Adhya bowed with both palms together to the man, showing deep respect. He returned the gesture and said towards me, "Miss Sandra Wonlecty, we were excited about your visit. I'm Kennis, mayor of Yudh. I propose we keep walking; people are waiting for you."

"Mr Kennis, I never imagined there were astral cities, people, and even a mayor…"

He smiled. "I have been the mayor since its foundation. According to the Gregorian calendar you are familiar with, it was precisely 701 years before the birth of Christ. Initially, it was a city with few visitors from Earth, but it gradually grew as we added new technological resources. Please call me only Kennis. It makes me feel younger." He laughed.

"Did you say 701 years *before* Christ?" That seemed absurd to me.

"Yes. Adhya was also here from the beginning, but she was reborn in Tibet nine years before Jesus was born to help him there."

"Helping Jesus in Tibet?" I asked. "I have little knowledge of religion, but wouldn't it be in Jerusalem or Nazareth?"

Adhya looked at me and smiled. Her eyes were like those of a patient preschool teacher trying to explain a complex subject to a small child. "Jesus was deliberately hidden for at least eighteen years of his life. He went to India and Tibet from age twelve to thirty before returning to accomplish his mission."

"There are documents of this evidence on Earth that have not been destroyed," Kennis said. "Unfortunately, this information has been kept secret for centuries by elites."

I remained thoughtful and felt ashamed. Besides knowing nothing about religions, the knowledge I thought I possessed as a scientist had become a tiny drop of water in a vast, unknown ocean.

"That enormous metal pyramid at the top of the city we are going towards," I said, admiring the colossal construction reflecting the sky's light, "what material is it made of?"

Adhya and the mayor looked at each other for a few seconds.

"You will have the opportunity to check it for yourself inside," Kennis assured me. "But first, there is a library that I want to show you."

Chapter 7

The Astral Library of Yudh

We walked towards the pyramid situated on the highest level of the city.

"Yudh has nine main streets," the mayor explained. "Eight of them, like the one we are on, converge into a wider circular one, within which is a square with the Great Pyramid on it. Looking from above, we would see that four converge precisely in the direction of the vertices and the other four to the centre of the sides. Everything has been carefully planned for the perfect circulation of cosmic energy. It is the pyramid that provides the power for the whole city."

We arrived at the main street that circled a vast, neatly wooded square. There were birds of different species and various colourful flowers in its gardens. In its centre was the gigantic metal pyramid without any doors or windows. Between the pyramid and the grassed area was a circular lake, more than thirty metres wide, full of colourful fish.

Many people walked in the square; some people were sitting on the vibrant green grass or on the benches, admiring the exotic landscape. Near the pyramid was the library. It was made up of three ancient-looking buildings in a U-shape.

We entered the library, and I was awestruck. It was huge and modern, surrounded by wide corridors lined with bookshelves. There were three floors down and three up from the entrance level, through its hollow centre. In its halls were countless tables where hundreds of people, out-of-body projected or not, of various appearances and ages devoured knowledge.

"It's immense!" I exclaimed, admiring the construction.

"This is the most extensive library in the astral on Earth," Kennis bragged. "Here, you can find books from the most diverse areas of knowledge, from all languages and ancient civilisations, such as Lemuria, Atlantis, Ancient Egypt, China, Israel, and others. Every book written on Earth has its astral counterpart. We can say that every book has its own life because it emits its vibration to the readers. We have selected only good books here. They must have content that brings meaningful learning. So, the most diverse consciences may study them for their evolution."

"Imagine authors arriving here after death," Adhya observed, "and seeing unimaginable people reading their books..."

Kennis laughed. "They are perplexed! Authors often realise that they have made mistakes on specific points in their works, defending some wrong thesis. When they come to this side, they get nervous with the need to fix their views immediately. It's common in books written by religious people, philosophers, or scientists. In these cases, they are allowed to make an addendum or corrections. The changes are automatically registered in all book copies in the various astral libraries of the universe. This is a very dynamic and precise process."

He paused for a moment, pointing at a section of old books.

"Unfortunately, several important books that revealed truths about life and death have been burned or destroyed on Earth in the past, as in the Inquisition. The good thing is that they are all around here, being read and studied by those prepared to receive this kind of information, which is never destroyed."

We walked down towards the lowest level. On the way, I saw many people wearing pyjamas walking like zombies.

"Some out-of-body people appear unaware of what is happening here," I observed.

"You're right," Kennis said. "They are deeply sleeping on Earth and exist here in total somnambulism. It is normal to absorb only a tiny fraction of the knowledge they seek. However, it is enough to generate new ideas and insights. Many famous people who have made significant discoveries on Earth have spent many nights studying in our library. But they don't remember."

"Where do you think great inspirations come from?" Adhya asked. "Scientists, doctors, philosophers, engineers, filmmakers, and writers study here."

"How does everyone get here when they sleep?"

"Good question. Our consciences don't rest, only the physical body, as yours is doing now," she replied. "So, they are always automatically attracted to the most diverse places in the astral plane with similar vibrations, either for good or evil. Some arrive in Yudh automatically when they sleep, but most on Earth are helped anonymously by other more advanced consciences. They have various names on Earth, such as helpers, spiritual protectors, masters, ancestral spirits, guardian angels, etc. Even dead relatives or old friends bring consciences to help them."

"Knowledge, used for noble purposes, is the best way to seek peaceful evolution for any planet," Kennis said. "This is why we receive thousands of consciences daily from various parts of the Earth and other planets. Each visit, each book, and each page read always has a specific evolutionary objective behind it. Those who plan to know for selfish purposes rarely get enough vibration in their astral cells to come here, no matter how much they wish to. It is a physical law of the universe."

After a pause, he said tensely, "Unfortunately, we cannot guarantee that all people who study here for noble purposes will subsequently use them for this purpose. Selfishness, hatred, exacerbated materialism, and the conquest of illusory power are deeply rooted on Earth. These make people not listen to their inner voice and mindlessly follow dark paths. For example, here we provide advanced atomic knowledge, but to use it to manufacture nuclear weapons is the free will of each person. By the law of the universe, we cannot interfere with any individual choices. But everyone will pay, somehow, for the consequences of their decisions in the future."

Some people kept their books closed on the tables but were reading them in different languages through a three-dimensional holographic image. The mayor invited me to sit at a vacant seat at one of the tables, took an old book from a nearby shelf, and put it in front of me. It was written in a strange language with symbols and letters that made no sense.

"This book is written in Senzar, a secret priestly language from thousands of years before Christ," he said, noticing my confused expression. "It was designed exclusively for the Initiates, who were prepared to know occult truths, to use them exclusively for the good evolution of humanity."

When I closed the book and left it on the table, an impressive three-dimensional holographic image appeared in English. I could handle and turn the image pages while the book remained closed on the table. I quickly read just a few sentences. It said something about the evolution of man, divine energy, primordial atoms, cycles of development, magic, and the destruction of races.

He looked at my astonished expression and stated, "I told you that the burned and purposely destroyed books are all available here. They may be read in whatever language you are currently most familiar with. It's an automatic process. The library's artificial intelligence has identified that English would be best for you now. It takes a reading of the vibration of your astral cells."

"Here on the astral plane, there are no language barriers," Adhya said. "Apart from books, if you concentrate, your mind understands what anyone is saying, except for secret languages or magical words."

Kennis took the book off the table; the image instantly disappeared. "I know you would like to search our scientific collection, but we have to go to perform the λ3 experiment, which is more important now."

He was right. I wanted to stay for months in that vast centre of knowledge.

A wooden door with iron frames was on the lowest floor between two unobtrusive bookshelves.

"The only way to access the pyramid is through this door. I'm staying here; you continue with Adhya. I hope your book will soon be part of our collection. It will help many to understand life beyond physical death."

"My book? What're you talking about?"

Adhya gave her girlish smile and said in an irritatingly calm voice, "In fact, you will not write it. Someone else will write it for you. You must relate to him all the experiences that you will have here in the astral plane. We will reveal where to meet this person if all goes well."

"A writer?"

"No, he is not. He is a spiritualist who knows much about magic, and you are a scientist. The book represents the union of two opposite consciences. The world's different religions have walked apart from science for centuries, and the time has come to start awakening this union and understanding of death. It will be safer for everyone this way."

"Your father will be proud to read your book, which continues his studies," the wise old man said in a tone of encouragement.

"Where can I find my father? I want to talk to him," I pleaded.

"Unfortunately, it is not yet the time to meet him. Your bond with your father is too strong, and the emotions of both of you could make the experiment fail."

"But—"

"We didn't bring you here for an out-of-body holiday. Your father has no idea that his beloved and protected daughter is here with us. You are going to visit the lower astral levels inside Earth's surface… Allow me to explain in another way. During the entire experiment, you will experience very intense emotions. You will discover harsh truths. This astral world of Earth does not have allegories of people happy in eternal rest, with the sound of angels playing the harps. Conversely, most places are increasingly sinister, dominated by sick consciences, and must be revealed for humanity to awaken."

After a brief pause, he continued, "Do you know why we have kept walls around the city since the Middle Ages? I will give just one recent example... During the Great Wars, the planet's vibration was so low that it affected this astral level. The brightness and blue sky you saw outside darkened with black clouds laden with storms. We were very close to being invaded by sick consciences that perpetuate hatred and do not want the Earth to evolve. We had to shelter people savagely killed in the wars along the corridors of this library. The astral hospitals, which are not few, no longer had enough space to receive them."

I realised the profound impact of human insanity on the astral plane. Our actions and behaviours affect each other and have a ripple effect that extends beyond our physical world.

"The vibration of the Earth is dropping frighteningly and continues to attract evil consciences from other dark planets, like Planet Z. The last and most dangerous astral planet of this galaxy," he explained. "The Earth's energy needs to rise to its evolutionary path towards peace. Without knowing it, humanity is heading for its destruction. Remember a main rule: we can only give the knowledge to show the right path, but unfortunately, we cannot intervene to change its direction. That's the law of the universe."

Adhya and I entered the door opened by Kennis that gave access to the pyramid. We headed towards the mysterious λ3 experiment...

Chapter 8

The λ3 Experiment

Adhya and I entered the Great Pyramid through a door into a long, modern hallway. It didn't match the ancient architecture of the city of Yudh. With its luminous grey hue, the metal used to construct the pyramid reminded me of aluminium alloys.

The passage was illuminated by lights embedded in the ceiling and on the sides. It seemed to be an absolute labyrinth, with many halls and metal doors. We went up and down stairs in different directions, guided by gates that rose automatically when we approached. Several others remained closed.

"There are confusing connected passages. How are these metal doors opening? I can't locate any sensors or cameras," I asked, looking in detail at one of the doors that had just opened.

"They do not exist. With artificial intelligence, the pyramid controls everything inside, including entrances and exits. It reads the subatomic vibrational of our astral cells. The pyramid knows exactly who we are and where we are going. The DNA, digital, or facial recognition methods used on Earth's physical plane are ancient for us."

We arrived at a massive room with high ceilings and a modern laboratory. Many men and women, all wearing white clothes, talked and handled three-dimensional holographic images on various tables. There was equipment and apparatus that I had never seen before. Some holographic images were of planets and stars, others of places I couldn't identify. Like Adhya, they all had diamond-shaped crystals in varied colours stuck on their foreheads.

Everyone stopped what they were doing and looked at us in silence as we walked towards the centre of the room. In its centre was a circular platform built one level higher, where Narquiamides was standing beside a woman waiting for us.

"Welcome, Miss Sandra Wonlecty." Narquiamides smiled. "It is rare that living consciences on Earth are allowed to enter here. Consider yourself privileged."

The woman accompanying him was impressively beautiful. She had long brown hair and light green eyes, highlighted by a light green shadow. She wore a diamond crystal of the same colour on her forehead and pearl earrings of a greenish hue.

"I'm Jade. We've been anxiously awaiting your arrival to start the experiment. Lie down, and we will explain how it works." She pointed to a metal table.

In the middle of the platform was an enormous, luminous cylindrical column. Its base, about three metres high, was clad in golden metal. From it came a bluish light, like a powerful searchlight, that seemed to pass through the ceiling.

As I lay on the table, I could observe the automatic appearance of holographic images with graphs and numbers beside me.

The woman carefully looked at the information and said to Narquiamides, “Silver cord vibration is at less than ninety-five per cent due to tension. Her mind is boiling; I will do an induction to calm her anxiety and shift her mental body, generating a stable gold cord. REM neurotransmitters are excellent at their maximum charge. She is at a good level of prana absorption, but the physical heart needs to drop the beats per minute below thirty-nine. Conscience is wide awake at seventy degrees; she will remember all the details when she returns.”

I was worried about my low heart rate. It was the only variable mentioned I knew about. Besides, I’d had that strange dream with the pianist, and something similar had happened.

“These heartbeats—”

“Don’t worry about your heart, Sandra,” Narquiamides said. “Please pay close attention to what I will tell you: the experiment has three phases, two of which have mental visions and the last one is in person. Let’s start with the first one so you can get used to the experience. Adhya has told me that you like movies.”

“She knows everything about me,” I mumbled, looking at her.

He smiled and continued, "Imagine that instead of watching a film comfortably in an armchair, you are immersed in it and can direct your vision wherever you want, in any of the multiple directions. You will move instantly through portals. A portal will open if you need to be on a mountain or miles away."

"Would it be like virtual reality games?"

"It goes far beyond those. In this immersion, all your senses will also be present. You will feel sensations of heat and cold, and detect smells in the places where you will be. All the feelings are very intense because it is not a game. All the scenes you will experience are not imaginary. They are 100 per cent real. They can be related to the past, present, or future."

"For the experiment to work," Jade explained, "we need your astral body to reach a suitable vibrational level. This way, we will be able to displace your mental body from this astral body of yours. We will induce you because you don't know how to do this. You will be so relaxed, in a state of catalepsy, that you will not be able to move; your mind will be awake and balanced. With your astral body still and motionless, you will move with your mental body. Do you see that golden metallic part at the base of the blue luminous pillar? You will go through it just as you went through your flat door with Adhya."

She said something about a mental body... That's also a mental Sandra inside me. As a scientist, I realised that the experiment would take me to other unknown subatomic levels. It was composed of atoms in a vibrational state, much more intense and invisible to the astral plane.

"For safety reasons, we need to bind your hands and legs on this table," the woman said, immobilising my limbs with blue energy rings. "You will go through such strong emotions that your astral brain may be unable to bear it. So instinctively, it will try to make you move your body to wake you up. It is like the mind does to get rid of a nightmare. If this happens, it will instantly return your mental body to this astral body. The process is so abrupt that, by cascading effect, there is a risk that you will wake up in your flat in London. If this happens, your physical brain will convince you that it was all a weird dream."

"Don't worry, Sandra, everything will be fine," Adhya promised, holding one of my hands, probably seeing my perplexed expression.

Jade picked up a small dark box resembling a jewellery box. On it were the λ3 symbol and inscriptions in a language I couldn't identify. She opened it, and inside, there were five tiny diamond-shaped crystals.

She picked up one and explained, "This crystal has been programmed to guide you on the first journey. It has the authorised information to access at different times and spaces. Remember that it is not a game. All you will see are real scenes."

She placed the crystal on my forehead between my eyebrows. I felt my forehead burn as it adhered tightly. Jade positioned herself standing just above my head and placed her hands on the sides of it so that her thumbs touched two of the vertices of the crystal diamond. Her eyes turned upwards. At that moment, I could no longer move my astral body. I also couldn't keep my astral eyes open.

Jade's voice echoed inside my mind. "Don't try to answer; just listen. Your mental body will detach in a few seconds. Enter the tube through the golden metal; do not try to look back to see your astral body. Otherwise, you will return and the whole experiment may fail. An energetic golden cord links both bodies. Only when the bodies are closer can it be visualised."

As soon as she finished her sentence, I was already standing looking at the metal base of the tube with my back to them. I crossed over and felt myself being pulled upwards by the bluish light. I saw stars and planets around me briefly, followed by complete darkness.

I felt like I was standing up without seeing anything. The darkness gradually dissipated. I was in a room in a house with baby decorations. I already knew that place. Through the window, I looked down the street of the neighbourhood where I lived during my childhood in Birmingham. *How is this possible? It is my old house!* People were walking on the pavements, and I identified our neighbour. She was very young.

Slowly, I approached a cot near the wall. When I looked at the sleeping baby, I saw it was me. Then the door opened, and my mother entered the room. She was younger and beautiful. My heart started beating fast.

She approached and smiled with a loving look that only a mother could give and said to the baby, "I had a beautiful dream. There were angels in this room and—"

She was interrupted. I heard my father's voice calling her downstairs.

My eyes were filling with tears. I tried to follow in my mother's footsteps. However, as I passed through the door, the scene changed completely.

It was night in the house's garden, at another time. I saw myself, a twelve-year-old girl, sitting next to my father. I could feel the pleasant temperature of the night and detect the aroma of his Irish tobacco. We were looking at the stars. My father always encouraged me to reflect on the universe, unlike my younger sister, who was never interested in these matters.

"Sandra, look how beautiful the stars are in the sky. They are so far away from us that they are unreachable by man. Some of them no longer exist. They have left only the beauty of their lights for us."

He remained thoughtful while looking at the starry sky and observed, "One day, we will all die, too; that is why we must try to leave our light, inspiring people with our brightness. This way, we can encourage them to leave their light to others. This is the beautiful and mysterious evolution that the universe teaches us. Just observe it to learn."

"Dad, do you believe there is life in these distant places?"

"Of course it exists. People who think life only exists on Earth within this vast universe are very naive. Imagine that now, on some distant planet, a little girl like you is looking at our sun and asking her father if there is life here. I am sure that in hundreds or thousands of years, we will, in some unknown way, be able to travel in space. Then, the distance between these two girls will no longer be insurmountable."

"All this is so fascinating!"

"I want to give you some advice. Life is short and passes very fast. We start dying from the moment we are born. I see that most young people today waste too much time with parties, dating, and nonsense things. The world would be much better if everyone reflected on these fascinating issues. I feel that you are special, so my advice is always to follow your intuition and not get carried away by the crowd. The important thing in life is to let your star shine for those who need it."

Unable to stand, I sat down beside him and wept copiously... Jade commented to me afterwards that many tears came out of my astral eyes, and certainly out of my physical eyes, lonely in my London flat.

~*~

I walked into a medical room through a new portal that opened next to me. I saw my father talking to a doctor. It was a few months before his death.

"Mr Wonlecty, I have good news. Your tests are perfect, and there's nothing wrong with your health."

My father sighed with relief. "That's good, Doctor. I didn't tell my wife about these tests so she wouldn't worry," he said.

"Have you been having those strange hallucinations or dreams that seem like reality?"

"They've disappeared for the moment. I haven't had them since I had the examinations."

"You've probably had some sleep paralysis, waking up in the REM stage, where the eyes move fast. Stress could be one of the causes." He signed a prescription and gave it to my father. "I recommend fifteen days of mind rest. I suggest you travel somewhere away from the big cities to relax. Don't take any of your technical books, just light entertainment… Don't read newspapers either. It's hard to find any good news these days. As for films, only comedies are allowed. Calls from work or your students are forbidden… I've prescribed you some medication to take before bed. Come back in a month."

~*~

A new portal took me to my parents' house. It was a few hours later.

"I nearly forgot. A package has arrived for you," my mother shouted from the kitchen. "I left it on your desk in the study."

The house was not spacious, but my father had created a comfortable and private area for his home office. The bookshelves were lined with scientific books, some of which he had written. He walked over to the desk where the shoebox-sized package lay. The sender, in various unfamiliar letters, indicated his origin in Tibet.

It was a wooden box carefully decorated and painted in gold, with symbols and the image of a Buddha in its centre. When he opened it, inside there was only a piece of paper the size of a postcard. On it was a replica of an old painting of Father José Archiolano at the time of the Inquisition. My father's eyes widened. On the back of the card was the following message:

What you are experiencing is real. You are not hallucinating. If you are seeking answers, please visit us at your convenience. We respect your decision if you choose not to come.

~*~

The house slowly vanished into the icy winds at the top of a mountain. I was on a narrow stone path that led to a temple set into its rocks. Cold? It was freezing! It was like being invisible in a film, feeling all the sensations. I ran along the stone path until I reached the corridors of the building, which were at a much more pleasant temperature. I followed a strong smell of incense coming from one of the rooms. Inside, at its centre, was a man lying on the floor, wearing an orange tunic, seemingly in a deep sleep. The room was stunningly decorated with golden and vivid colours. A few metres before him, seated motionlessly in a meditation posture, was an elderly Tibetan monk with a shaved head. He had white-grey eyes, and there was a cane by his side.

My heart was beating fast; the man lying in the centre of the room was my father. He was on his last trip to the East before his death.

A portal opened in front of the old monk, and my father, with his astral body, emerged fully conscious, accompanied by Father José Archiolano. My father stood with his back to his body, addressing the blind monk.

"I don't know how to thank you, Master," my father said. "Father Archiolano has taken me to unimaginable places. Millions of euros are spent on gigantic subatomic particle accelerators, and millennial science has a way to be inside, present, and aware for free. This is the secret to studying various worlds, formed by the atoms and molecules invisible to the physical man."

"Mr Wonlecty, you have nothing to be thankful for. Your experience has been authorised by higher consciences, who are concerned with the current course of the planet. Your out-of-body experience is not for entertainment. Unfortunately, modern science does not have an interest in these subjects. You will face many obstacles in transmitting this ancient knowledge. As we talked about before, you will need help to overcome them. Now is the moment to immediately involve your eldest daughter, Sandra, in this research. We need to prepare both of you fourteen days before the next solstice. You will have a secret mission together. We will reveal the details at the appropriate time."

Unlike when I first met Archiolano in the church, his expression was now rather tired and worried. He stepped forwards and commented, "Master, I have talked to him a lot, but he is reluctant. He has given up on involving his daughter."

"You know we don't impose anything, Mr Wonlecty. We cannot intervene or force you to include your daughter. It will always be your free will. Please keep in mind that, ultimately, you are the one responsible for the decisions you make. It is the universal law of cause and effect, and no one can escape it. This is my final warning: your daughter's involvement is essential for you to succeed. The probability of succumbing is very high if you choose a solitary path. The meeting is over."

The elderly monk slowly stood up with his cane. At the same time, the priest placed his hands on the back of my father's neck, waking him up immediately, and then disappeared into the still-open portal.

My father remained on the floor, still a little dizzy, and shouted to the old blind man leaving the room, "Master! I can't involve my daughter in these experiments. Everybody will call her crazy. She will lose her reputation and ruin her life! I am already a certain age, and I don't care what people will say about me. She is brilliant at what she does. I want her to have a normal life, like any woman, marriage, children, grandchildren…"

Ignoring my father's pleas, the monk continued his slow walk with his cane, leaving the room through one of the doors. Only my father was left, sitting thoughtfully on the floor.

I sat next to him. I wished I could talk to him at that moment. So much protection for his daughter for what? I was alone in this strange λ3 experiment, a road with no return…

A woman's voice broke the silence through a new portal that had just opened behind me.

"Tomorrow, Sandra is coming." I heard my mother's voice. When I turned back, I saw my sister's house in Italy. The image of the temple disappeared as I entered the kitchen.

"I will make a surprise for your sister. It's her favourite dish: the vegetarian lasagna she loves," my mum said.

"I'm worried about her, Mum! Since Dad's death, she has been working too much. I feel she is getting a bit depressed. Look what happened to Dad... She is so clever; why not try something around here... Giovanni's partner at the travel agency said that they need people who are fluent in English. It could be a good start. She needs to be closer to us. We must help her."

"I am worried too... You're right. It would be nice for her to move to another country and make new friends. We will try to convince her, but it won't be easy, because she's stubborn like your father. Everything must always be her way, and she refuses advice."

"What she needs is to fall in love. She loses interest in her boyfriends, and they were all magazine cover stars," my sister exclaimed.

This dialogue between them provided me with a delightful feeling. *What a privileged person I am to be loved by my family...*

~*~

Suddenly, a massive portal opened, and that pleasurable scene slowly faded. I was alone on a lawn. Thunderous roars came from a scary grey sky. In front of me, a metal pyramid glowed with lightning. When I looked to the side, I saw the library. I realised that I was in Yudh. The city was different, now surrounded by darkness...

Chapter 9

The Prophecy

I walked across the lawn towards Yudh's library. There was a cold and strong wind. The blue sky I had seen before was now grey, laden with thunder and lightning. What had happened here?

No one was on the streets, and all the bookshelves in the library were empty. I couldn't see anybody around.

Suddenly, I heard voices coming from the lowest floor. I slowly went down the stairs. To my surprise, Kennis and Narquiamides were beside the door that accessed the pyramid.

"What is happening here?" I shouted, unable to think clearly.

They didn't answer and couldn't even see me. I realised I was inside another vision, now accessing the future.

"How long before they storm the city?" Kennis asked, looking at the empty building with deep sadness.

"A couple of minutes. Enough to take all the books away from Earth's astral plane."

"So, let's go, Narquiamides. Everyone is ready to depart, just missing us."

"I've decided to stay, my friend. I am joining up with one of the rescue teams from the east. You know I have personal reasons for staying."

"Yes, I was already anticipating it." He looked at the library's empty bookshelves. "There have been so many books and so much noble knowledge. Where did we go wrong?"

"We didn't do anything wrong; the Brotherhood of the Golden Circle defeated us. This time, evil won and took over this planet. Let us remember the 24,000-year elliptical cycles of the races of Earth. From Atlantis itself, they went from apogee to extermination. History repeats itself…"

"I know, but in this case, it is different. The Earth is on an upward cycle of 12,000 years. I have never known a decline at this stage."

"We reached the limit after doing everything we could. Unfortunately, humanity had mindlessly chosen to live the following millennia in darkness. The Earth will remain ailing until a new cycle brings new hope for the consciences that are not wiped out. In any case, we will work around here to redirect it well before that."

"I must go now. Yudh will be a new astral city of knowledge from another blue planet like this one. It will have its ascending elliptical cycle towards the Central Sun in a millennium."

"May the Infinite Spirit of Love illuminate our steps."

They smiled and shared a friendly farewell hug.

I heard cries of hatred and footsteps from an angry mob entering the city streets. They were getting closer and closer.

"Go, my old friend! Now!" said Narquiamides.

Kennis walked through the door, which then closed. I followed Narquiamides, who came out of the library rather hurriedly. There was a loud bang, and the building began to crumble into ruins. As we ran outside, the walls and ceiling collapsed. On the way out, back on the lawn, we could see the city, which lay below the slope, being consumed by flames. A crowd with horses and carrying torches were setting fire to the houses. I was deeply depressed when I saw Yudh, a city of knowledge, being destroyed. Their cries, mingled with the roar of thunder, could be heard in the darkening sky.

There was no longer a pyramid. It became a light moving at high speed in the grey sky. In its place was a gigantic crater. The most impressive thing was that it was much more extensive than the pyramid. I looked again at the sky, and the light was already disappearing towards a new destination… I had been suspicious of those corridors I passed that looked like they were made from aluminium alloys. It was a giant spaceship. From the size of the crater, the pyramid was only a tiny part of it.

Narquiamides sat in the garden leading to the library. He appeared calm, as if he were waiting for the arrival of friends, not invaders. *What is he doing?* My heartbeat accelerated.

About fifteen men, all wearing black tunics and mounted on huge horses, approached. There was a strange symbol on the back of their clothes: a golden circle with an inverted pentagram inside it and an inverted triangle of bright red colouring in the centre. At the front came the group leader, a white man with a shaven head and dark eyes. They stood with their horses in a circle, leaving Narquiamides in the centre, who remained seated on the grass.

"You there. Get up!" the leader shouted.

Narquiamides ignored the request and continued sitting, with the semblance of someone on a beach holiday.

Visibly annoyed, the leader turned to one of his men. "Let's not waste time. Send this old, worthless man to hell. I think he was the only one left in this dirty town. The others, instead of fighting, ran away… All cowards."

A burly white man with a long red beard gave a sinister smile, moving only part of his lips. He got down from his horse and removed his sword from its sheath.

"Goodbye, Grandpa! Your soul will take a long journey. But without your head," he taunted and snickered. All the other men laughed at the wicked remark.

How could Narquiamides sit there without reacting? At that moment, my heart beat even faster. I was going to explode with tension.

Holding the sword with both hands, the man made an abrupt movement towards the still neck of Narquiamides, but as he reached a few millimetres from it, the sword no longer seemed to obey his command. The executioner struggled to move the sword while another powerful, invisible force controlled his hands. The blade suddenly turned against him, the point of the sword facing behind his body. It was coming closer and closer to lacerating his neck. His face began to sweat. He glanced sideways at the blade, just millimetres away from being beheaded himself. This force ceased only when it lightly touched his neck, where he finally managed to drop the sword. It fell to the ground.

"He is a devil wizard," the man shouted, pointing to Narquiamides, who remained motionless and quiet. The other men on their horses looked startled, agreeing with him.

The shaven-headed leader of the group got off his horse. His great height and muscular body were noticeable behind his black tunic.

"You fearful fools. Let me take care of this old wizard myself."

The big man withdrew his sword from its golden scabbard, decorated with precious stones. Unlike his soldier's blade, his seemed to have been carefully forged from a unique material.

When he threatened a blow with his sword against Narquiamides, he was interrupted by another knight arriving quickly on a horse.

"Stop, Petrus. Not him!" he shouted from a distance.

Petrus stopped and looked at the man sceptically. But he continued holding his sword close to Narquiamides.

The new knight joined the group. The hood of his black tunic covered his face.

"You realise he doesn't react, Petrus."

"And what?"

"He can decimate you and your whole army if he wants to—"

"Nonsense lies."

"Listen to me. Please don't touch your sword on him. This is precisely what he wants. Without attacking him, he will not have a chance to defend himself. We must use the laws of the universe to our advantage. We have more astral cities to conquer. Here, the mission has already been accomplished. They took the books away, and we no longer need to burn them."

Petrus frowned, but then he shrugged and lowered the sword. He put his sword back in its scabbard and got on his horse.

Before leaving with his soldiers, the boss said, "A new portal, opened at the city's entrance, will take you to another town. Take the energy and kill the astral bodies of those who do not cooperate. Don't destroy the hospitals. They will all be ours. Go now. I'll meet you soon!"

After the army left, Narquiamides, who remained seated, broke his silence, "You arrived on time, Bogat."

The man got off his horse and removed his hood. Although he had strange, clear orange eyes, he was handsome. A perfectly symmetrical face, and long blond hair. He was wearing a golden medallion with the same inverted pentagram symbol and an inverted triangle with red colouring in its centre.

He looked at Narquiamides, who now stood up.

"I don't understand consciences like you," the blond man objected. "Sacrificing yourself, trying to save this rubbish world that never wanted to be saved… Finally, we have sixty-six leaders in six different regions of the Earth. The Brotherhood is united for the first time; several have already been reborn. My turn is near."

"The world is only in chaos because of the influence of sick consciences like you, Bogat, which have stimulated dictators, politicians, and murderers, spreading hatred on Earth. Men destroy each other mutually without knowing that they are influenced by evil. You were responsible for turning Petrus from the good path he was following. He would have been an example of regeneration for thousands of men trapped in the lower astral by their psychic experiences with wars. You knew who Petrus was in other lives; he had no pity, but his conscience transformed in his last life on Earth. Now, he is the opposite example."

"I had to do this for my survival. For now, he is handy. He gives me much power, security, and respect, to be one of the sixty-six chosen leaders. It is power that opens the doors of this world. I no longer use black magic with the nature spirits. Instead, I formed an army of dead men, old warriors, and war soldiers with Petrus's help. They were in the mud, with their bodies and faces disfigured. I helped them, and they are all grateful to me. I gave them enough energy to return to a dignified appearance."

"Energy stolen from innocents, you mean..."

"Stolen from filthy consciences who went to the lower planes... they didn't deserve a drop of astral water. Every week, I send the soldiers to recharge their energies on Earth. Invisible, these imbeciles go to many places and return energised and happy. They worship me. I am God for them."

"This is ridiculous, Bogat. Don't you realise that power has blinded you? You and Lyha should be concerned with the welfare of the nature spirits, which was your dharma, your true mission on this planet."

"Do you think I'm not worried? These imbecile humans have polluted the seas, rivers, and atmosphere. For this, they deserve to be enslaved. I am the avenging god of the nature spirits. We are winning. We know the Creator's law of balance. The Earth will be our paradise; we will enslave humanity, but nature will be protected."

Narquiamides gestured with his hands, opening a portal. I could see mountains through it.

Before entering, he objected, "You are wrong, Bogat. It's the power of love that opens the door of the world. The power of evil that is leading you… it won't be long before you sixty-six leaders of the Brotherhood on the six continents fight among yourselves. Gaia, the Mother Earth that you are supposed to serve, will destroy you, and that will be the end of your conscience forever…"

Bogat shouted just before the portal closed, "It won't happen. The Brotherhood knows the laws of the Creator…"

~*~

Suddenly, I felt the ground of the lawn open up. The sensation was of my body falling from a great height. I opened my eyes, my heart beating fast as if I were returning from a nightmare. I saw Jade with her hands on my face beside Narquiamides and Adhya.

"How are you feeling?" Jade asked. She offered me a glass of a light green liquid while Adhya released me from my restraints. I sat on a chair beside the table. "It is energised water made from a powerful astral plant, which will rebalance your chakras. The effect is quick. You will be more peaceful and willing for us to continue in a few minutes."

Jade removed the crystal from my forehead and walked away with Adhya. Narquiamides sat down beside me to talk to me alone.

"I know you are confused," he observed, looking at my expression.

"Everything happened so fast—"

"As a scientist, you know time is relative," he said. "Centuries or millennia can mean a fraction of a second to Infinity. Past, present, and future have a direct and permanent relationship."

"The scenes I saw were so real! How was this possible?" My voice was that of a doctor of physics knocked out by an unimaginable experience.

"The individualised lives of each conscience are stored in registers called the Akashic. These contain their evolutionary history, diverse lives, loves, fears, and conquests. Everything is inserted in a universal memory. When someone remembers something from their childhood or previous lives, they access these registers, and the memories appear."

"You guys can access anything? This is magnificent! It would be the key to unlocking the most diverse mysteries of humanity."

"There is much restriction on what each can access. Yours was limited by the crystal on your forehead that Jade programmed. The more developed the conscience, the more allowed and deeper the accesses. It is a vibrational state. Earth's humanity is still in preschool, and children should not risk themselves... Because of its immaturity, it would use the information exclusively for dark and selfish purposes. But it is gradually being matured to understand its proper role in evolution."

"I witnessed Yudh being invaded, and you were there... Was that access to the future?"

"Yes. You were in the future."

"Our destinies, then, are somehow already programmed?"

"No, they aren't. It would be illogical to have a programmed future. Past, present, and future happen simultaneously in the Akashic field, but with significant differences. The past is unchangeable and is recorded. On the contrary, the future is the result of our present actions. It is composed of multiple probabilities. Unlike the past, the only future scene you have seen is the invasion of Yudh. It will not necessarily happen, but at this moment, there is a strong probability that it will. In other words, despite being only one of several possibilities, this is the future recorded today, but there is still time to change it. We can choose a different path if we know a dangerous drop after the turn."

"Are the various prophecies, such as that of Nostradamus, just probabilities?"

"Yes, exactly. This is why many don't happen: humanity takes a different course. Some are also misinterpreted. Authors sometimes have difficulty describing exactly what they saw in the Akashic field in the distant future. For example, imagine you are a researcher in Europe living in the Middle Ages, and one day, in a deep sleep, your conscience leads you to have a vision of the technology of today's Earth. How can you describe and explain the internet, satellites, quantum computers, drones, and artificial intelligence if your brain cannot understand or find adequate nouns?"

"I had never thought of it this way..."

"The same happens when having visions of other worlds more advanced than Earth."

"This prophecy about Yudh... Who were those men with that symbol drawn on their backs?"

"Except Bogat, the rest are human beings who died on Earth. Most of them were killed in wars and battles over many centuries. They have no idea what they are doing... The golden circle with the inverted pentagram within it and the bright red inverted triangle figure in the centre are symbols of the powerful Brotherhood of the Golden Circle. It symbolises the union of diverse forces of evil."

After a pause, he continued.

"If humanity does not wake up now, most countries will soon be dominated by dictators and tyrants. The countries of the European Union will all be separated, just as happened with the United Kingdom, but in a violent and bloody way. Others will invade the weakest. Hatred will be increasingly driven by fake and manipulated news and become out of control. It will cause disunity between people, even in more solid countries. Democrats and Republicans, for example, will be so unthinkingly inflamed by mutual hatred that they will cause the downfall of the United States, with the United Kingdom and Australia also being ruled by tyrannical dictators."

"And how do you combat this? What must humanity do to prevent this?"

"We cannot intervene directly. It is a cosmic law. Knowledge is the key. Humans need to know that invisible forces are manipulating them. The λ3 experiment is the first step to correcting the course... However, everything will depend on humanity's behaviour. It is the only one responsible for designing its future. It can be light or darkness."

He winked and whispered, "We have a powerful secret weapon that we will use. I will reveal it to you soon."

"A secret weapon. What—"

Jade and Adhya approached, without giving me time to get more information.

"It's time," Jade said, inviting me to lie on the table again. "Now that you know how this experiment works, let's continue with the second stage."

My hands and legs were bound again with blue energy rings.

She opened the dark box with the symbol λ3 and placed another crystal on my forehead. Three remained inside it. They started the same procedures to induce the expulsion of my mental body.

Before the detachment, Jade mentally warned me, "In this phase of the λ3 experiment, you will be allowed to access the lives of other consciences. The main ones are the three persons who died in the car crash in London. They went to dark lower astral planes. Take care of your emotions."

I again went through the metallic part at the base of the blue luminous pillar, which led me into unimaginable scenes...

Chapter 10

First Life – Dino

I was in a cold autopsy room. There were four bodies covered with white sheets on different tables. A doctor with black hair and glasses was filling out forms when he heard the door open.

"Inspector Hunter. Please come in."

Hunter was tall, with trimmed hair on the sides, and looked around forty-five years old. He wore a dark blue suit and tie, contrasting with his white shirt.

The doctor opened the top of the sheets covering two bodies. One was a fat white man in his fifties, while the other was a young black man.

"I believe this is the man we talked about on the phone, and this young man was driving the car."

"Yes, that's him. That's the end of Bernardino, or Dino, as he was known. The boy is Joe, his driver," Hunter observed. "Dino was a brilliant man with an endearing and pleasant personality. Most people doubted that he could be involved in illicit transactions. Unfortunately, he used all his intelligence to generate a fortune from smuggling gold, diamonds, and jewellery. His import–export company has always made suspicious money-laundering operations between several countries and has been heavily investigated. I tried to arrest him several times but never gathered enough evidence to convict him."

"I know the story: a lot of money, influential friends, and the most expensive lawyers… Does he have a family?"

"He was adopted. His adoptive fathers are deceased. They were very wealthy, and already involved in money laundering. Dino had a good education, never married, and had no children or siblings. His lawyer is taking over the company and told me he will close it. Dino was lonely and lived in one of the most expensive neighbourhoods in London. Important people always surrounded him. He was always present at high-society events. I believe his greatest pleasure was to feel powerful and invincible. Indeed, he was. He managed to beat me many times. He used to make fun of me, telling me, staring straight into my eyes, that I wouldn't be able to catch him. Now it is true… What was the cause of death?"

"He had a fatal head injury; he wasn't wearing a seatbelt. This young driver was protected by his seatbelt and airbag. That's why he had only light scratches on his body, but unfortunately, he suffered a cardiac arrest… I believe he could have survived if he had been revived quickly. Who was the driver at fault in this tragedy?"

"We are still investigating. The strangest thing is that even looking at statements from different witnesses, we concluded that at the time of the accident, for just a few seconds, all the traffic lights were green for vehicles and red for pedestrians."

"That's weird."

"Yes. There is a technical team working on it."

~*~

An enormous portal opened on a wall of the room. I went through it to a forest with pale and colourless vegetation. Some trees seemed almost lifeless. The sky was grey and cloudy. In the distance, lightning bolts cut the sky, followed by a loud crash of thunder. Around me, the silence was broken by the noises of insects in the forest and the wind that shook the poor vegetation.

I heard a groan further ahead… There was a fine mist that made it difficult to see. When I got closer, I saw Dino lying on the ground. He was wearing an elegant suit covered in bloodstains. He opened his eyes, making an expression of pain. Without the strength to get up, he crawled to a large tree where he rested, leaning his back on it. He noticed the bloodstains on his suit and ran his hand behind his head. He felt a lesion, but there was no bleeding. Visibly confused, he took out his phone from the inside pocket of his suit and tried to use it. It didn't work. He checked his wallet. It was intact, with cash, credit cards, and ID. He struggled to get up and staggered until he reached a dirt road.

At that moment, I realised that everything is a physical phenomenon. After death, the astral cells are automatically directed to a place with strong magnetic attraction. So, what would make this man, after his physical death, be attracted to that strange place?

Dino walked along the road as if searching for something. Voices and footsteps came from the opposite direction. He stopped walking, waiting for people to approach him. The illumination of the grey sky, added to in some parts with mist, made it challenging to identify details of people in the distance. He stood in the middle of the road, signalling with both hands upwards.

"Help! Please help me! I think I've had an accident! I don't know where I am."

Two men and two women with cadaverous features were approaching. Their faces were wholly disfigured. They were wearing old, dirty clothes with torn parts.

"Folks, my name is Dino. I have money," he said shakily, showing his stuffed wallet. "I propose we talk and negotiate."

The two men promptly knocked Dino to the ground and held him down, ignoring his stuffed wallet, which fell on the roadside.

"You don't know who you are dealing with," he screamed. "I have influential friends, and if anything happens to me, you will suffer, and they will send you all to hell."

The men laughed loudly as if it were a funny joke.

One of the men instructed the woman wearing an ancient dress. “Take the tube and draw his energy. Let’s all have fun today on the surface of the Earth.”

From within her dress, between her breasts, the woman took out a cylindrical metal object with a small needle on the tip, resembling a syringe. She got down on her knees and put the tube close to the back of Dino’s neck; he was totally immobilised, shouting for them to stop. Suddenly, they heard the loud noise of approaching horses.

They looked at each other, and one of the cadaverous men shuddered. “There won’t be time! We need to hide quickly. Everyone help get him off the road now!”

Dino, realising the uncomfortable situation of his current enemies, began to shout louder. “Help! I am being kidnapped.”

“Quiet, idiot! You don’t know what you’re doing,” the man whispered, covering Dino’s mouth tightly.

In total silence, the four dragged Dino into the woods beside the road, and hid behind some large stones. The loud clatter of the horses’ hooves came closer and closer, and the cylindrical tube carelessly fell to the ground.

“The tube!” one of the women exclaimed with utter despair. “If they see it, we’ll be in trouble. We’d better run away through the woods and leave this man here.”

“No way!” one of the men whispered. “We can’t lose that tube. It was too hard to get it. Even more, we need this newcomer’s fresh energy. Stay hidden and quiet. I’ll sort it out.”

He stood up and ran towards the road. There, he quickly threw the tube to his companions, where one of the women grabbed it and remained hidden.

The man realised the riders had already spotted him. He remained alone on the road and pretended to be walking in the same direction. Quickly, two sturdy black horses reached him. Their riders wore black clothes with hoods covering their faces.

At first, it looked like they would continue, ignoring the man walking. However, one turned back and called his companion when he spotted Dino's wallet lying on the ground beside the road. They got off their horses. They were enormous, just over two metres tall.

One of them called out to the man pretending to be walking. "You there, come here now. Where is the owner of this thing?"

The man looked back and saw one of the black riders holding Dino's wallet. He obeyed the order and returned.

"Thing? What thing? I don't know. I'm just walking."

They drew their swords, and both stood looking around, trying to find its owner. Their blades glowed and contained inscriptions and symbols of an unknown language.

Both riders lowered their hoods. I could see their big white faces, hairless and deformed. *Who are these scary monsters?* My heart beat faster, especially when I noticed their orange eyes exuding an energy of evil.

"What are you doing walking alone in the opposite direction of the city?" the monster asked in a thick and hoarse voice.

"Why? Is it forbidden to walk now?" He skilfully replied with another question.

"You know that no one can take away the energy of the newcomers in this zone without Bogat's permission."

"Yes. We all know, of course. Bogat is the boss in charge around here," he replied in a firm voice, while his hidden companions silently admired his courage.

Dino was lying immobilised by the other three colleagues, unable to see those sinister riders. He started to emit several sounds, even with his mouth covered.

"You lie!" the monster exclaimed, showing his enormous, crooked teeth.

At that instant, he lifted the man by the neck with just one of his big hands. His face and orange eyes reflected his anger as his sword pierced the man's body. His friends ran into the woods, leaving Dino behind. The wounded man fell to the ground. A small round black portal opened below his body, which sucked him in and quickly closed.

Dino was still lying down. He had not seen that horrible scene, but he heard loud footsteps approaching him. He looked relieved, probably thinking some help had arrived to save him. But as he was about to get up, he froze, looking at the two monstrous beings. They caught and gagged him, and then dropped him behind the saddle of one of the enormous horses, lying face down, and continued along the road.

And now? How can I follow them?

At that moment, a portal opened beside me. Upon entering, I was on the same road about three kilometres ahead of the riders.

The road made a ninety-degree curve where I stood, continuing between two parallel mountains. When they made the curve, they were surprised by a high barrier of burning wood. The frightened horses stopped, raised their front legs, and knocked one of the riders to the ground. The other, carrying Dino, managed to stay mounted.

A tall, muscular white man came running out from behind a rock next to one of the mountains. He had shaved hair, was barefoot, and was wearing only a pair of dark black trousers that looked like a sportsman's trousers. Several tattoos covered his muscular body, including on his arms and chest. He was carrying a wooden spear made from a tree branch. He thrust it, with agility, into the fallen rider's chest, just before he could get up.

The monster cried with pain mixed with rage, which echoed off the parallel mountain walls, and fell unconscious on the ground.

I looked in detail at the man's face, which seemed familiar. It left me with no doubt: it was Petrus. According to the prophecy, he would invade Yudh in the future. However, at that moment, his eyes and expression did not bear the evil I saw. It was milder, even exuding an air of simplicity.

The other monster got off his horse calmly. His disfigured white face reflected much hatred. Orange eyes stared at Petrus, who was beside his fallen colleague. The creature drew his sword from its sheath, which glowed even brighter in the flames' light.

"I will send your soul to a place that will bring agony, day and night, for a long time," the monster said with a raspy voice.

Bound and gagged on the saddle of the great black horse, Dino was watching the whole thing. His eyes were wide open. He was trying uselessly to escape from the ropes that were holding him. I confess that he was not the only one frightened. *What is all this? Who are those horrible creatures?* I needed urgent answers...

Another man was hiding behind the stones on the opposite side of Petrus. He watched every detail of what was happening, like an animal waiting for the best moment to grab its prey. He was a young man with light skin and short black hair, of medium height, wearing jeans, a leather jacket, and an earring. Keeping a distance, the young man threw two stones at the monster.

"Come and get me. Idiot from hell," he taunted. "I'm the one who planned it all."

The stones seemed not to make any scratches on the creature's body. The monster turned to see who was challenging him.

"You are cowards," the young man screamed. Then he threw another stone towards his enemy's chest, who broke it with his sword as easily as tearing a thin sheet of paper.

While the rider was distracted, Petrus took the sword from the sheath of the other. With brutal force, he ran and pierced the blade through the back of the monster, who fell like a heavy tree trunk.

The two men hugged each other.

"We did it! We did it!" the young man exclaimed. "We got the swords, and look at our transport over there waiting for us." He pointed to the two big black horses standing a little away. "Let's go far away from here. Surely, there must be better places in other regions in this hellish place."

Dino was still tied up on the horse, sweating like he was in a sauna. He saw the robust and tattooed man carrying the sword approaching him. Then he closed his eyes. However, his ropes were cut, and he got off the horse and collapsed to the ground.

The giant riders lying on the ground began to dissolve into a fine dark dust that disappeared with the wind. Two tiny men stood in their places, little more than a metre tall. One was wearing a dark green jumpsuit. He had long white hair and light brown eyes. His nose, ears, and feet were gigantic, disproportionate to his height. The other was very similar to the first, except that he had a long white beard and no hair.

A transformation also occurred with the two swords, now just two long wooden sticks. Petrus threw his on the ground in fright, where one of the little men ran to catch it. One of the tiny beings gestured with his hands, opening a sizeable hexagonal portal. In contrast to the grey sky and rocky landscape on this side, there was a beautiful sunny field with green trees and birds. With their sticks, they stood at the portal door, took one last look at the men, who stared in amazement at the spectacle of magic, and stepped inside. One whistled with his hands, and the two great black horses followed them.

"Oh no! We need the horses!" the young man pleaded.

He tried vainly to enter that portal, but intense energy stopped him like a glass wall. The two horses on the other side were no longer so giant. One was white and the other brown. Both were running loose and happy through the field. The portal closed, leaving only the three men on the road.

The young man put his hands on his head in despair.

With a voice that mixed anger and frustration, Petrus complained to his friend, "What the hell is this place, Michael? We planned everything to get horses and guns, and now... Nothing. All we got was a useless, fat old man."

Dino was still sitting on the floor. His face showed he was trying to understand where he was and what had happened.

What he didn't know was that this was not a nightmare. His new life, his new home on the astral plane, was beginning.

Chapter 11

Second Life – Mrs Stephanie Puizhant

I was taken to a small stone-built room about nine metres square, with very high walls. There was an old iron door closed with bars. On the opposite side were two small vertical windows too high to see out of. Through them, flashes of lightning dimly illuminated the room.

On its damp and cold floor, a woman was lying unconscious. She appeared forty years old, and had dark hair tied behind her head. She was dressed elegantly in a grey woman's suit and white shirt, but there were some bloodstains. Her accessories, such as earrings, jewellery, shoes, and a small handbag on the floor, showed her great wealth. When I looked at her face, a portal opened next to me, inviting me to enter.

Then I could access her most profound memories…

I left that cold stone room behind the portal, which was now closing, giving way to a children's room carefully decorated with several dolls and stuffed animals. Sitting facing a small table, a little girl in a dress played alone with her dolls and happily sang a song. The girl was carefully cutting and pasting coloured fabrics. They were little outfits for her dolls.

The door opened, and a woman appeared and said sweetly, "Stephanie dear, I've called you to dinner twice already. Your daughters can wait for their little dresses."

"I am coming, Mum. I'm just finishing this new model for Christmas. But I am already thinking about the spring collection. What do you think?"

The mother looked thrilled at those beautiful little clothes, carefully handcrafted from her daughter's imagination. She took one of the dolls in her hand.

"They are getting more and more beautiful. That's amazing how you can create with such perfection and so little material," she exclaimed, in a voice that mixed admiration and pride. "It is time to let you use my sewing machine."

"Really?" the little girl said, opening her blue eyes with a beautiful smile.

"But on the condition that you use it only under my supervision. What do you think?"

Stephanie hugged her mother with the happiness of someone who had just won the lottery.

"When I grow up, I want to have many children, and I will make clothes for them all."

The girl's face did not deceive me. She was the same woman I had just found unconscious.

I heard a slight sound coming from the room's wall, and when I turned around, a new portal appeared. It was a double metal door that opened for me to enter.

~*~

It was in a modern lift, and Stephanie stood alone, wearing the same elegant outfit as when I found her unconscious in the stone room. Unlike the adorable little girl I saw, her countenance now, with her blue eyes behind the glasses, exuded a dull expression.

The lift opened on the highest floor.

A young woman with glasses was waiting for her with a folder and a tablet.

"Good morning, Mrs Puizhant!"

She returned the good morning without looking at her secretary and continued walking until they entered a modern office. On the elegant reception desk was a sign: Steph Baby.

Walking alongside her boss, the secretary reported, "I have placed the information you requested for the board meeting in this folder."

Still without looking at the woman's face, Stephanie exchanged her handbag for the folder and continued walking through the office. As she passed through the corridors, all the employees were silent in a military posture, reflecting the severe authority exercised by that executive, who barely looked at them.

The assistant, walking and holding the boss's handbag, was reading the agenda on her tablet.

"For today, lunch is scheduled with the Spanish investor group. Then, at 15.50, you will have a presentation from the suppliers of the new German sewing machines. Your driver will be with Mr Puizhant at the end of the day, who will go to the doctor and then for physiotherapy sessions. Would you like me to book a car to take you home?"

"No, tell the driver to bring my car. I will drive back myself today. Is everyone in the room?"

"Yes, except for the new marketing director, Mrs Alison Wenery. Her children have taken ill, but she is already on her way and will arrive a little late," the young secretary explained nervously.

"Delay? Due to the children?"

"Yes, they are cute identical twins! She said she spent the night without sleep, finishing the presentation and caring for the children. I go almost crazy with just one. Imagine two simultaneously," the secretary said, ignored by her irritable boss.

They arrived at the meeting room. Nine people were sitting at a large table and stopped talking at the arrival of the executive. Professional photos of babies and small children in various outfits were on one of the room's walls. In the background was a dark-coloured world map, with little dots of white light showing various Steph Baby shops in different countries.

About ten minutes after the meeting started, Alison arrived with apologies. Her hair was badly combed and her make-up that tried to disguise her fatigue was badly applied.

A hush fell over the meeting room.

Without giving time for justifications, the chairwoman looked at her luxurious watch and scolded, "Mrs Wenery, you are new to our organisation and have an excellent résumé. But let's get one thing straight right away: just because our company works with children's clothing, it doesn't mean that I will tolerate delays from an important director due to sick little children. Here, time is money, so you must choose between business or family if you want to stay with us."

Everyone was now looking at Alison, who was visibly surprised by the rebuke from her new boss.

"Understood, Mrs Puizhant," she replied in a trembling voice.

After the meeting, a man sat next to Stephanie.

"Stephanie, today we are having lunch again with the Spaniards. They will certainly improve the proposal, which was already great. I speak now not as a vice president but as a friend who has helped you build this empire from the beginning… They are a solid group that wants to include a winning children's line for their brands. You have been working for years at a breakneck pace. This is an opportunity to sell the company, slow down, get a seat on a board, and enjoy life better with Edgard."

"John, the only reason I didn't cancel this lunch is your insistence. You are the best in finance, and I am the best in children's fashion. We are a team, and you already know my position." She got up and left the room without looking at the man, who remained seated with a look of defeat.

On the wall beside me, a portal opened in the shape of a staircase. As I climbed it, I entered a room with décor that indicated it was a doctor's office. Stephanie was on a sofa, and next to her was a man wearing a fine suit, sitting in an electric wheelchair. On the wall, there was a modern light grey digital clock that included the current day and month. It was two days before the accident.

A nurse opened the door.

"Mrs Puizhant, you and your husband may come in. The doctor will see you."

After the formal greetings, the doctor addressed the couple seriously.

"As agreed at our last meeting, I have sent all your tests to three of the best fertilisation laboratories in the world: one here in England and the others in France and the United States. Unfortunately, I do not have good news. As we have already discussed, Mrs Puizhant, the quality of your eggs is not good. You were born with a problem of morphology and genetic load. The more years go by, the worse this situation gets. The solution could be an egg bank, but in your case, we do not recommend it because you have already had several miscarriages in the past and—"

With a look of disgust, the woman interrupted, holding back tears that begged to come out. "I've been told this! I never wanted donated eggs. It must be my eggs." She took a deep breath and continued in an authoritative voice. "I've been looking for a solution for over ten years. I pay England's best and most expensive doctors to bring me solutions. Fertilisation medicine has evolved so much. I know women who have already done it at an advanced age. But no laboratory in the world can solve my problem. It is too much incompetence..."

Her husband, Edgard, with the patient look of someone who already seemed to know his wife's strong temperament, held one of her hands and interrupted the conversation in a serene voice.

"We know you have tried, Doctor, and we are grateful. We don't always like the news we get. See what happened to me... a few years ago, I had to have my legs amputated after a car accident, but soon, I will experience a new technology of mechanical legs made in

Switzerland. I thank God that I survived, and today, I see life with different eyes. I have told Stephanie for years that we should go for adoption—"

"Thanking God?" his wife said furiously. "God doesn't exist, Edgard. If He existed, we would have children, you wouldn't be in a wheelchair, and there wouldn't be children abandoned in the world by cruel mothers… I will not adopt any children. Let your God take care of them."

~*~

That woman was distressing me. I was glad when a portal opened at the doctor's office door for me to escape.

I was back in the strange stone room. Stephanie was starting to move slowly. She sat on the floor, looking at this unknown place. She put her hand on the side of her head and made a pained expression. Seeing bloodstains on her clothes, she began to move quickly. She grabbed her handbag and tried to use her phone. She checked her belongings, which were all intact. Then, she looked over all her jewels and her expensive watch, which was not working. It read precisely nine o'clock.

She picked up her handbag from the floor and stood, confused and staggering. The small windows in that room were too high, and she couldn't reach them… Lightning illuminated the room, and thunder rumbled from outside. She slowly opened the iron door that led into a damp, partially lit stone corridor. The place seemed deserted. Its walls were imperfect and worn, reflecting its antiquity. She walked carefully. To her right, there were other empty rooms with iron doors, just like the ones she had just left. It looked like an ancient prison.

Further ahead, a girl was singing in one of the rooms. It was the same song Stephanie had sung while playing and sewing for her dolls as a child. She trembled as she moved towards that well-known song from her childhood. She opened the iron door, which was already a few centimetres ajar, and could see a little girl with her back to it. The girl had long white hair and was sitting in front of an old sewing machine driven by a pedal.

Two fire torches, embedded in the walls, lit the room. Two small vertical windows were very high up, identical to the room she had been lying in. All you could see were flashes of lightning and an icy mist outside. Some rustic wooden shelves, supported by iron bars, were on one of the stone walls, holding several dolls made of cloth and ceramic. They all had expressions of sadness, anguish, or despair. Some were missing limbs. The girl stopped singing.

“That is very strange,” the girl said without looking back. “We are not expecting your arrival, Mrs Katharina Keller… I think someone has advanced the process of your death.”

“Mrs Katharina Keller? Death? I don’t know what you are talking about. Where am I, and who are you?”

The girl replied, "I am Elisabeth. Come closer. I am sewing clothes for my dolls. I learned from you when you were still alive. As a child, you could see me sometimes in your room. You called me your invisible friend."

Stephanie took small steps, very slowly, into the room, keeping some distance from the strange girl with long white hair. The flashes that entered through the high vertical windows illuminated her even more.

"What a pity you couldn't have babies. Do you know why?" the girl asked, holding a doll with a black dress. She rose and turned towards the woman. Although her voice and stature were those of a girl of about fourteen, her face was wrinkled, and she looked like a very old woman. Her eyes were a whitish-grey colour. The doll's face, handmade from porcelain, was a perfect copy of Stephanie's face, with a frightened expression.

Stephanie was terrified. Her eyes widened as she saw a large red needle going through the doll's little tummy towards the uterus.

With a sarcastic smile, the girl concluded, "Because we did not let you."

Petrified, as if she were living a nightmare and unable to wake up, the woman left the room. She closed and locked the door from the outside with a horizontal iron bolt and sprinted through the cold and damp corridors of the building. Then there was a loud sound from an animal horn that echoed everywhere, signalling an alarm.

Stephanie opened some doors along the corridor to look for an exit; however, all the rooms, like the previous ones, were empty and had small high windows. To make matters worse, she began to hear voices and footsteps coming behind her.

She saw an iron gate in the corridor to her left. It was a darker and different passage that could lead her to another place. She desperately put her trembling hands inside and opened the iron bolt. Before entering, she ran further ahead and threw her handbag and shoes on the floor, as far as possible, to throw off her pursuers. She hurried back, closed the barred door, and went down the new dark corridor.

She walked quickly, groping its damp walls, until she spotted flashes of light ahead. They were lightning flashes that went through a hole in one of the walls, just above her eyes' height. Besides the lightning, from the crack, it was possible to feel a strong wind, proof that was the way out of the place.

Footsteps and voices echoed through the corridors. They seemed to be getting closer and closer. The wall was damp, and despite being tall and barefoot, she couldn't find the strength to jump up to the gap. She slipped back to the ground.

With great effort, she finally made it through to the other side, hitting her head on a spiral stone staircase. She held back tears, forced to remain completely silent as she listened to the voices of her pursuers.

"Where did she go?"

"She arrived ahead of what we expected..."

"We will catch that murderer." Different voices echoed through the corridors.

With a mixture of fear, pain, and despair, she climbed the spiral staircase towards where the constant flashes of lightning originated. Thunder and a strong wind could be heard. When she reached the end of the stairs, she was at the top of a ruined, U-shaped, three-storey building. It surrounded a huge stone-floored courtyard. In its centre was a tall wooden stake about six metres high.

"There she is! On the roof. Up there," a boy shouted, standing in the courtyard.

Before long, about fifteen of her pursuers appeared in the courtyard. They were all teenagers, likely between thirteen and sixteen years old. Their clothes, reminiscent of the seventeenth century in Europe, were dirty and torn. Some had no arms. Others were on wooden crutches and were missing one of their legs or feet. Some of them pushed their friends on carts made of rustic wood.

They were all watching her at the top of that building while walking in silence. Their expressions exuded hatred.

They stopped in the courtyard's centre, right around the wooden stake.

Standing out from the group, the leaders were a couple: Elisabeth, the old-looking girl she had met a few minutes ago, and a boy missing his left arm. The girl was holding a large wooden stick, leaning on the stones. Her long white hair swayed in the wind.

Stephanie tried to find a path to run away, but both sides of the roof of the building were partially destroyed. The only way out was to return by the spiral staircase. It was too late; some of her pursuers were coming up it. She was trapped. Her body froze, facing that crowd of hateful teenagers in the courtyard.

The leading boy in the yard signalled everyone, stretched out his only arm, and pointed his index finger at the woman on the roof.

"Revenge. Revenge. Revenge," he shouted.

All the other youngsters followed the same gesture, shouting together. The word echoed.

Elisabeth uttered a few words in a strange language, striking the ground with her wooden stick with great force. At that instant, the wind increased, and black clouds gathered in the sky with thunder.

Stephanie fainted.

In the aftermath, the pursuers quickly caught her...

Chapter 12

Third Life – Dr Vincent Gitumed

A portal led me to a well-known London pub. Four men sat at a round table, chatting happily over their drinks. One of the men caught my eye. He was wearing an elegant navy blue blazer and a white shirt. He seemed to have little interest in his friends' conversations. His eyes were directed exclusively at a woman sitting at the counter. I could understand it. She was stunningly beautiful, with long, straight black hair, light brown eyes, make-up on, and a red dress that clung to her perfect body. She returned his gaze, smiling at him seductively.

One of the men at the table, wearing a suit and tie, raised his glass. "Before we go, let's make a further toast to Dr Vincent Gitumed, an internationally renowned physician joining our Brotherhood of the Golden Circle. With the sponsorship of our pharmaceutical company, we are sure that he and his future wife will be the most powerful couple in England. And it is power that opens the doors of the world!"

The man who was looking at the beautiful woman turned to the others. "Thanks again, Charles."

Realising no more drinks were in front of him, he raised his arm to call the barmaid, who ignored him. When he moved, he noticed some bloodstains on his blazer. He passed his hand behind his head; his fingers were covered in blood.

He stood up immediately, apologised to his friends, and left the pub just as a person opened the door to enter.

When he tried to use his phone, it seemed out of battery. While he was waiting for a traffic light to cross the street with other people, a medium-sized dog, leashed by its owner, kept barking in his direction. The owner only managed to control the animal when Vincent ran to a nearby hospital at full speed.

As he entered the emergency room, he bumped into a tall, fat man, barefoot and wearing a hospital apron. "Watch out! There are sick people here!" he shouted.

Apologising, he hurriedly continued to the reception desk, where there was a long queue of people. He went straight to the counter and addressed the attendant in a gasping voice. "Please, it's an emergency. I am a doctor and need to be attended to now."

The receptionist ignored him completely.

Suddenly, he heard a voice calling him. "This way, Doctor. Come quickly to room number seven in this corridor."

It was the voice of a man in his thirties wearing a British Army uniform from the First World War. Visibly unsure but with no better alternative, he followed the strange soldier, who walked with difficulty. As he entered the room, unlike a hospital ward, he found himself in a room in a London residence, decorated in the second decade of the twentieth century.

"Please, sit down, Dr Walter," the soldier said, pointing to one of two armchairs near a lit fireplace, separated by a small wooden table.

Remaining standing, he looked at the soldier. "Look, Nurse, my name is not Dr Walter. I'm Dr Vincent Gitumed..."

"I know who you are—"

"Please listen," Vincent said. "I know exactly what is happening to me. I am going through a process of delirium that is now escalating. My brain is seeing absurd things here in this hospital room. You will think I am going crazy if I describe it. I know that it is just a hallucination created by my mind. I have bloodstains. Something has happened in my head. I need to do a tomography scan urgently because I am afraid it is severe... There are patients with similar symptoms." He held his phone with trembling hands; it did not light up. "Please urgently call Dr Sutherland, a neurologist friend of mine. I know he works in this hospital. My phone must have run out of battery."

The soldier standing next to him listened patiently.

"My name is Thomas, and I understand perfectly what you are feeling, Dr Walter. It is not delirium or a dream. Everything here is real." He held Vincent by the arm, pointing to one of the armchairs. "Please sit down. I will explain it to you."

"No... You don't understand, Nurse." He forcefully removed the soldier's hands from his arm and returned to the door. "I'll get Dr Sutherland myself."

He opened the door, but it no longer gave access to the hospital. Only fog, accompanied by a strong icy wind, entered the room. His eyes widened; he was on a high mountain. He looked down; it was an abyss without end. The soldier went to the door and closed it with great force and difficulty because of the strong wind. Dr Gitumed was paralysed in shock.

With Thomas's help, he took slow steps until he could sit in the armchair.

"I'm delirious, Thomas," Vincent said, worried. "I urgently need help..."

A tiny golden pyramid was in the centre of the table that separated the chairs by the fireplace. The soldier took the object, turned it anti-clockwise, and opened it. Inside was a small ball that resembled a pearl, which emitted a very intense bluish-white light.

"Take this pill, Doctor. You will feel better." Thomas had to help put the pill in Vincent's mouth, holding his trembling hands.

From this moment, Vincent fell asleep. A portal opened beside me, and I entered inside his memories...

Dr Gitumed was driving and arguing on speakerphone with a crying woman.

"What's going on, Daphne? Are you drunk?"

"I heard everything, Vincent. I went to your office late this afternoon. I wanted to give you a surprise visit. Your secretary had just left, and I decided to wait for you. The door was ajar. I overheard you talking to some men from a pharmaceutical lab who want to hire you. I was waiting, distracted by my phone, until I heard my name. So, I started listening attentively to everything. One of the conditions of the contract was to end our relationship. You agreed because I am a nurse from a poor background. After hearing this, I left and—"

"Calm down, Daphne," he said. "I am going to your flat now. So we can talk like adults…"

"Don't come! You have thrown our future in the bin," she scolded, crying.

"I have never made you any promises."

"Oh, no? What about everything we talked about, living together in a beach town? I am drunk, and you have lost your memory…"

"I like you very much, but I have bigger personal goals. You don't understand the ways to obtain power in this world."

"Power? I love you, Vincent, and I thought you loved me too. Deep down, I think you always used me as a sexual hobby. Oh…

God! My friends warned me that our relationship would have no future. Why didn't I listen to them? I kept insisting on sailing in a leaky boat... How foolish I was!"

"Let's not talk on the phone, Daphne. It is almost nine o'clock now. I am on the way to your flat. I will explain all the strategies. We will find a way to keep meeting. The contract is only for five years. After that, we will be so rich that we can live in a beach house of your choice anywhere in the world."

"Strategy? I'm going to be your hidden lover for five years? This is ridiculous!"

"It would be ridiculous not to accept this opportunity. We will be wealthy."

With a mixture of pain and hatred, she continued in tears. "I never wanted your money or to be a millionaire. I only dreamed of building a happy family with you. You never realised this because you are a selfish, ambitious monster, Vincent! You love and think only of yourself."

"I'm sorry. I don't want to have a mediocre life. I have the right to dream big. This is a unique opportunity not only for me but for us."

"You ruined my life. My dreams. Our relationship is over right now. I will make sure you can never come near me again."

The woman hung up the phone. A few minutes later, Vincent would be dead in the accident...

His memories continued in an old war car, with two men pulling into an army camp somewhere. They wore the same uniform as Thomas, worn by the British Army in 1915 during the First World War.

"Dr Walter, this is the makeshift medical centre we have set up." The soldier pointed, after parking the car. "We are happy to have a renowned doctor like you to run our centre. Our human resources are scarce."

"Well, I'm not in the army. I just accepted the invitation from the British government because I want to help our country somehow."

When I looked more closely at the doctor's face, behind his round glasses, I noticed that it was the same conscience that today was Dr Vincent. I had never imagined that strong traces were kept in our eyes between lives. Perhaps this is why some wisely say they are the mirror of our souls.

Upon entering the medical centre, the depressing scenes visibly shook the doctor. Dozens of wounded people were arriving from the battlefield, most of them in agony. Several nurses were running around to help with the heavy demand.

One of the nurses showed Dr Walter around, who could not hide his startled expression, observing those scenes that were undoubtedly new to him.

"Dr Walter, there is another case of a soldier who came from the trenches with a serious foot infection." The nurse pointed to a man on a stretcher. That man was Thomas, visibly ill, sweating, and muddy.

"Another case of foot infection?" Walter asked with utter indignation. "When I came here to contribute my work, I was only waiting for those wounded in battles."

"Well, I think it was the same for all of us here, Doctor," she said rather awkwardly. "Unfortunately, the infections are caused by the poor hygiene conditions in the trenches. There are faeces and urine, and rats eating the deceased's bodies. This is causing unimaginable chaos. This soldier is just one more; we must amputate his feet and hope he survives."

"I never imagined that. Sending men into these filthy trenches is murder. Is anyone seeing this? We are killing these young men," he protested.

"We have alerted our superiors several times about the hygiene conditions of these trenches, but so far, we have no solutions..."

"I have contact with the highest authorities in England. When the war is over, I hope to God we win, I swear I will make an extensive report to denounce all this. Those responsible, aware of these conditions, who send these young people to their deaths, must be severely punished. The whole world must know about this," vowed the doctor.

"Thank you, Doctor. Everyone here is counting on you."

~*~

That distressing picture was disappearing. Dr Walter was walking alone in London after the war, and a young journalist approached.

"Dr Walter, have you got a minute? I work for an independent magazine. I am doing a long report on the inhuman conditions of the war, especially in the trenches, which killed or injured thousands of young British men. You coordinated the improvised medical centre near the battlefield and were decorated for your great work. I want to set up an interview with you to give us all the details. It is an opportunity to expose the truths they try to hide from the public. Your testimony will be fundamental for those responsible to be judged and punished."

Dr Walter continued walking and said, turning his back to the journalist, "This matter is closed. We have conducted our work and saved many lives, that is all. I have nothing more to contribute. I am sorry."

The journalist walked with him and angrily asked, "Apart from the political position they gave you, how much did they pay you to keep quiet, Dr Walter?"

Dr Walter stopped, turned, and stared at the man. "You journalists are all inconvenient. Stop writing about the Great War. It only creates more suffering. It is already over, and we won." He turned his back on the man and kept walking. "Leave me alone. All of you," he shouted.

"Can you sleep peacefully? Many people expected more from you, Dr Walter. Your love for medicine has been bought by power," the man yelled in the distance.

The scenes disappeared.

I was back in the hospital.

The doctor opened his eyes. His face was drenched with sweat. He stared at Thomas, who remained seated in the other armchair near the fireplace, silently watching him.

Vincent exhibited a fearful expression. He begged for answers…

Chapter 13

Llyn Din: The Astral City

First life – Dino

The plan to acquire guns and horses had failed, and Dino was visibly confused. He sat on the dirt road and looked at the strong, tattooed Petrus and his friend Michael.

"We can't stay here on the road standing still, Petrus. Let's find another place," Michael suggested. "We better take him with us. With three, we are stronger."

Petrus looked at the man sitting on the ground with undisguised contempt.

"Hey, guys. Where am I?" Dino asked. "What is this strange place? I think I fell and hit my head, and I'm hallucinating. This—"

"You've died, stupid," Petrus said.

"I'm dead." He snorted sarcastically. "No way! How did I die if I'm talking to you guys?"

He looked at the serious faces of the two men and smiled.

"I already know what is going on here. I have found out," Dino said, now quite confident. "Someone is trying to fool me. It's a TV show. All those special effects of those monsters and those tiny beings… Today, technology is spectacular…"

Dino looked in various directions, searching for hidden people, and shouted, "Congratulations, everyone, you are all great actors. But this has gone far enough. Put away the hidden cameras. Let's wrap it up!"

The two men looked at each other and laughed.

The younger man held out his hand to Dino. "You are funny! I'm Michael, and this is Petrus." He opened his jacket, showing his bloodstained shirt. "This has been like this for a few days. I don't understand why it still hurts a lot. I got stabbed in a fight while selling drugs on the streets in London. My last memory was of me lying on the pavement. I watched some people around me trying to help and heard sirens. Then I blacked out. I was in the bush near this dirty road when I woke up. I saw newly arrived people being carried away by these monsters. Then, I found a safe cave to hide in on the top of this mountain. From up there, I analysed their movements and devised a plan to get their horses and swords, but I lacked a buddy. That was when I spotted Petrus from afar, beating and knocking down four men who wanted to steal his energy. This is the right guy! Luckily, I carried a pocketknife, which helped us make wooden spears. The fire was not easy to make, but I remembered my school camps."

Dino was now thoughtful, listening.

Petrus vented his frustration. "I didn't have much luck with jobs when I was alive. Before I died, I fought to make money. There was a bookmaker near London. I fought and beat the Thunder, who had been undefeated for three years. With this victory, me and my agent, Robert, earned enough money to start a better life—"

"Robert? Robert Cox was your agent?" Dino interrupted him. "What a coincidence. He's a childhood friend of mine. We met at an orphanage. He always loved games and invested in these street fights for some time. With my contacts' help, I got him released from prison once for involvement in it."

"I don't know about Robert… But I'm sure I was robbed and killed. When I arrived at my flat with a briefcase stuffed with money, I believe someone was waiting for me there. I was very sleepy and tired. So, I lay down on the sofa and blacked out. When I woke up, I was in this hellish jungle. Then I met Michael, who planned to steal the swords and the horses that seemed to be the only transportation around here. We want to search for other, better regions, if they exist."

"I remember now," Dino said. "I was in the back of the car talking to my driver, Little Joe. He must have lost attention when he turned around, offering some sweets he had prepared. He has such culinary talent." He put his hand behind his head and felt the back of his severed skull in detail. "It was a car accident. This is why my head hurts so much… Why do I have this pain if I am dead?"

After a brief pause, he continued, "Well, guys, I'm Bernardino, but you can call me Dino… What the hell is this place?"

"We're still trying to figure it out, Dino," Michael said. "It feels like we are in an eternal Halloween party. People here are horrible-looking. Some approach because they want our energy, while others wander around on the road. Not to mention those monsters in black on their horses. They appear occasionally and seem to dominate the area…"

Michael looked at Dino's clothes and commented, "You must have been wealthy, to have your nice suit and watch. But money, gold, and your expensive watch, which no longer works, are probably worth nothing around here."

"Please don't underestimate me. I am an experienced businessman. Surely, a boss must be around here, so I can talk and negotiate. Who knows, maybe we can offer something in return to get out of this nightmare and go to better places. As you said, Michael, with three, we are stronger. Let's help each other and find a way to get out of here."

"From up where I was," Michael said, pointing at the top of the mountain, "I could see a town at the end of this road. I was afraid to go alone without horses and swords because I would be easy prey. But now, I believe it is our only alternative… If we walk through the woods in that direction, we'll make a safe path and won't be noticed."

They walked through the woods to the town's entrance. The cobblestone streets, with their houses and various small old buildings, recalled London in the late nineteenth century. Many of them were in ruins.

Several people walked through the streets chatting. Most had disfigured or aged faces. Some behaved strangely, laughing loudly, crying, mumbling, or wandering the streets. The most varied clothing showed how long ago those people had left the Earth plane. Ancient clothes from different times and centuries mixed with more recent ones.

Suddenly, nine men appeared in the street, carrying wood, stones, and machetes. They approached the three newcomers and stopped them in their tracks.

"Gentlemen. We don't want any trouble," Dino said, raising his hands. "I am a very influential person, with possessions and strategic contacts… Please, I would like to talk to your leader."

All the men laughed loudly.

Petrus stood in a fighting position and taunted, "You're all ugly runts from hell. We've just liquidated two of those monsters. You are like little children to me."

The men looked at each other, startled, when the fighter mentioned the defeat of the monsters.

Michael positioned himself in front of Petrus. "Gentlemen, put down your weapons. We come in peace."

A man in an antique priest's tunic quickly approached the group, shouting, "Calm down, everyone. Can't you see that these men don't want confusion? Let's not create discord unnecessarily."

The men immediately obeyed the old priest. He seemed to have specific authority in the city.

"Welcome to Llyn Din," the priest exclaimed, with a kind smile behind his white beard. "We are in another dimension just below London." The three men looked at each other in disbelief. "I know you all look astonished, but if you're here, it's because we all have much in common. In other words, it is the same atomic vibration. There are several places where souls go after death, and yours came here."

The priest, who seemed to be of advanced age, looked at the three men. They were thoughtful and stood like statues. Then he suggested, "Let's go to our church, and I will explain better."

He took the new arrivals to a large church nearby. Inside there were no images or paintings of saints, just several improvised wooden benches and a large handmade wooden cross at the back. Despite everything, there was an atmosphere of absolute peace inside. Some people were sitting on the benches in silence. Others were kneeling, murmuring their prayers to themselves.

What was surprising was the dome at the church's top, which gave off a white light with pastel shades of blue and violet that illuminated the church as if a sun were behind it.

"Priest, where does this light come from if the sky is always grey? It's a kind of magic?" Michael asked, admiring the beauty of its colours.

"It's an egregore. The energy comes from higher planes through a portal. On Earth, all serious places of prayer, no matter the religion, have egregores, but they are invisible to human eyes. Occasionally, the strength of an egregore in a small chapel or religious temple is much more powerful than in large buildings. The visitors with their prayers of love are the ones who feed its vibrational force."

A strange man caught my attention. He was medium height, with a long, unkempt grey beard, wearing a dark grey tunic that was old and dirty. When he saw the new visitors enter, he quickly put on his hood and remained at a distance in silence, just listening to the conversation.

"Let's not waste time, priest," Dino said. "I'll get straight to the point. There must have been a serious mistake in my death. I always made generous contributions to the church. There must be an accounting record somewhere. Is there a superior of yours around here that I can talk to about how we can get out of this horror film? I want to negotiate our passage to more pleasant places with beautiful and elegant people."

"You can't choose where to go. It's a physical law. The energy from the Creator," the priest replied in a calm psychologist's voice. "All of you have been drawn here, and—"

"Creator?" Michael said. "What is a religious man like you doing in this filthy place?"

"There are beautiful cities in the astral, but this place is yours for now," the priest stated.

"So… this is hell. Isn't it?" Michael asked worriedly.

The priest laughed, grinning widely. "Gentlemen, we are the ones who create our hells. Without realising it, we are drawn to them. There are thousands of astral cities, and I assure you that Llyn Din is not so bad. I have been in much worse places than here for many years. You must know what is hidden behind appearances, even of religious people. I've been around these lowly regions since 1605."

"Since 1605? That is a long time in this nightmare," Dino commented worriedly.

"I passed away on the Earth plane five years after ordering the burning of living people, those with heretical theories, for that time. For some of these people, the mind of God was infinite and was present in all creatures. We should not look for it in churches but in ourselves. The Earth was also not the centre of the universe as the church preached and many other thoughts that—"

"But you are innocent," Dino said, unconvinced. "You followed what the church ordered you to. The church is like a company where employees are obliged to obey its business rules, even though it may not be what they would like to do."

"Nonsense! That is not how the universe's laws work," the priest explained. "If the person knows the path is wrong and follows it, the consequences will come eventually. That is a personal decision. In my case, I knew that all the theories considered heretical were correct. It was a conscious decision by my colleagues and me. I belonged to an ancient secret brotherhood called the Golden Circle that exists even today. They are controlled by sick souls here in the lower astral plane. We had vast knowledge of magic, radiesthesia, physics, astronomy, and ancient rituals. The few members from countries like England, Italy, France, Germany, and Spain exchanged confidential information. We studied copies of books burned in the Inquisition in secret libraries. Manipulating a spiritually ignorant population is effortless. The dissemination of knowledge has always been a threat to the church's power in Europe. Unfortunately, I made my decision consciously without measuring the consequences. Today, I deeply regret it."

The strange man, with his dark grey hood covering his entire head, was sitting closer. He wanted to listen to the conversation but disguised it, looking ahead as if praying silently.

"But if you have already regretted your actions, why do you remain here in this dreadful region?" Michael asked, concerned.

"Good question, young man. Things don't change so quickly with a simple regret. I have hurt many people in the past. This is engraved in my soul or conscience."

He remained thoughtful for a while, sighed, seeking unpleasant memories, and continued, "One day, I decided to leave the Brotherhood, and they killed me. After I died, I went directly to dark places. I spent months in torment with great mental suffering. My mind was out of control. People that I killed or their relatives persecuted me. Then, I was tortured for years. There are intelligent evil beings who control different territories in all these regions. Knowing who I was, they offered protection and enough energy to free me from that suffering. In exchange, I would have to visit as a ghost, influencing the leading religions and politicians, stimulating limitless power, conflicts, sexual perversion, and domination. That's how the Brotherhood works in both planes."

"Ghost? How can we go back?" Petrus asked, showing much curiosity.

"They have advanced methods to approach those still alive, frequenting their homes and families without noticing. With so much suffering, I almost accepted the offer, but fortunately, I managed to be stronger than the temptation because I knew it was not the right way. I saw some members of the Brotherhood accepting, and today they are like spiritual ghosts who stimulate the minds of several powerful people of the world to obscure paths."

"What do these evil intelligent beings get out of this?" Michael asked.

"Time to be reborn. These regions, like the one we are in, only exist because men themselves, with their spiritual ignorance, kill each other on Earth. Hatred keeps them stronger and stronger until the day comes when the chaos will be so great and the Earth's energy so low that they will manage to be reborn. If there were peace in the world, these regions would not exist. They would all be automatically purged from the planet to others or disappear forever. It's a law of physics."

He paused briefly and continued, "After years of unspeakable suffering, there was a real regret coming from my soul and begging for a chance. One day, in an extremely cadaverous state, I was immersed in a swamp with many others... my mind was going wild. I could not stop thinking about my stupid actions and getting rid of those images. Like a film, they came back from the beginning thousands and thousands of times. I don't know exactly when I felt a hand pulling me, but I was finally rescued from those regions. Bha, an enlightened woman, recovered part of my energy. I would have the mission of going into lower astral cities, spreading the truth about the Golden Circle, and influencing everyone I meet for love, peace, and growth."

"So, this is your mission... that is why you are telling us your experience..." Dino said.

"Yes. I've been doing that ever since, but it isn't easy to convince people to go against their deep-seated dogmas... Contrary to what people think, hatred and addictions don't disappear when we die! Getting rid of our inner demons when we die can take many years or even centuries. What I am proud of is that I have managed to help many people go to much better places. The secret is the simple exercise of thinking differently with our heart and knowing the truths."

"Priest, your story is interesting, but I don't think I deserve to be here," Petrus said, his countenance exuding indignation. "If God exists, he makes unjust laws."

"Well, as I said, you are not in these zones by chance. There is no divine injustice, not even the allegory of an angel who judges your actions. Heaven and hell are within you. Each of you is automatically attracted to a particular place according to the vibration of your astral cells, which are connected to the most profound memories of your soul. It's like a powerful magnet; nothing can change this powerful force of attraction, only you. Follow my advice and reflect deeply on the real reasons for being in these regions. Many people who have listened to me are now in much better places. It may take a few years... but remember that only one person can get you out of here: yourselves!"

The three men stood thoughtfully, looking at the priest, trying to process all that information.

The silence was broken by the sound of horses' hooves coming from far away.

For the first time, the face of the priest showed great concern...

Chapter 14

Katharina and the Witches of Germany

Second life – Mrs Stephanie Puizhant

Germany – seventeenth century

A portal opened beside me, leading me to a forest lit by the moon on a cold night. I could hear voices behind the trees.

I walked a few metres and saw twelve women of various ages sitting in a circle on the grass. Their clothes were from the early seventeenth century. In its centre was an incredible translucent and luminous image of a very tall, thin woman wearing an Egyptian dress from centuries before Christ. The other women were projected out of their bodies. On the ground in front of each of them were long wooden sticks.

"Dear Merit, we are all terrified!" one woman said towards the Egyptian. "The church is persecuting us all over Germany. They are inventing stories that we talk to the devil."

Another woman agreed. "She is right. They also say that the problems with the crops and natural disasters are our fault. They savagely torture women, who confess absurd lies to escape suffering and die faster. The cities of Bamberg and Würzburg are insecure."

"My dear students! Who is afraid of whom?" Merit asked. "Here you have learned to make conscious astral projections, work with plants for healing, and understand the constellations and their influence on life and destinies. You have learned techniques to help other women with their births, even the most complex ones. Women give life to spirits that need to be born on this planet. These will be, at their core, grateful to all of you. You have understood the power of thought, candles, and prayers. The knowledge you have is powerful. It is always directed towards the good and the evolution of this planet. With this wealth of knowledge, in truth, the church is afraid of you all."

"What are they afraid of anyway?" another woman asked.

"Love. They are afraid of love. The Infinite Spirit is pure love. It is the opposite way with men who dominate by force, conflicts, killing, or wars. These attitudes only generate hate. The woman is the true symbol of this great love on Earth. Just look at the mammals, and you will see how a female instinctively loves her offspring. Now multiply that seven billion times. You will still be far from the powerful, loving force of a woman who instinctively welcomes the arrival of a spirit through her womb, which is nothing more than a powerful natural gateway between planes. You have the portals within your bodies."

"They hate us, Merit!" a woman exclaimed.

"Misogyny, unfortunately, was and still is stimulated by powerful dark consciences. Look, for example, at the allegory that the woman was created from a rib. A misrepresentation provokes guilt and inferiority in the woman from a fanciful original sin. Women who helped to celebrate church services were banned, including the celebration of baptisms, which became the exclusive preserve of men. They imprisoned religious women, with restricted access to teachings, developing sexual repression beyond the limits of human nature. They made most women illiterate, with rare opportunities to study, because the noble knowledge leads them to think, especially the most fearful, to teach their children and grandchildren to love."

After a brief pause, she continued in a calm voice, "Ignorant people believe in dogmas. The devil is a dogmatic invention of the Western church to cause fear and thus exercise domination. He has become the perfect personification to create a false relationship with women like you, who are here learning things that a perverse elite does not want you to know."

"But they will kill us!" the woman screamed.

"Die? Nobody dies! Am I dead? The herb mixture I taught you worked, and you're all here now, talking to me in spirit. It is your flesh and bones that sleep in your homes. Death is merely the definitive disconnection from a perishable body made by the elements of nature on Earth. Death is the main fear of humanity, and the lack of clarification about it is a great opportunity for the church to create its dogmas and thus dominate it."

"How does the Infinite Spirit allow this persecution if we only do good things?"

"He allows the total free will of men. This persecution results from the momentary ignorance of the majority, who must understand what is happening on Earth. Many powerful people are influenced by invisible beings from the lower astral, an ancient brotherhood called the Golden Circle. The members of this brotherhood should have been automatically banished from Earth in the early centuries. Unfortunately, they managed to change the course of human history by influencing the free will of powerful men. They are behind a lot of the blood that has been shed so far. The more negative energy, the more power they gain for sixty-six of the evilest souls to be reborn in six different places in the future."

Merit fondly looked at the woman and continued, "I understand you. But if we analyse only the beginning of these first years of the seventeenth century, where you are now, we will think that something is wrong with divine justice. However, what are 1,600 years in an ascending period of 12,000 years of an evolution circle?"

"When will there be peace on Earth?" a woman shouted.

"We don't know. But certainly, Initiates will come many years before the end of the Virgo-Pisces Era to put this world on the right path of love. Many evil souls will be automatically expelled from here by their low cell vibrations and suffer unimaginably. Some will disappear forever. At the same time, with a high vibration of love on Earth, noble souls from other planets will be reborn here to push the revolution even further. Divine justice is simply perfect if we look at the long term. In the distant future, I am certain that most of you will want to be like me, helping other women. Perhaps on another planet or here on Earth, when initiating new races in a new ascending cycle."

She took a moment and then said, "In the distant past, no distinction was made between magic, religion, and science. The segregation was carefully planned by an elite who knew more about the power of magic than you can imagine. The Brotherhood keeps and studies copies of important ancient, burned books in secret places."

"So, the clergy know that our encounters exist, how we come out of the body, what we learn, and that there is no devil?"

"Yes, a small group who belong to the Golden Circle know. This is why they persecute you. The others unthinkingly follow them like a flock of sheep."

"Merit. You have taught us to read the stars and the signs of nature. We already know that dark times will come in the coming days in these southwestern regions. The problem is that most of us have nowhere to hide and nowhere to go—"

"Whatever happens," Merit said, "I will be with each of you in spirit. Remember that good and evil will always be latent within your souls. Using magic for one side or the other depends on each of you; do not succumb to the temptation of following the path of darkness. May the Infinite Spirit always be present. Now you can go back to your bodies." She pointed to a woman and ordered, "Except you, Lydia. I need to talk to you in private."

The women placed their hands behind their necks, cutting the energy from their silver energetic cords so that it would instantly return to their bodies.

Merit looked at Lydia with a serious expression and said, "I am forced to reveal a big secret to you. Unfortunately, this is not the best moment. Your daughter, Elisabeth, is not here with us yet because she is just a few months away from her fifteenth birthday, and she probably never will be. She is a millennial Initiate. If we add the power of you all together, it is only a grain of sand of what your daughter can do if she awakens and develops her abilities. She doesn't realise that her powers are dormant in her soul, and it is safer to stay that way."

"Why?" she asked, astonished.

"The attitudes of humanity in the present entail future consequences. It is they who design their destiny. More than 1,600 years after Christ's death, the Earth was supposed to have a milder vibration, with less hate and much more love. It was planned for your daughter, as an adult, to play an important role in slowly building peace. But the course is heading down the path of darkness. She will be reborn when she can be more useful."

"I don't understand... If she has so much power, why can't she fight against these sick people?"

"Because we don't have time to prepare her. So far, the Brotherhood is winning. Through torture, she may succumb, awaken her powers, and work for the evil that has taken over this world. She has the image of the moon, a tiny birthmark, on the back of her neck. It can only be seen clearly with a lens. However, do not underestimate the bishop's intelligence. If he finds out, he will use her in his evil plans. That is why Elisabeth can't be alive when they capture her. Am I being clear?"

"Yes, clear, Merit," the woman replied, with watery eyes.

"I am deeply sorry for that. Her astral body will remain dormant in a secret place in the Cave of Zugarramurdi. You can visit her there after you die, but she will awaken only when she is needed for the good of humanity. Now you may go, Lydia."

The woman took her wooden stick and put a hand on her head to wake up in her home.

I felt the intense energy of these poor women's anguish, faced with such powerlessness against evil. My eyes were drenched, and my mind invited me to deep reflections.

Merit's luminous image disappeared as a new portal opened beside me. I entered a large room with a high ceiling, beautifully decorated with furniture and paintings. The seventeenth-century decoration showed that this was a noble place. Sitting in the room, in comfortable chairs, were a man and a couple facing him. He had a large wooden cross on his chest, fastened by a cord that matched his dark religious robe. The couple's clothes showed their wealth. She wore a white dress with many embroidered details in beige and gold that went up behind her head, ending in a tiny hat highlighting her delicate face. The man wore a brown shirt with gold buttons and a decorated navy blue jacket.

"Prince-Bishop, as we have already talked to the vicar, my wife wants to denounce someone as a witch who, unfortunately, works in our house. She is also a midwife for these unfortunate and dirty country women."

"I am at your service, Mrs Keller. Please tell me everything you know."

At this instant, I was awestruck when I looked into Katharina's eyes. It was indisputable that, in the depths of that physical body, the conscience that is now Stephanie was alive.

"I was at home when I overheard Lydia, one of my maids, talking to another about her nightly encounters with other women. The door was ajar, and I could hear everything without them noticing… I was terrified of what I heard. She said that the group talked to a woman from Egypt who was adored by all of them."

"It's the devil, Mrs Keller," the bishop said without surprise. "The devil takes different shapes, and the witches worship him." The man moved closer and whispered, "These women even have sex with him… at the same time."

The couple's eyes widened.

The religious man continued, "The midwife witches of the countryside are the most dangerous. They kill some babies to serve as offerings to the devil. We have accessed several reports and confessions from different regions of the continent. You see, the last harvests were a disaster. We have never seen weather conditions so severe. All this is the fruit of witchcraft to overthrow our church and impoverish the population. We must kill them to return to peace."

The woman was wide-eyed and trembling.

"Did she comment on where this meeting was?"

"Somewhere in the woods and sometimes in the hills. But the most frightening thing is that I understood that they fly through the sky in spirit while they sleep after passing something in their bodies."

"Nonsense! It is always the same story. They are very cunning; they talk these fantasies to throw off our church, and we can never get to the right places to arrest them." After a brief pause, he continued. "Does she have a family?"

"She has been a widow for a few years, with two children, a boy and a girl."

"Forgive my indiscretion, but I know you don't have children…"

"We have been trying for some time now," the husband sadly replied, "but Katharina can't give me a child. She had a miscarriage in the first weeks of pregnancy a few months ago. Until then, we were delighted. The doctor, Dr Weyler, said it was normal for this to happen."

"Normal? Of course it is not normal! You are examples of good Christians but with a representative of the devil working in your house. These people are very jealous and will take all your wealth." He took a breath and looked at the couple seriously. "It was witchcraft. She is the one who killed your child before it developed in the womb."

"I imagined it. Murderer. Murderer of children," the woman exclaimed. "What can we do to break the spell?"

"We're going to follow church witch protocol endorsed by the Pope. First, we will torture her to try to find other witches. Then we will burn them alive. Regarding her children, although they are children of the devil, we are pious. We will kill them first, then cut off some limbs before burning them. It's to avoid the suffering of the pain of the flames. Regarding the spell, just as the crops of the last harvest destroyed by the witches will never be born, I do not guarantee that you will still have children. But the most important thing is that faithful people like you, who always make large monetary contributions to the church, are legitimate servants of the

Lord. You are standing here today before the highest ecclesiastical authority in Bamberg and denouncing the devil. This is invaluable to God. I guarantee you will have a special reserved place of peace in heaven."

"Thank you so much, Bishop," the man said, holding up one of his wife's hands. "We'll be much more reassured when this devilish woman is dead."

"Right now, I will talk to the judge to issue an immediate arrest warrant for this witch, Lydia. We will carry out the execution as soon as possible. She will pay for the death of your poor unborn child. I insist that you watch her death."

Katharina nodded with furious eyes. "Yes, we will be there."

I was emotionally disturbed by the dialogue I witnessed. There was a mixture of ignorance and boundless cruelty.

I entered a new portal. What I did not know at that moment was that the worst part was yet to come…

Chapter 15

Dr Gitumed and His Death

Third life – Dr Vincent Gitumed

Vincent came back to his senses. His face was sweating and his eyes were wide open.

He looked at the soldier sitting in the armchair before him and babbled, "Nurse, this medicine you gave me caused a narcotic effect. I had a terrible nightmare. I remember the details of the First World War... I was physically different; I can't explain it... Do you know what I saw in this crazy dream with this drug?"

After a brief pause, he whispered, "I saw myself amputating your feet. Now, I know exactly what the effects of drugs are on those who ingest them. This one I took made my brain believe I died and was born again. This is simply impossible. It would be a cycle of insanity."

"No, Doctor, these are cycles of evolution of our souls. All the experiences of these cycles are recorded in the Universal Intelligence, in a place called the Akashic field. We only have access to those with a true purpose, and always when we are prepared to understand and accept them."

He snickered. "And who provides this access? Your hallucinogenic drugs?" he asked with solid sarcasm.

"We have access as we evolve. It is a physical law. However, in your case, some specific access has been authorised to accelerate this process. This is what happened to you, through the pill I gave you. These images that you have seen are real and have happened."

"Real? It seems very fanciful to believe all this..."

"If you were not here, you would probably still be wandering the streets of London like that man you met at the hospital entrance, deceased two days ago, but still thinking he is alive. This is quite common. There are several of them in all parts of the city. But I have learned that everyone has time to get help."

"It is absurd... But supposing this is true... Why have you stayed here, for so many years, since the First World War, and not come back like me?"

"Good question. I am being more useful around here. I have helped, over these years, those killed in wars and terrorist attacks who arrive confused or with much hate."

"Nonsense... England is not at war."

"There is a team of dead soldiers acting all over the world. We help enlighten souls who leave the Earth in war conflicts... no matter the country, race, religion, or sex, we are all connected to a single Infinite Conscience. The great secret is to love and help each other."

"All over the world? It seems like an impossible, Herculean task."

"Well, the few successes make up for many failures. It is not easy. We must light the flame of love. Thousands of people remain trapped in spiritual ignorance. Only true love buries hate, selfishness, and the evil we create in ourselves without knowing it... By the way, I never had the opportunity to thank you for amputating my feet." The man took off his boots, and there were wooden prostheses a little below his knees. "They could have already repaired them around here in the astral plane, but I keep it like this to show the soldiers who arrive mutilated that I am also one of them. Thank you, Dr Walter."

"Thank you? Sorry, Thomas, that's enough of this nonsense. Please call Dr Sutherland urgently."

"You did an excellent job, Dr Walter. There were no antibiotics or penicillin at that time. I returned home and had the opportunity to be with my wife and see my children grow up for several years. Not only that, after I returned, I was sleeping one night and left my body. When I saw my body there sleeping on the bed... I was dead! But no, in the room was a Chinese man wearing the ancient armour of his army. He told me I was once one of them and that my spiritual mission was beginning—"

"Now a Chinese man appears in your crazy story." Vincent snickered. "This is ridiculous," he mumbled and said to himself, "As far as the fantasy of my mind goes. I must wake up from this hallucination…"

The soldier continued, "He would always come when I was sleeping, take me to visit homes of enemies I had killed in the war. Their families were suffering in their homes, small children were without their parents, and many were in need because of my gun. I realised that I had destroyed the homes of dozens of people. I was emotionally very shaken. Then, I begged him to teach me something to help me make up for my wrong. After this day, he took me to fantastic astral cities. I learned techniques of energy manipulation and detachment through portals. I helped many men who were once my enemies escape dark places where they were trapped. We became friends, and some worked with me in groups of former soldiers. We help those who leave the Earth in these insane war conflicts."

"Nurse… soldiers don't do evil. They obey orders and defend their countries…"

"I thought so, too. It took me a while to understand that soldiers are sent and massacred at the front solely to satisfy the egos and power of a few men. If both sides understood this, there would be no more wars. What power does a tyrannical dictator have without an army? What is worse is that without knowing it, powerful evil consciences manipulate powerful men. If we continue with wars, hatred and violence, the energy of the Earth will be so low that the evil consciences will all manage to be born here and enslave humanity for millennia."

Vincent laughed loudly and shouted, raising his hand, "Stop! That's enough, Nurse… that's enough…" He put his hand on his head and said, "I have fully understood what has occurred to me. I am a doctor. I know that I am in a hypnotic state after being heavily medicated. And most probably, I'm in a deep coma after an injury to my head. This is why I cannot wake up from this dream, which is the most unbelievable I have ever had. I will get up, walk out that door right now, and jump into that abyss, which is a figment of my imagination. It does not exist. And you don't exist, either. Nothing of what I am seeing here is real. I will jump and wake up from the coma."

"I will not stop you, Dr Walter. It is your free will. I have already fulfilled the mission Narquiamides gave me to try to enlighten you."

"Narquiamides? Oh, let me guess… It's your Chinese friend," he said in an ironic tone.

"No, he is a wise man. He is the one who provided me with the pill. He even predicted that you would probably jump after our conversation. But I understand. We had to speed up your memories a lot. I know there is a lot of information for your brain to process in such a short time."

"That's enough! I am alive… Alive!" he shouted, going to the door. "One last observation, Nurse: my name is Vincent. Dr Vincent Gitumed."

Vincent jumped into the abyss, disappearing into the mist. Next to me, a portal immediately opened to follow him.

~*~

I entered somewhere. The fog was making it difficult to see anything.

A few seconds passed, and the fog gradually cleared. I was in a doctor's office in a hospital. Dr Gitumed, wearing a medical apron, was sitting in his chair, sleeping with his arms resting on the table. Suddenly, he was awakened by a tall, grey-haired man wearing a medical apron, who had just entered the room.

"Vincent! Vincent! Wake up! Come with me. I need to show you something."

"Mr Lambert?" He opened his eyes, visibly confused. "I'm sorry, I think I fell asleep! I had a horrible nightmare… what time is it?"

"It's quite late. I want to show the different work I do with patients here some nights."

They chatted as they walked through the corridors of the hospital.

"I did not know that you, as hospital director, still had time to act as a doctor at night."

"Well, I try to balance my time in the twenty-four hours," he said, laughing. "It is love for others that makes us doctors."

Some nurses hurried past, greeting them both.

"Many new people are working at night. I haven't got to know most people's faces," Vincent said.

"It is true; there has been a massive increase in demand at night, and we need more and more people to help."

They passed near a ward, where three nurses were crying, when he heard Daphne's name. He was about to talk to them when the director grabbed him by the arm.

"Let's go. Daphne has had an accident."

"Daphne? An accident? Where is she?"

"She fell from the balcony of her flat. You will be able to see her. She is with other patients in this special work we do."

They entered the upper part of a large room. Sitting on chairs in a circle were fourteen people, seven men and seven women interspersed, of various ages, dressed in white clothes, with eyes closed, backs erect, and palms open on their legs. In the circle, there were about twenty adults of various ages, some standing, others sitting on the floor, some wearing hospital patients' clothes, and others wearing ordinary clothes. Several nurses prevented people from leaving. They complained, wanting to go home.

Without giving Vincent time to question that strange scenario, the hospital director pointed out a woman sitting on the floor in the circle, covered with a blanket on her head. Only part of her face could be seen. A young nurse sat next to her, holding her hand. Her eyes were open but with a faraway look.

Vincent ran and crouched down next to her with tears in his eyes.

"Daphne! What happened?"

Without looking at him, she replied, as if in a deep trance, "Vincent? I'm glad you are here, darling. It's freezing. I think I have a fever. Can you prepare some tea for us in the kitchen?"

The young nurse beside her explained, "She is in a trance. The fall was huge. It is normal after suicide."

"Suicide?" he said, widening his eyes.

Vincent examined part of Daphne's body, where he found bloodstains and obvious injuries from a fatal fall. He looked in more detail at those people in the room, supposedly sick. He saw the man he had bumped into when he entered the hospital.

I recognised the older man in the suit, with his cane, that I knocked over while running with Adhya around the corner from Seikatsu, the Japanese restaurant.

Vincent stood up and looked, startled, at the director, who was watching from outside the circle. The soldier, Thomas, had just entered the room and greeted him from afar… Vincent promptly removed his medical apron and noted his bloodstains. His face now reflected uncontrollable despair. At this instant, a circular white light opened on the room's ceiling, and all the patients floated towards it. The magnetic force was so great that there was no chance to return. Some complained and screamed. Others just let themselves go. Daphne called his name in tears, and he was also sucked towards the light.

The director shouted from afar, “Vincent. I’m so sorry. Many can’t believe they physically died. This is my second job while my body sleeps back home. We assist souls who are stuck on Earth to move on. Physical life is very brief. May God enlighten you on your new journey.”

With great effort, Vincent stretched out his arms and grabbed Daphne’s feet. They were all sucked through that portal of white light, which closed instantly, taking them to different destinations…

Chapter 16

Petrus the Great

First life – Dino

A man entered Llyn Din's church. "Father, the black riders. There are many of them, and they are coming towards the church."

The priest addressed the three newcomers. "Stay here! Do not leave. I will try to solve it in the best way."

He stood outside the church, near the door. The streets were practically deserted. A few people were still running to hide when they heard the horses approaching. There were twelve enormous riders dressed in black from head to toe. They followed two leaders, visibly smaller. They stopped before the church, and one of the two smaller riders removed his hood, showing his face. I immediately recognised him: his long blond hair and handsome look hid a deep evilness. It was Bogat, whom I visualised in the prophecy when the soldiers led by Petrus attacked Yudh.

With his orange eyes, he faced the priest without getting off his horse. "How are you, priest? I've heard you have new arrivals in town… Ah! Let me guess… They are listening to your beautiful stories of love and forgiveness. Confessing their crimes to a murderous priest who betrayed humanity… This is pathetic."

"Bogat, your insults don't get to me. We agreed: inside the city, we are at peace."

"Peace? I decide who gets peace here. Yes, we have an agreement. I protect the city against invaders who could enslave you all. But it lost value when two of my men were annihilated."

"Men? You use black magic on nature's little beings, transforming them into monsters. Soldiers of darkness. Their magic sticks become swords."

"I'm a generous soul," he said sarcastically, getting off his horse and approaching the religious man standing in the church doorway. "Who is the helpless one here, priest? The Earth, the great Gaia, is today the only helpless one! She is the mother who gives life to this imbecilic humanity. And what do they do with their mother? They pollute the air, rivers, seas, burn forests, and explode bombs everywhere. Seeing their Gaia destroyed, I give a real gift to these little beings. I give them the power of revenge."

"Revenge? They are at a different stage of evolution, with no idea what is right or wrong. Using black magic on them is to transgress the universal laws."

"I do this because I know the universal laws." He snickered. "By the way, you are always teaching these ignorant people too much. What a waste of astral time… They don't understand… You know we will soon be reborn and dominate the planet before they destroy it… I want to take the new arrivals hiding inside your old church. Then I'll leave, and we'll get back to our deal."

"The door is open, Bogat; they are inside. Go in and get them yourself."

Bogat headed towards the church door. He took a step to try to enter, but there was such powerful energy coming from within that he could not continue. He took a step back and gave a signal to the other shorter rider coming in front. As he got off his horse and took off his hood, to my surprise, I saw it was a beautiful woman with long black hair. She had white skin and light orange eyes, highlighted by a strong shadow. Between her eyebrows was a red crystal shaped in an inverted triangle.

She looked at Bogat and smiled as if she was communicating with him by thought. He nodded and said, "Priest, we propose a fight. The strongest of them against the best of my riders. If he wins, they will all be free. If he loses, they will all go with me."

The priest was astonished. "A fight? What do you and your witch want with this?"

"My beautiful Lyha and I want to give these primitive men a chance. As I said, I'm a generous soul."

Lyha shouted, “The big guy has already fought for his freedom in another life, and his subconscious knows this. He’s the only chance they have.”

“You are both sick. We are no longer in the Middle Ages. Go away with these bewitched monsters. The newcomers will be protected inside the church.”

“In that case, we’ll take others instead.”

Three monsters appeared on the street nearby, holding three screaming and frightened townspeople.

Petrus, who had been listening to the conversation from near the door inside the church, came out and shouted, “I will fight! But without weapons. I don’t know how to use these swords.”

At this moment, the strange man with the long, unkempt grey beard had come out of the church. He sat down near the entrance.

Bogat looked at Lyha, who smiled mischievously. They went to a square just in front of the church. There were a few ugly trees and colourless grass. A crowd from the town approached to watch the fight. Bogat called over the leader of his monsters. The monster lowered his hood and was hideous like the other two I had seen: bald, big, white-faced, deformed with crooked teeth and orange eyes. He struck a winning pose in the middle of the square with his two strong arms up, and his colleagues shouted euphorically. He was taller and more muscular than his opponent.

The priest approached Petrus and whispered, “Young man, pay attention to what I will tell you before you begin this astral suicide.

These monsters have brutal strength but no agility. They are quite slow. There are two vulnerable points on their bodies: one on the forehead that connects their vision, and the most important one is the nape, where the dark energy enters. Wounding them with objects of astral nature, like wood and tree branches, will help to expel the black magic from their bodies, freeing the little nature beings."

"Thanks for the tip, Father. I will defeat him," Petrus said, looking at his opponent like an enraged bull.

Petrus entered the square and raised his arms, and the townspeople who had approached shouted in support.

The fight began. First, they separated, looking at each other in a fighting position. The monster stepped forwards, moving closer to Petrus, who tried to punch his adversary in the chest, but he did not seem to feel the impact of the blows. Instead, the monster laughed debauchedly and retaliated with a straight punch to Petrus's thorax, with such force that it threw him far away. He fell backwards on the ground. The creature's companions celebrated while the people of the town stood in silence, watching Petrus get beaten. Once again, he was thrown to the ground at the side of a tree.

The monster lifted a gigantic stone. Petrus lay still on the ground, but just before the stone was thrown in his direction, he rolled to the side, letting it crash down. Quickly, he stood up and began to punch the monster in the face, aiming exclusively at its forehead, as the priest had instructed. The habitants now shouted Petrus's name in euphoria, encouraging him to fight more bravely. Everyone could see the determined face of the fighter, who managed to bring his fists to the place indicated by the priest.

The monster began wandering, punching the air instead of hitting his opponent. He ended up hitting a tree, which shattered. Petrus picked up one of its branches from the ground, and he stabbed the branch into the monster's nape. The being of darkness stopped and, like a giant tree being felled, toppled to the ground, making a loud noise.

The crowd of the city shouted in celebration. Petrus raised his arms in a victory pose. Then everyone fell utterly silent as attention turned to the fallen monster. Exactly like what happened to the first two, he turned into black dust, blown away by the wind. A little white-haired man, with a big nose, big ears, and big feet, appeared in its place. With a peaceful countenance, he opened a hexagonal portal with his hands where a beautiful garden could be seen. However, before entering, he looked around, searching for something.

Lyha went towards the loser's horse. She took a wooden stick, which a few seconds ago was a sword, and handed it to the little man. He stepped into the portal, which instantly closed.

I was stunned to witness the unexpected attitude of that perverse woman. What had she done? I realised that in the laws of the universe, there are situations where wickedness, when overcome, must respect certain limits.

Petrus looked at Bogat and shouted, "Get out of here! We won. We are free of you and your witchcraft."

Bogat gave a slight smile. At that exact moment, Lyha approached Petrus. She ran her hand over his muscular arms and said seductively, "Of course, this was the deal, dear. You are a warrior, strong and brave, who has lived many lives. You were a Roman gladiator, one of the Crusades' commanders, hailed by the Pope, and took part in other fights and wars… But your last life was so mediocre… You won a great fight and earned lots of money but were unfortunately murdered and robbed…"

"Don't listen to her," the priest advised. "Lyha is a powerful witch."

"Murdered? What else do you know?" Petrus asked curiously.

"I know everything. You beat your greatest opponent, called Thunder, but you were robbed. Your poor little son, so beloved, will be left without a penny. Here in this dirty city, your strength will grow weaker and weaker, your energy will diminish, and your astral body will slowly rot." She put her mouth close to his ear and whispered, "Every day and night for tens of astral years, you will wonder: who killed me? It's a pity you won't have any chance for revenge…"

"Let's go, my pretty one. He is a loser," Bogat said, turning her back and heading towards his horse. "He doesn't want revenge. Let him stay there and pray and rot with this priest. It is a pity. I also thought we were facing a great warrior, but I was wrong."

"Don't fall for this, Petrus," the priest shouted. "It's a trap. They want to use you, forget what happened on Earth. Whoever you need to forgive. That's—"

"Forget? Forgive?" Petrus exclaimed. "Look at you. Look at these people living in this ugly city. Where is your merciful God, priest?"

"You don't understand. We are not here by chance; it is a process—"

Petrus interrupted the priest again, turning to Lyha. "I want to know what happened to me and get my revenge. What do I have to do?"

The witch smiled and explained, "First, you must bring an object from the Earth plane. We can send you back there for a short time."

"What object?"

"You will know. Just follow the instructions you will receive when you arrive there."

"I will go alone?"

"We can't go to the Earth plane yet; only dead people like you or a few witches and wizards with specific powers can go. When you come back, we are going to plan your revenge. You will love it… Let's start your journey now."

Many people in the city were watching. The black riders positioned themselves in a circle, leaving only Lyha and Petrus in the middle. Bogat, with his sarcastic smile, was following the ritual from outside.

The fighter lay on the ground with his eyes closed while the witch sat by his head. She took a vial with red liquid from her pocket and drew a circle with a triangle inside pointing downwards on Petrus's forehead. She held the man's head so that her thumbs were positioned at the top two vertices of the triangle. She uttered words in a strange language. Then, the monsters raised their swords to forty-five degrees and repeated the words.

The priest turned to Michael and Dino. "Unfortunately, the black magic ritual has begun. So, it was Petrus that Bogat and Lyha wanted all along… They can't go to the Earth plane any more because of the dense vibrations of their astral bodies, much less their monsters. That's a physical law. But they can send our astral bodies to work for them. Nothing is better than conquering an atheist newcomer with strong energy, egocentrism, much war experience, and a thirst for revenge. He is the ideal link they need for their nefarious plans."

Dino asked, concerned, "What are these plans?"

"To be reborn and dominate Earth. After rescuing me from the swamp, Bha told me that Bogat and Lyha were from an old, distant planet with Earth-like conditions. Here in the Earth's astral, they promised to use their advanced knowledge of magic to help the little beings of nature in the evolution of our humanity. Unfortunately, when they witnessed the Earth's population destroying nature without limits, they gave up their noble mission. They sought power by joining the Golden Circle and expect someday to be reborn."

After pausing, he continued, "I, unfortunately, cannot criticise them. The temptation of power has blinded me, too."

Dino became thoughtful, his expression mixing astonishment with an inevitable self-reflection. He seemed to understand exactly what the priest had just said.

Meanwhile, the ritual of magic continued. The witch sat motionless in a state of meditation. Her orange eyes were turned completely upwards towards the red crystal on her forehead. Her hands remained on Petrus's forehead. The fighter's body began to disappear and became translucent.

The priest explained to Michael and Dino, "Your friend is no longer here. What you see is just a sort of double of his astral body. He is already somewhere on Earth, receiving Lyha's commands."

Michael was wide-eyed. "We are just watching passively. Can we do anything to stop this?"

"No, young man. We can't interfere in this way. The evil won one more time," the priest replied.

A portal opened beside me to follow Petrus on Earth's plane in his mysterious mission...

Chapter 17

The Execution

Second life – Mrs Stephanie Puizhant

After going through the portal, I found a stone spiral staircase. As I climbed it, I could hear the voices of a crowd of people outside. When I reached the top, I realised I was in the same spot where Stephanie had passed out and been captured, but in another era. It was the seventeenth century, and Katharina stood beside her husband, the bishop, and the vicar of the city of Bamberg. Unlike the storms of the astral plane, there was a feeble sun, which hid behind some clouds, illuminating the courtyard. The crowd of people wore simple clothes. In the centre of the square was a tall stake, with several pieces of wood leaning on it in a forty-five-degree position.

A soldier with a uniform and swords joined the group. The bishop looked at him and whispered, "How did the interrogation end?"

"She did not denounce her witch friends, even under the severest torture, but she confessed exactly what Mrs Keller exposed to you. Insisting that she was part of a group of good people who believed in God and that there was no devil. We didn't believe a single word."

"Yes, she is possessed. It's the devil talking inside her, trying to make a fool of us. Have you found any birthmarks?"

"No, we searched her entire body and didn't find any."

"What about her children with the devil?"

"We found the girl, Elisabeth, hiding in the back of her house. However, she took a poisonous liquid on seeing us, falling dead almost instantly. As for the boy, we did not find him. He must be hiding in some house belonging to these country people. We are hunting him. At the same time, we've already identified other witches and children."

"That's good news."

"We are torturing the witches to get more information and have already killed their children. We will throw their remains into the flames immediately after the new witch is burned."

The crowd's attention in the square turned to a woman with a headscarf, wearing a simple outfit covered in bloodstains. She was barefoot, limping slowly towards the wooden stake. It was Lydia, with her hands chained, escorted by two soldiers, one carrying a long lit torch. She was followed by a religious man holding a large cross and an elegantly dressed man with some papers.

At that moment, I cried copiously, witnessing such cruelty. But Lydia's physiognomy impressed me most, which transmitted an incredible peace. Her eyes turned to the sky, ignoring the crowd screaming "death to the witch", which began incessantly.

Hidden among the crowd, I could identify a few people struggling to hold back their dangerous tears, as they might give away their affection for Lydia. The woman was tied to the stake, and her gaze, which had been focused on the sky, suddenly turned to Katharina, who was watching the ceremony.

"I forgive you, Mrs Keller!" Lydia shouted; the crowd became silent, listening to her. "You don't know what you are doing. There is no devil. We don't kill babies. The church is the real killer. We are not evil. We—"

Furious at those unexpected words, the bishop shouted, "Don't listen to her. She is possessed. The devil is speaking to deceive us." He looked at the soldiers in the square and ordered, "Shut this witch up and set her on fire immediately."

Obeying the order, one soldier gagged Lydia with a piece of cloth. Seconds before the other soldier, with the torch, could set fire to the wood around the stake, a boy emerged from the crowd with a piece of wood in his hands. He struck the soldier in the face, who fell to the ground, dropping the lit torch.

"Leave my mother alone, murderers!" the boy shouted.

Unable to speak, Lydia looked at the scene with emotion, making a few sounds and head movements in disapproval.

Soldiers grabbed the boy and immobilised him, with the help of other soldiers who had just arrived.

The fallen soldier's face was bloodied. He got up, staggering with rage, and picked up a nearby axe with a wooden shaft and an iron tip. The boy was restrained on the ground by other guards. With a shout of rage, the man cut off one of the boy's arms.

With a face of immense pain, the boy, lying on the ground, looked at the fire that began to consume his mother's body; she did not utter a single moan. As if it were a trophy, the soldier lifted the boy's amputated arm with his hands and threw it to be burned with his mother.

Most of the crowd watched this brutal scene, shouting, "Death to the witch." The boy unexpectedly stood up, but with difficulty without one of his arms. His eyes showed an intense hatred. At that instant, a silence reigned in the place.

With the same gesture I had witnessed in the astral world, he pointed the index finger of his only hand at Katharina, who was now watching with her eyes wide open. "Revenge! Revenge!" he managed to shout twice, before falling unconscious to the ground.

The bishop stood up again in significant irritation at the scene, which shocked the spectators, and ordered, "Bring all the dead children's bodies now, friends of this son of the devil. We will send them to hell with him."

Katharina watched all that calmly, exuding a specific relief. She couldn't imagine that the anger of those young people would last for centuries.

At that moment, I wanted to get away from there. Knowing truths about our world history, reading a book in a quiet café in London, or watching a film in a cinema is impactful enough. But being immersed in history, living and feeling up close to this human suffering, knowing these were all scenes with real people... That was too much for me. That was enough! I wanted to leave that place immediately. I couldn't watch children's bodies being burned...

~*~

As if someone had read my pleading thoughts, I entered a room beside me through a new portal, leaving that stage of barbarism. I was on the upper floor of a finely decorated mansion with seventeenth-century paintings and tapestries. Seated in a comfortable armchair before a large window, Katharina enjoyed the sun, which fed the plants in the house's front garden.

"Mrs Keller, here's your juice. You need to feed this growing baby," the maid said, leaving a glass on a small table next to the woman.

Without looking at or thanking the maid, she stretched out her arm and reached for the glass. She continued her relaxation, taking the drink. Her maid showed a certain nervousness. As soon as the maid left the room, she closed the door, and a man was in the hallway.

"She's drinking, Dr Weyler," she whispered.

"Take it. I won't need this any more." The man handed her a small, dark cloth bag. "You have enough money for your family to escape safely to the south. Go now!"

The man entered the room quickly without knocking, locked the door, and put the key in his pocket. Katharina looked back, her eyes widening in fright.

"Dr Weyler? What… what a surprise." Her expression was a mix of fear and tension. "I thought you were travelling."

"I came back ahead of schedule," he stated, with a hateful face.

Katharina got up and tried to run towards the door, but she fell to the floor, without strength, remaining with her eyes open and unable to speak. The doctor approached the window. Through it, he could see the maid, with her husband and two children in a cart pulled by two horses, leaving at high speed.

"Do you know what poison is, Mrs Keller? It's a kind of medicine with the wrong doses." The man took two small glass bottles out of his pocket; one was empty, and the other was full. He placed them both next to the half-full glass of juice. "This one I gave you affects the brain. It gives a temporary paralysis in the body; you cannot move, speak, or scream, but you can hear me for the few minutes you have left before you die."

The man stood near the window while talking to the pregnant woman lying on the floor. She was making meaningless sounds with her mouth.

"You and your husband knew about my journey, but you may not have known all the details I will tell you now. Because I am a doctor, I had free access to the prison. My hidden personal goal was to understand what was going on with this insane persecution of dozens of women the church called witches. I saw up close their suffering, cruelly tortured. I took down the statements of several of them before they died. They swore they knew nothing about devils, macabre sexual encounters, or flying brooms."

He took a breath, looking out of the window, and continued, "For their death to come faster, they were obliged to confess the most absurd things. There were cases of some who ended up denouncing friends and neighbours, even though they knew it was a lie. In tears, they were sorry and asked God for forgiveness because the tremendous pain of torture was what allowed such irrationality."

The woman groaned and tried in vain to crawl slowly to the door. Her wide-open eyes reflected dread and despair, while the man beside the window kept talking.

"I prepared a long report about everything I had heard and presented it to the judge of Bamberg. To my surprise, he was furious and asked me to burn it immediately. Otherwise, there would be serious consequences for me. Even though I was threatened, I travelled to take the case personally to the Emperor. I aimed for all the guilty parties to be judged and sentenced by the highest court. Unfortunately, he did not receive me, but after much insistence, I managed to speak to his representative, who only said that he would analyse my report… At that moment, I realised that my long journey had been wasted. Nowadays, those imbeciles are only concerned about whether you are Catholic or Protestant."

After a pause, he looked more intently out the window and continued.

"Well, I came back ahead of schedule. When I got home, a neighbour told me my wife and daughter had died. They were accused of witchcraft and killed, and I had to flee as soon as possible because I had also been sentenced to death for having made a pact with the devil. Desperate and without knowing where to go, I went to the house of a friend I trusted to get more details. And what did I find out? I found out that you and your husband were the key witnesses. You said witchcraft probably killed your baby right at the beginning of your last pregnancy. I had already explained that it was just a miscarriage and that it was normal… With this testimony, the court concluded that it was me, with your ex-employee Lydia, who was burned, plus the devil – that we killed your foetus. To compensate for your loss, half of my goods will remain with your family and the other half with the church. Finally, I realised how naive I had been and decided to take justice into my own hands."

At this moment, through the window, he spotted soldiers who had arrived with her husband. "He's up there!" one man shouted.

The doctor gave a little smile as if he wanted to be seen. He took a surgical instrument from his pocket and crouched down near the woman. He grabbed his victim's hair, lifting her head, making her neck more visible, while shouts could be heard from the soldiers entering the house and going up the stairs.

"I don't believe in the devil, Mrs Keller, but if he exists, your house is one of his homes."

He cut the woman's throat, dropping her to the floor as the soldiers tried to break down the door. He took the other small, full glass vial on the table and drank from it. Then he opened the window, with difficulty. The strong dose of poison was already acting fast. As soon as the soldiers entered, he let his body fall, hitting the ground in front of the house.

All those sequences of scenes since poor Lydia's execution had shaken me deeply. I managed to remove the crystal from my forehead. For the first time, I ignored a portal that opened beside me.

I saw Katharina lying dead in a pool of blood… pregnant, and her husband crying in despair. The crystal was in my hands. Instead of entering through the portal, I hurried out of the house. Near the front door, I saw the doctor's body; his beloved family had been killed. My heart was beating so fast that I could feel it…

Then, I continued running through the field without direction until I stumbled and fell into the grass. I wanted a few minutes before I put the crystal back on my forehead to continue the λ3 experiment.

I needed air, the sun, the wind…

I sat down and looked up at the sky.

I cried…

I cried for the atrocities of humanity in the past…

I cried for the atrocities of humanity nowadays…

I cried for all of us…

Chapter 18

The Proposal

Third life – Dr Vincent Gitumed

One week before the accident

A portal led me to a large auditorium in a famous Paris hotel. Doctors and scientists applauded Vincent for his lecture from his field of oncology. He left the hall and sat in the hotel bar with his friend.

"Congratulations, Vincent! Let's celebrate. I am happy for the recognition of your work."

"No, Charles, I should be the one to thank you. I would not be here without your company's financial help in my research."

"It's the business world, Doctor. We need each other to grow, and more importantly, millions of patients taking our medicine worldwide." He laughed loudly. "Listen, the company wants to open a high-relationship executive position, and the board is unanimous on your name." He took an envelope from his pocket. "Here is the proposal. The remuneration and benefits are spectacular, certainly much more than you earn today in that hospital."

"Executive of a pharmaceutical company? I had never thought of such a position before..." he said, opening the envelope.

"Then start thinking."

"It is a tempting remuneration. Do you want to retire me early?" Vincent said, not hiding his smile as he visualised the figures. "It's quite a lot of money. What specifically do you expect from me?"

"Well, we need a recognised doctor who interfaces with governments, regulatory agencies, and opinion-forming local doctors."

"That's it?"

"It is not so simple. We have new anti-cancer drugs to be released, and their components and effects are a challenge for approval by regulatory agencies. There is also a secret new drug related to exposure to nuclear weapons."

"Nuclear weapons? That is weird..."

"It is a billionaire market. We have the drug to give immunity to and a cure for nuclear radiation. A famous physics laboratory in London helped us develop it."

When I heard this, I remembered that where I worked, in the laboratory's basement, there was a shielded area with restricted access because of tests on equipment that emitted radiation for medical use.

"This drug will be only for NATO countries, I suppose."

Charles gave a little smile and said, "Not necessarily. Regardless of the country, every little child in the world deserves protection. Your mission as a doctor is to save lives. Do you agree?"

"Yes… sure. Sorry, I just—"

"Our business has no borders. You will travel to any country that pays for our medicine. You will have a senior team that will arrange the meetings, lunches, and dinners… We always find ways to thank the people who help us, in private, if you know what I mean…"

"Yes… I understand. I can imagine how the business at this level works…"

"Exactly. A lawyer will always travel with you. He will act behind the scenes… That's what I can tell you for now. You will find out the details after signing the NDA."

He took a slow sip of his drink and continued, "Vincent, we met a few years ago. You are a successful, intelligent, articulate, and charismatic man. You have all the potential to become a millionaire with us, mainly because you have a great quality: ambition for power. Power is what opens the doors of this world."

"Then towards power," Vincent replied, raising his glass, not hiding his contentment.

Charles looked around, checking to see that there were no other guests nearby at other tables in the bar. Then he said in a low voice, "There is a delicate matter that we can't put in the contract. But I need to know if you agree before we proceed." He took the proposal out of Vincent's hands and stored it back in the inside pocket of his suit. "If you disagree, no problem. Our friendship remains the same. I tear up this proposal, and we never had this conversation..."

"Delicate matter?" he asked with curiosity.

"We are talking about a big business, and we don't waste our money, Doctor... I know that you are in a relationship with a nurse at the hospital. Unfortunately, we don't see her as up to accompanying you on this new journey. You must start a relationship with an important, cultured, socially known woman, project yourself like a rocket beside her, and be a compelling couple. We can arrange this romance. We already have a name, and she has already approved you. She is divorced, without children, and we are helping her in her political career that is on the rise."

Vincent made an astonished face upon seeing the photo of the woman, whom he already seemed to know, on Charles's phone. "Wow. Is that her? She's always in the media spotlight giving interviews—"

"Yes," he said. "It won't take long for her to be tipped to be the prime minister of the United Kingdom. She will have a lot of our financial support. But she also urgently needs a husband accepted by society for her ascension. We cannot have a divorced prime minister. And the most essential thing is that she approves of you. We sound out women first; they are very sentimental, you know." He laughed loudly.

"Would it be a fake marriage?"

"Yes. But this is up to you… This verbal agreement is precisely the length of our contract, at least five uninterrupted years together. With her, the door to any country will be open for you. After this period, if you like, you can divorce… I don't believe it. She is an attractive, intelligent woman, and you have great ambition in common. I think you'll get along within the four walls…" He winked maliciously.

"But, Charles, if something occurs, and we have to divorce—"

"Vincent, we're old friends, and I'll be straight to the point. Much of your success is thanks to us. We helped build your excellent image… Please don't take this as a threat, but our board of directors gets angry when any verbal agreement is broken ahead of time. We are part of the Brotherhood of the Golden Circle, with connections in many countries. To destroy your image, or this woman's, is easy. She also knows that. All it takes is one phone call to a hacker company that works for the Golden Circle. They control thousands of fake social media profiles all over the world. Any little false story will become a truth quickly… The most interesting thing is that people love these stories, like vultures after carrion. Your fortune will be eaten up by lawyers trying to defend you. At the very least, it will end your career as a doctor. A great deal of money is on the table. We need to protect ourselves. Do you understand, my friend?"

“Yes, I understand… I’m in. This opportunity is way beyond my relationship with Daphne. Five years go by fast…”

“Excellent. Next week we will go to your office to close the details… Towards power.” He smiled, raising his glass again.

They were interrupted by the approach of a young man with long brown hair and a thin beard. With the anxiety of someone who cannot miss a golden opportunity, he said, “Dr Gitumed! Dr Gitumed! Do you have a minute? I want to talk to you about my research.”

Vincent looked at the boy, who spoke English with a strong French accent.

“What is your name?” the doctor asked. “Are you a medical student?”

“My name is Ethan. I am a physics student. I came here in person because I have already sent many emails to you with no reply, and I also tried to contact you by phone, and—”

“I receive a lot of them,” the doctor said. “Maybe my secretary has filtered them out… but what can I do for you?” He pointed to one of the chairs at the table for him to join them.

“I am developing studies that directly link to the area of oncology in which you are a specialist.” The young man gave a sigh, accessed some images on his phone, and continued, “Look at this map, for example. I have identified, through radionics, water veins in the ground—”

The man from the laboratory interrupted him. "Radiesthesia? Sorry, Dr Gitumed has no time for pseudoscience..."

"Let the boy finish, Charles..."

"Thank you, Dr Gitumed." He sighed again. "From what I have studied, there is a subatomic degree where diseases start. It can be detected through radiesthesia before it manifests in the physical body. I have verified that the contact of radiation from contaminated water on the ground hits these subatomic particles, and they develop initial tumours, which are impossible to detect by any traditional examination—"

Vincent stopped him with a sceptical look. "Tumours from contaminated water on the ground?"

"They are in many places, especially in big cities. To build cathedrals in the medieval era, right here in France, they were already measuring the energy of the waters even before they were built. It is ancient knowledge that has been lost."

"Sorry, I am not interested." Vincent snickered. "That's the most absurd thing I've ever heard..."

The young man quickly took a photo from his pocket. "Do you remember this boy, Doctor?"

Vincent looked at the photo without touching it. "I'm not certain. I believe it was one of my patients..."

"Nathan is his name. He is my younger brother; he came to England last year for treatment with your team. After weeks in the hospital, they sent him home and gave him a maximum of two months to live."

"Yes, I remember it perfectly now. I am sorry to hear of your brother's passing—"

"Nathan," Ethan shouted. A boy of around fifteen, who had been sitting in a far armchair, approached the group.

The boy looked remarkably healthy. Vincent's eyes were wide.

Ethan continued, "When he returned to France, I convinced my parents to stop your costly medicines because they caused a strong side effect… We had to sell our family house to pay for your whole treatment. I took several measurements and used metallic stones, crystals, and radiesthesia charts to isolate the telluric energies. Finally, I started my 100 per cent natural energetic treatment with specific food supplements such as vitamin D. Last week, he went to a doctor in Paris, and the tumour has disappeared. He is 100 per cent healthy."

Seeing his future executive's astonished expression, Charles intervened. "Young man, this happens in medicine daily. Some get saved, and others die following the same protocol. We are not gods to judge who should or should not live. Doctors do not make miracles. They only provide diagnoses based on science, which is exactly what happened to your brother. Isn't that right, Vincent?"

Vincent didn't answer. He just kept looking at the boy as if he were seeing a ghost in front of him.

"Dr Gitumed," Ethan said, "nobody wants to listen to me here in France. I want to share my discoveries with you, a recognised authority on the subject, who is the key witness to my brother's cure. I don't want fame or money to tell the world that sometimes natural solutions are better than expensive medicines. Could you please help me?"

Charles answered while Vincent was thoughtful. "Ethan, I know exactly what happened. These homemade experiments certainly provoked a strong placebo effect in your brother. The power of the human brain is a still unknown universe. In rare cases, people mysteriously heal themselves. Every day, we see people around the world cured only by prayers. What you have done is esotericism or witchcraft. True doctors must defend science. They cannot go along these lines of alternative medicine, and they will certainly have their career and reputation destroyed; isn't that right, Dr Gitumed?"

"Yes… he's right, Ethan. I'm sure it was a placebo effect. I'm pleased to see your brother healthy, but I can't get on board with miracles…"

"Now, please excuse us!" Charles stated in an authoritative voice.

The young physicist stood and said, before walking away with his brother, "You were my last hope, Dr Gitumed. At the very least, I had hoped that you would take an interest in reviewing my notes. I thought you cared about saving people…"

A little later, Charles asked to be excused for a few minutes because he needed to make a private call. Outside the bar, he talked on his phone to someone else. "It's me. We have one more who has discovered an alternative cure. It's a boy, a meddling French physics student. He managed to cure his sick brother, a terminally ill patient of Vincent's. After our conversation, I think he'll give up. Anyway, I'll get his data and send it to you as soon as possible. We need to monitor him and act if necessary..."

When I looked for the hotel bar, it had already disappeared. In its place was a portal that provided access to a narrow cave, which invited me to explore it.

I walked forwards. It was cold and humid, and there was an unpleasant smell. The lighting was dim, coming from some rocks that seemed to glow. There were other paths in various directions, like a labyrinth.

Suddenly, I heard Vincent's voice coming from one of them. As I approached, I saw the doctor kneeling beside Daphne, trying to communicate with the her as she lay on the rock floor, entirely still, wide-eyed as a scarecrow.

"Daphne... I'm so sorry..." he wailed in tears.

Footsteps and voices were coming towards him. He got up quickly and hid in a hole behind a rock.

It was a couple pushing a silver trolley containing a sizeable cylindrical tube made of a material that resembled aluminium. Both had white skin and orange eyes and were wearing black aprons. The symbol of the Brotherhood of the Golden Circle was drawn on their clothes. They stopped before Daphne's body, and the man said to the woman, "We're in luck today. Another suicidal newcomer. I'll hold her while you draw power from her."

The woman, wearing black gloves, picked up a small silver cylindrical tube with a needle on the end. It had a hose connected to the large cylinder on the trolley. The man held Daphne, sitting on the floor with her head forwards.

As Vincent watched the scene, a hand grasped his heel. When he looked back, he saw a young man lying there. His mortal body was infested with astral worms. With trembling effort and in a low tone, the man managed to whisper a single word: "Help…"

Vincent released his leg from the cadaverous young man's hands, jumped, slipped, and fell on the damp stone floor of the cave. The couple with Daphne immediately saw him.

"We have an intruder in the suicide caves. Intruder!" The man's shout echoed.

The doctor got up and ran aimlessly through the labyrinth, chased by the couple. He reached the end of one of the pathways but there was no way out. It was in a gigantic underground mountain, at a height like that of a twenty-storey building. An abyss divided the two parallel hills. On both sides were hundreds of caves connected by these narrow paths, as if they were an extraordinary beehive.

The couple had already spotted him; he was cornered.

"You'll regret being here," the man said, walking towards the doctor.

Vincent looked more closely down, and about five metres away, a small ledge provided access to another cave. It was his only chance. He knelt and hung by his hands until he got loose and managed to fall, but he twisted one of his feet. He got up with a pained expression and continued walking fast, but with incredible difficulty. Sinister voices and laughter came from different directions and got closer and closer.

"Someone help me! Please! Please! Thomas!" the doctor begged desperately.

An intense light appeared in the tunnel where he was standing, about 300 metres ahead. He went as fast as he could towards it, and I followed him. His pursuers, now several of them, were getting closer and closer. He made it through the light. It was a portal that closed instantly behind us.

We were in a city in ruins, which seemed to have been destroyed during a war.

He walked down the street. The city appeared to be completely deserted, but it wasn't…

Chapter 19

The Astral Sword

First life – Dino

Even after Petrus's astral body disappeared, leaving only his translucent image, Lyha remained seated, as motionless as a rock. Her orange eyes turned upwards, and she held the fighter's head firmly.

I entered a new portal, and I found myself next to Petrus. It was night, and he was lying on a path next to a river. The witch could communicate with him through thought, and I could hear her.

He stood up and said, "Where am I? I am alive again." He smiled. "I'm back. I'm reborn!"

"No, my dear, only your astral body is temporarily travelling on the same frequency as the physical plane."

"Same frequency?" he asked, confused.

"Never mind... Hurry because I cannot keep you with this vibrational level long."

"It doesn't feel like London here..."

"No. It is Paris at 3 a.m., and you are near the Seine River, next to the Louvre Museum. That is where we will go now. A warrior must first prepare for battle. I cannot explain now, but you will soon understand. I will guide you. Make sure you follow my instructions exactly. Otherwise, your revenge on your murderer will never happen."

"OK, what do I have to do?"

"Climb the stairs at the side and walk towards the museum. The few people awake on the streets or human guards cannot see you. The power to see dead people is rare on Earth. However, you must be careful with astral protectors."

When Petrus made his way to the museum, he saw an impressive scene: a sleeping crowd clustered near the glass pyramid where the museum's main entrance was. Some were wandering the large square.

By the small lights on their necks, I realised that the majority were projected out of their body, sleeping deeply somewhere on the planet, totally unconscious of where they were.

Some vibratory affinity attracted these people to this famous museum when they slept. There were also dead people. Some wore old clothes from different times, and they wandered around everywhere with their ugly faces.

The clothes of the sleepers were the most varied possible. Many were in pyjamas, others in social clothing, suits and ties with work bags, sportswear, and shorts. Some laughed loudly in small groups;

others shouted that they wanted to enter to get their objects, and others said they had an important job to do inside…

"You can pass through glass and walls if you fix your mind to it," Lyha instructed. "Remember that your body is no longer solid with Earthly atoms."

"I'm a ghost." He laughed.

"Yes… Unfortunately, all the museum doors and walls are energised by the protectors. Everything is carefully blocked, from the side buildings to the entrance of the main pyramid. This prevents all these out-of-body and dead people from entering the museum. But the smaller pyramid, on the right-hand side, which acts as a skylight, will be your entrance door."

Indeed, with the walls and doors energised, most of the sleeping people, with their bodies projected, would give up entering and walking around the square, grumbling and disappearing, probably going back to bed in their homes. Those who remembered something would perhaps find the experience to be some absurd dream.

Near the main entrance, two protectors dressed in white stood out. They were very tall, one with white skin and long hair and the other black with a shaved head and a beard. Both stood near the entrance door in total silence, just watching the crowd that tried in vain to enter the museum from all sides. It seemed that they were used to that mess every night.

Petrus followed the witch's instructions, mingling with dozens of people walking around the square.

When he approached the small pyramid, he touched the glass. "I can't go through," he whispered. "It's solid."

"Keep calm. A friend who lives on Earth will help you. Follow his instructions," the witch said.

An old man, projected out of his body, with a long beard and a black hooded cloak, approached, came very close to the fighter, and whispered, "We have been expecting you, Petrus. You will go through this pyramid – jump inside after my signal. Your astral brain is still conditioned, and that's why you cannot get through glass or walls. But you are no longer solid on this physical plane. Not even me. My physical body is sleeping in Scotland. I'm now projected like these imbeciles walking around in pyjamas. The difference is that they don't know that. Now place one of your hands on the glass and repeat in a low voice without stopping: 'I am not solid; I pass through walls.' Repeat until I give the signal."

"I am not solid; I pass through walls," Petrus said falteringly.

"Where's the warrior inside you? Repeat low, but with more vibration, for sure. Let's go. Do you want your revenge or not?" the old man said, looking into Petrus's eyes like a coach encouraging a competitor to take to the field and defeat his opponent.

"I am not solid; I pass through walls," Petrus kept repeating, with increasing conviction.

The white-bearded man took out a necklace from inside his clothes. It was a round golden talisman about nine centimetres in diameter. On the object was the symbol of the Brotherhood of the Golden Circle: the inverted pentagram surrounded by a golden circle. In its centre, there was an inverted triangle of bright red colouring. He kept it hanging around his neck, holding it with his left hand and placing the other on the glass next to Petrus. He began to utter words in a strange language. His eyes turned whitish and upwards. The triangle glowed brightly as if it were a light.

"Jump now! Now!" the man ordered.

Petrus's hand went through the glass and he jumped into the museum. The man hid the talisman around his neck and continued walking, blending into the crowd and leaving the square.

Some people walking nearby saw Petrus go through the glass into the museum. They shouted in fright and drew the attention of the protectors. The white-skinned protector with long hair ran towards the small pyramid and examined it; it seemed to be in order. Some people even pointed to it, saying that someone had entered. He signalled to his shaved-haired friend and entered through a part of the pyramid's glass.

I entered a portal that opened beside me. I was in the museum, running with Petrus.

"Run as fast as you can," Lyha ordered. "I see through your eyes."

The witch guided Petrus through the vast museum, passing through several rooms and going through walls. He reached a room where a beautiful sword stood out in a glass dome. Its silver blade contrasted with its carefully decorated golden hilt. The scabbard was also golden, with nine precious stones, which had undoubtedly belonged to someone important.

"Take the astral sword and its scabbard."

Petrus put his arm through the glass and pulled out the astral sword: an identical replica, invisible to human eyes.

He looked carefully at the astral sword in his hands. I could see images arriving in his mind: an avalanche of memories from other lives was now like a snapshot download of countless films with struggles and wars. There were so many scenes that I could barely follow the details.

He felt the sword's power; it had found its owner again.

"A great wizard forged this sword. The astral one lay dormant for centuries beside the physical one. Only a true warrior who has used it before could free it. You are the chosen warrior, Petrus. You will lead our future astral army."

The most impressive thing was that Petrus's face was transformed. It showed a calmer, more mature countenance but with an air of cruelty. He was now fully aware that he had already spilt much blood for ideals in previous lives; the thirst to continue his conquests, for the allure of power, resurged.

With the skill of a seasoned warrior, Petrus made some quick movements in the air with his sword. He sheathed it in the scabbard at his waist.

"Let's get out as quickly as possible. My friend will open a portal nearby for you to return."

Footsteps approached the room and he drew his sword. It was a museum security guard making his nightly rounds. Petrus remained motionless while the guard, not noticing his astral presence, continued his walk.

At the door, he spotted the long-haired protector. Petrus went towards him with his sword. The protector deftly took an astral replica of an exposed shield from a display case beside him and defended himself from the powerful, enchanted blade.

The protector took a great leap to the side, slamming the astral shield into Petrus's arm, and his sword fell to the floor. Petrus started a hand-to-hand fight with his opponent, who was also strong and agile. I noticed that the wise protector tried to punch Petrus in the back of the head.

"Be careful with your nape," Lyha advised, "you could disappear and return anywhere in the astral plane."

The fighter defended himself with the skill of many fights in many lives.

"Petrus, you won't be able to beat him," the witch said. "The protectors are not human. They have a different evolution and are highly trained for fighting. Take the sword and run away, right now, through the window. The enchanted sword will break the energy, allowing you to pass through! Go now!"

With brutal strength, Petrus managed for a few seconds to push and distance himself from his great adversary. He picked up the sword from the floor and went through the window, falling into the courtyard outside. The protector jumped out and began to chase him. Petrus was running across the square, where several sleeping people were still wandering.

A few metres ahead, the other protector awaited him. He was cornered.

"Take the girl next to you," Lyha ordered. "Aim the tip of the sword at the middle of her forehead. This could cause damage to her astral brain that will directly affect her physical body. It can cause dementia and is difficult to reverse. Protectors are trained to protect humans first. They will not approach you if you have a projected hostage."

Petrus embraced the girl with one of his strong arms while the other held the sword, almost parallel to the young girl's body, where the blade's tip almost touched her forehead. The young girl was trembling and crying with fear. She was unaware she was out of her body, sleeping somewhere.

"Now, go with her towards the garden in front of you. When I give the signal, let go of the girl, run, and cross the Arc de Triomphe du Carrousel. My friend will open a portal and take advantage of the strong energy there. You will return here as soon as you go through it."

The man in a black hooded cloak who had helped Petrus enter the museum was near the Arc de Triomphe du Carrousel.

The standing crowd now watched the scene of the protectors following Petrus from a distance as he headed with his hostage towards that arch. Lyha gave the signal. He pushed the girl to the ground, ran through the portal, and disappeared.

One of the protectors hugged the frightened girl, who was crying. He placed one of his hands on the young girl's forehead, where I could see a bluish-white energy that immediately calmed her down. He put his large hands behind the girl's neck, destabilising her silver cord, and she disappeared.

It was a shame I couldn't see her after-scene, but I knew she woke up instantly. She was probably relieved, thinking that it had been a nightmare, or, on the contrary, laughing a lot because she was saved by a Prince Charming dressed in white. I have learned that many of our dreams are true astral experiences. Sadly, most of humanity can still not comprehend or recall everything that happened on this fantastic plane, where we are transported almost every night. However, some experiences could be traumatic...

I was back in Llyn Din. Everyone watched Petrus return with his sword. He didn't look like the same man. He now had a transformed expression, of someone who has a great power in his hands. Then, he drew his new weapon upwards, and all the monsters in a circle did the same, in reverence to their new leader, with euphoric shouts.

The priest, Michael, and Dino stared at that scene of the awakening of a secular conscience, sickened by conquest and power.

Lyha was now smiling.

Bogat looked at the scene and said, “Finally, after Earthly centuries, a true warrior has arrived. He has been drawn to us. The law of universal attraction is now in our favour. Petrus will be our great link between the Earth and the astral planes. He will form our army of surface dead.”

“No!” the priest shouted at the fighter. “First, they will use you. Then, after they no longer need your services, they will discard you like rubbish.”

“No, priest.” Bogat snickered. “Petrus is proof of Earth’s low energy. The cosmic energy in action has allowed him to come here with this sword. The biggest culprits were your friends, who still hide the great truths. More than 2,000 years after Christ, nothing has evolved regarding morality. So, my only choice was to join the Brotherhood to survive in this jungle. For the first time, during a rising cycle, we will take the power of a planet.”

“Don’t invert the positions,” the priest shouted. “The Golden Circle still influences the people on Earth. They have done so since before the dark years came. Evil minds like you are responsible for the chaos the planet is going through today.”

"No, they are not. It's a matter of free will and allowing yourself to be influenced by someone. I think you are not the best person to approach this subject... By the way, after Petrus has assembled his army, we will free all the little beings of nature... Lyha and I are good souls. There is still time for you to join us."

"Never!" the priest exclaimed. "I'd rather be decimated in a black hole."

Lyha looked at Petrus and said smoothly, "Good job. As we promised, you will now understand what happened to you. You will have the chance to take revenge on your killer."

She raised her arms and uttered phrases in a strange language, and an image like a 3D film flashed into the open air. Robert, his agent, was in a room backstage at the big fight that had ended. He opened a small bottle of beer with utmost care. Then he removed a small vial with a white powder from his pocket and poured a portion into it, before closing it again. He put the bottle in the nearby fridge.

Petrus entered the room, and his agent congratulated him on his victory with a forced grin. They were interrupted by a man in a suit with thick glasses and grey hair entering the room with two personal security men. They put a large bag on a table.

The man looked to Petrus, ignoring the presence of his agent, Robert. "Congratulations, young man. You did a fantastic fight. This is one of the biggest prizes our house has ever paid to a new fighter. Enjoy this money and prepare for the next season after summer. We want you back here in our house. Take my card; message me directly if you need anything, including a new agent."

He glanced with a look of some disapproval at Robert and left the room with the two men.

"What did he mean about a new agent?" the fighter asked.

Robert took two beers from the fridge and offered one to the winner, replying, "Business stuff. No one believed in you. Now everyone wants you. Let's toast to your victory." They raised their bottles and toasted. "I'm taking you home! You can't be walking around in the street with all this money."

"Thank you, Robert! And your share, where is it?"

"I've arranged to come by tomorrow to pick it up. I have some debts here with them to adjust… accounting arrangements."

"Thank you for getting the fight with Thunder and trusting me. I will give half this money to my son. I love that boy, and I want to help him. The only thing I know how to do is fight. But now I will stop this and get a real job. I want my son to be proud of me – not as an underground fighter. He is the only precious thing I have in this world."

"You already told me you'd give up fighting when you made a lot of money. It's a shame, because fighting is inside you. Let's go. I'll take you home."

The image now was of a small and old flat. The door opened, and Petrus entered, looking very dizzy. With one of his hands on his chest near his heart, he left his bag on a small table and fell on the sofa. He managed to get out his phone. He reached for the card he had received minutes before from the man from the fight house but dropped both to the floor without strength. His physical death came first.

The flat door opened. It was Robert wearing gloves and carrying a copy of the flat key. He approached Petrus, verified his physical death, and asked the dead body, "How did you beat him? We had only been together for a few months when I saw you fighting in the street… I knew you had potential; I first scheduled some relatively easy fights, but you insisted on fighting Thunder immediately without any technical preparation. My only fear was that he would kill you in a few minutes. Then I would still have to pay the house to dispose of your body… Where did this brutal strength come from? Well, I lied. I didn't expect your victory, either, and I bet everything I had against you and lost. I'm left with nothing and have many debts. This money will solve it. You don't have a family like me, just a little son who lives happily with his mother…"

He picked up the card and the phone and put them in his pocket. Holding the bag filled with money, he left the flat, and locked the door from the outside.

Petrus watched the scenes with perplexity. He was incandescent with rage and was thirsting for revenge.

"Calm down, warrior!" the witch exclaimed, seeing the fighter's face. "You will meet Robert soon. It will be quite amusing. Imagine that you will take your revenge while invisible to the eyes of that traitor. First, you will haunt and dement him. After he suffers a lot, who knows, maybe cause a stroke…"

After a pause, she looked directly at Dino, who was watching those scenes, and continued, "But first, I believe you wish to start your revenge here. Right now, with his friend."

Dino widened his eyes. Something terrible was coming…

Chapter 20

The Revenge

Second life – Mrs Stephanie Puizhant

I exited a portal and observed Stephanie in front of me. She was tied to a stake in the centre of the square.

Lightning and the crashing of thunder mixed with the hateful cries of youths. They occupied the square as spectators in the astral plane. Next to her were Lydia's son and daughter. Elisabeth was holding a large wooden stick.

The crowd of youths shouted: "Revenge! Revenge!"

The boy raised his one arm upwards, and everyone fell silent. At this moment, a man wearing a black toga walked towards the centre. His pale skin contrasted with his long dark hair, and his greenish eyes were outlined with black paint like a mask.

A glow came from the centre of his chest. It was from a necklace with a round golden talisman on its tip. It was identical to the one worn by the man in France who had allowed Petrus into the museum, with the symbol of the Brotherhood of the Golden Circle.

As he approached, he looked at the old-looking girl and said in a proud voice for all to hear, "My young witch, Elisabeth. This is a special day for you. You followed my instructions and sacrificed your astral appearance to use your millenary powers, and now, for the first time, you will be the great protagonist."

He looked at the youths in the square and shouted, "For those who do not know me, my name is Zorufh. I am Elisabeth's mentor. What do you all want from this murderer?"

"Revenge! Revenge!" everyone shouted euphorically.

He smiled wickedly and raised his arm. "You will finally have an unprecedented and historic revenge today. I will explain why. I found poor Elisabeth many years ago. She had been lonely and asleep for centuries in the depths of the Cave of Zugarramurdi. Someone hid her there after she took her own life. Why would a beautiful little girl kill herself? She was her murderer," he pointed at Stephanie, who was watching, "she caused Elisabeth's death. Katharina was the name of her conscience in that life."

After a pause, he continued, "Elisabeth told me her story; her memories were still not so clear, but with the help of friends of the Golden Circle, I could locate her lovely brother here in this astral region. Since then, she has been studying my books, which finally awakened her knowledge and powers that were hidden. She has the moon mark on the back of her neck." He pointed to the girl. "She is a powerful Initiate of Ancient Egypt. One of the most powerful consciences I have ever met!"

"Elisabeth! Elisabeth! Elisabeth!" they all shouted.

Zorufh again pointed to Stephanie. "By the law of the universe, misfortune had already been predicted for this murderer in her other lives on Earth. However, you made it even more complicated and did a magnificent job. You threw deleterious mental forms into her brain, causing fears, illnesses, depression, and even suicide in one of her previous lives. In her last life, you had Elisabeth's help for the first time. With her powerful magic, she left this woman sterile and caused a car accident for her current husband that left him in a wheelchair."

The man looked at Stephanie and said, "Deep down, her husband was a poor wretch. He was the only person in this vast universe who still had feelings for this shrew, the richest, most hated, and most unhappy woman on Earth."

He looked at the youths and stated, "I declare this woman guilty. What do you think?"

"Guilty! Guilty! Guilty!" they repeated without stopping, tapping their feet and gesturing with their hands and fists.

Zorufh raised one of his arms again, asking for silence, and turned to the woman. "Stephanie, you have suffered little in this life; Elisabeth was carefully manipulating a powerful dark energy of hate to play on your brain so that you would quickly absorb your misfortune. We use the simple law of attraction of the universe to our advantage. This would make you mentally ill and suffer in a mental institution for several years. We don't know why you came sooner than we expected. But it doesn't matter; this time will be your end. Your soul will disappear forever."

"I'm so sorry. I didn't know. Please," the bound woman pleaded. Tears dripped down her face.

"Shut up. That's nonsense. It was always there within your conscience, but your arrogance never allowed you access. Now it's too late."

The man asked the youths to position themselves in a circle around the stake, keeping about ten metres apart and alternating between boys and girls whenever possible.

Elisabeth remained close to Stephanie, with her eyes closed, holding her wooden stick in concentration. The man asked Elisabeth's brother to stay beside him, outside the circle formed by his friends: "Young boy, let's watch the black magic that is about to begin."

The old girl opened her eyes, which were now orange, and her wooden stick began to release a red pigmentation at its end. Very close to her friends' feet, she drew a circle on the ground around the prisoner. When she had finished outlining the figure, she looked at the wizard, who nodded in agreement.

Zorufh ordered the youths, "Now, I want you to remember the tragedy that happened to you and your families. Remember it using as much strength of thought as you can. This is the most important moment; come on! What do you want for this murderer?"

"Revenge! Revenge!" the crowd repeated.

"I want it stronger. Remember your loved ones who have died. What do you want?"

They all shouted revenge in anger and beat their feet on the ground. A dark mental form of astral fluids began to emanate from their heads. It formed a dark cloud ring about ten metres above them. It became denser and denser as they repeated the word revenge with hate.

The little witch girl looked up, raised her arms, uttered some strange words, and hit the stick hard on the ground, exactly where she had finished drawing the red circumference. A bang shook the ground. A thin, circular crack of only one centimetre opened, very close to her friends' feet. Although it was tiny, a mighty wind emanated from it. Everyone was now silent, admiring the black magic show. Some came closer out of curiosity and their hair stood up.

The rift slowly began to move towards the prisoner.

Standing beside Zorufh, the boy looked startled at his sister's power. "I have never seen anything like this. What did Elisabeth do?"

"I discovered that your sister is a powerful Initiate of Ancient Egypt. It was a pity I didn't find her sooner," the man said proudly. "Rare consciences can generate the black hole portal. I never knew of anyone who could. This portal gives access to black holes, formed by dying stars in distant galaxies."

"Black hole?"

"Yes, it is the only place where a conscience can be destroyed. After she goes through it, it will destroy her astral body and, by cascade effect, the mental body, and other complex cells. They will all disintegrate until their primordial atoms mix with the cosmic Ether. In other words, Stephanie's soul will disappear forever, and she will never again be born or have life anywhere in the multiverses."

The boy widened his eyes. He remained silent and thoughtful.

The young witch began rotating in the air with her wooden stick. The dark cloud, emanated by the children in the audience, followed the action in a circular anti-clockwise direction. She spun around, causing an extremely circular wind. Still, it was not enough to dislodge her friends from their positions, who shouted happily, watching the spectacle.

From within the abyss, more dark clouds began to rise and join with those of the youths, like a large, dense, spinning tower. Finally, it remained hovering many metres high, circling like an immense dark cyclone. The weather was intensified with strong wind, lightning, and thunder.

The prisoner watched in terror.

The wizard Zorufh looked at Elisabeth and shouted, "Now, my little witch, as we agreed, send this wonderful mental form of hatred to London. We want chaos with uncontrolled bloody protests and murders. The Golden Circle needs revolutions throughout countries around the world. Then, soon, we all can be reborn."

The girl concentrated, rolling up her orange eyes, uttered intelligible words, and raised her arms, her staff in one hand. The mental form began to move slowly to its destination.

Zorufh smiled and said to the crowd, "I am proud of all of you. You will all be part of our brotherhood that will dominate the Earth. We will protect you all. Soon, we will plan your rebirths with fresh DNA, health, and power. Remember that power opens the doors of this world."

He looked at the dark cloud with satisfaction. "Now, everybody sit back and enjoy the greatest spectacle of your astral lives. See the eyes of the important and arrogant Stephanie begging for forgiveness." He laughed, followed by everyone except the witch's brother. "Elisabeth has achieved for everyone, finally, the ultimate revenge. It will take quite some time for the rift to open, and with it, the shrew will be wiped out, swallowed through the portal of a black hole forever. She will never be born anywhere again. Enjoy, because she must suffer a lot. Make yourselves at home, throw stones for her to scream in despair. That's how you make a great and last revenge."

Elisabeth's brother was standing away from his companions. Unlike his friends, he looked worried about everything that was happening.

I turned my face to the cloudy sky. I saw that dark cloud going towards its destination. This way, I avoided seeing Stephanie being stoned to the sound of laughter.

Hoping for a new portal to open to escape this cruel scenario, I reflected on our internal monsters. They are fuelled daily by hatred across the globe, and they remain alive and more ferocious in the astral plane after death. It's not easy to get rid of them.

It's an endless cycle between those who do evil and their avengers. The hatred and evil on Earth hinder eradicating our internal monsters and ending the cycle…

Chapter 21

Aphasya

Third life – Dr Vincent Gitumed

Vincent walked along the deserted street, frightened and thoughtful. Daphne had been left behind in those strange caves. The sky was grey, and it was pretty cold. There seemed to be no one around.

He walked down the street, dodging the rubble and observing small, destroyed buildings on their sides. There were shops with old signs written all in French.

A young soldier appeared on the street in a filthy French uniform from the First World War, missing his left arm and holding an 8 mm pistol in his remaining hand. He pointed the gun towards Vincent, who raised his hands with trembling arms. "Don't shoot! I'm a doctor… English doctor."

The soldier approached slowly, keeping his gun pointed at him. Suddenly, he started running towards Vincent, shouting in English with a strong French accent, "They're coming! We must hide."

With his gun, he pushed Vincent towards a destroyed shop on the side of the street and said, "The Germans are everywhere."

The man began to shoot across the street, but no one was there, and no bullets came out of the gun. Inside the shop, he was crouching down and protecting himself from something that existed only in his mind.

He looked at the doctor and whispered, "They almost hit you. Quiet." He raised his head and looked carefully out, placing the gun into his waistband. "They're leaving. We're going to stay here for a while."

Vincent looked carefully outside, and no one was there. They continued to sit on the floor.

The soldier gave his only hand in greeting. "I'm Jean Baptiste."

"I'm Vincent."

"Your clothes are strange for a doctor in a war. You're a long way from England."

"Yes, I am…" Vincent admitted in a sad voice.

"I lost my arm, Doctor… Sometimes I feel a lot of pain, and sometimes I don't feel anything. What do you think?"

"The same thing happens to me, Jean," Vincent answered, showing the wound on his head. "I can't explain why. Medicine doesn't have answers for everything… By the way, what is the name of this town?"

"Verdun." The soldier laughed. "You are lost in France, Doctor. I think war is driving you mad." He pointed to Vincent's head.

"I thought the war was already over."

"It's not over!" he shouted with widening eyes. "When it's over, I'm going to marry Camille. I miss her." He shed a few tears and took a black-and-white portrait of a beautiful woman in an old dress from his pocket.

"Oh. She is a beautiful girl."

"And you, Doctor, is a woman waiting for you?"

"Well, it's complicated—"

A female voice from across the street interrupted him. "Vincent, darling! Let's go!"

There was the beautiful woman in the red dress whom he had observed in the bar. She stood inside a small, rounded portal of a dark orange colour, about two metres in diameter. Her long black hair was swayed by a strong wind coming from inside. With a confused expression, Vincent looked at the beautiful woman who did not match that landscape. She raised her arms slightly, with open palms, pronouncing words in a strange language. The wind began to blow; the earth and sand from the rubble rose, mixing with the remains of trees and dry leaves that were blown away by the force of the wind.

"Come quickly. I can only hold this portal open for a few seconds."

With his eyes now tearful, the soldier gripped Vincent's arm tightly with his one hand.

"Don't leave me here, Doctor! Please."

From Vincent's expression, I noticed that the soldier's words aroused a sudden memory of his life as Dr Walter.

"Vincent, dear, we have no more time. I am your salvation and inspiration within your dreams, achievements, and pleasures. Come quickly. The energy to keep the portal open is running out. It's your last chance."

"Don't leave me here, Doctor," the soldier cried in maddened wails, still holding the doctor's arm.

"Vincent, darling. In the astral or on Earth, we must make choices. I chose you a few years ago, and you can lose me forever. The portal will close, and you will be left in this filthy astral city in the rubble with these war freaks," the beautiful woman shouted. "Make your choice now. I'll count to three. One—"

Vincent, in despair, shook off the soldier and headed for the portal as quickly as possible, which closed instantly. At the same time, a new portal opened next to me to follow him.

~*~

The portal provided access to an impressive modern laboratory with large rooms and high ceilings. Several men and women worked on modern apparatus I had never seen. They were all wearing black clothes or lab coats, with the symbol of the Brotherhood of the Golden Circle. Most were physically dead;

however, some were projected, wearing ordinary clothes or even pyjamas under their lab coats.

Vincent was walking with the woman and asked, "Who are you? What is this place? It feels like I've been here before…"

"I am Myrah, dear, and you are correct. You have been in this lab two times. Gradually, you will remember."

"But how?"

"While you were alive on Earth, sleeping, I brought you here. Lately, I have accompanied you in absolutely everything." She gave a mischievous smile, linked her arm with his, and whispered in his ear softly, "In your best moments of pleasure, I was also present, without you seeing me, but your conscience could feel me."

Vincent expressed astonishment. They were interrupted by a grey-haired man wearing trousers and a long-sleeved shirt with the same symbol as the others.

"Vincent. Welcome to Aphasya's lab." The man smiled.

"Dr White?"

"More alive than ever." He laughed loudly.

"I will leave you with Dr White," the woman said. "He will remove your astral scars from the accident, heal your head, and give you a new outfit. See you later."

They entered a room with an enormous machine like a CT scanner.

"Dr White, I'm confused; it all happened quickly. I have many questions: What is this place? What are we doing here? What—"

"I know, my friend," he said. "Accidents cause instant deaths and make people stunned. From now on, please speak only a few words and don't move your body."

Vincent lay down on the table below the machine. As they talked, it began to scan him slowly with a dark green light.

"I can imagine you are perplexed. Let this marvellous machine work on your body. I will tell you what happened to me, which should help you clarify something."

Dr White controlled the machine via a holographic panel.

"You know, I had a cardiac arrest in the hospital where we worked. Then I realised I was in a horrible place: an old city with a cold and grey climate. There was a stinking river that I saw bodies immersed in. I was pursued by people who stole part of my energy. With it, they can return for a short period to Earth, sometimes to try to get revenge on someone or to continue their addictions."

"Addictions?"

"Yes. Here, there are no drugs, cigarettes, drinks, and no sex. Even though they are invisible to human eyes, they hunt down places on Earth where they can feel these pleasurable sensations. I know it sounds bizarre, but it is something quite common."

"How long did they stay there?"

"From minutes to a few days. It depends on how much energy they can dredge up to stay there. With low energy, they come back instantly with the magnet attraction. Then, they look for more energy to return. It's a circle."

"What is this energy?"

"Energy of our astral bodies. It is the money here. I look better now than when I was alive, but that is not the universe's law. After my death, months passed, and I looked like an indigent, with torn clothes, thin, long hair, a long beard, and my face aged. One day, a black lady appeared, with a white dress, colourful necklaces, and a headscarf. Her name was Bha. I remember her beautiful smile; she passed her hand over my face like a mother adoring her child; she looked like an angel. She told me I needed to reduce my hatred and put love in my heart. Only then could they take me to better places—"

"And you did it. Here you are," Vincent said.

"It wasn't quite like that... You know me, I never believed in God or any religion. I don't even know how to pray. But pray for who? For a kind of unfair God that put me in that situation... No, I couldn't. I felt a strong hatred for everything. I hate the life that I left and living so little. I hate that my wife, who is still alive, is enjoying everything I attained... spending all my money... certainly having sex with another man. Do you understand my feelings?"

"Sure. And then?"

"One day, I was lying on the floor inside an old house. There were rats and insects. The door opened, and two people from this laboratory came in. They knew everything about my past and asked me if I wanted to work here. In exchange, they were going to give me protection, give me back enough energy for my body to return as it was just before death, even a little younger." He passed his hand over his face and laughed. "With nothing to lose, I accepted the proposal and have been around ever since. I had to learn how to operate these machines. We have nothing like them on Earth. They are impressive."

"How great to be together. I see you are pleased here."

The machine stopped, and all the scars and injuries of the accident had disappeared entirely. Vincent's face was spotlessly clean, and his hair looked like it had just been combed. He touched his head and face and noted the magic transformation. His friend gave him a dark outfit with the Brotherhood symbol.

"This astral body has plasticity," Dr White explained. "Working here, I have found that all illnesses on Earth begin first in our astral body, to a subatomic degree, long before they manifest in the physical. When people are out of body, being brought here, we can cure or minimise the effects of their diseases."

Vincent remained thoughtful and said, "A young Frenchman at the medical congress told me that, but I did not believe him... Where does all this energy come from to keep the lab and these machines running?"

"That is a good question. The energy comes from the centre of the Earth. This laboratory is well below sea level. Below this ground is a gigantic, inverted pyramid of metal whose composition I don't know. It takes the energy and powers everything around here, including this energised water." He took a jug of water from a table, and poured some into a glass. "Drink it; you'll feel better."

They continued walking around the vast laboratory as they chatted.

"Here, we have doctors and scientists from various nations. Most of them, like us, are physically dead. The ones with a tiny light behind their heads are asleep back on Earth. Those with orange eyes are our teachers. They are not like us; some come from other eras or planets. Their knowledge is far above ours."

"All this is still something fantastical for me..."

"I understand. In a few days, you will remember being here twice while sleeping. You were here with Charles from the lab and other people the night before who made the job offer to you. Everything was set up for you to become an influential executive and marry the future prime minister of the United Kingdom. I was glad when they wanted to give you so much power... Unfortunately, you had a car accident. They must think of another name but keep it a secret now."

"But how is this possible? To come here while I was sleeping..."

"Myrah brought you here through portals. She seems to like you a lot. If sex worked here, wow..." He winked and laughed loudly. "The only way to go to the surface is by the energy of newcomers or from this inverted pyramid. You know that energy only transfers or transforms. Fortunately, we have a big energy bank in the city. With a small charge injected into us, we can go to the surface of the

Earth. We can, like ghosts, go anywhere on the planet through portals that they open."

After a brief pause, he continued, "These orange-eyed people here have a strong vibrational incompatibility with Earth. Like us, they cannot get energised to the surface, except for the beautiful Myrah, who has certain powers. They are dependent on us for everything."

"Will we return to Earth? I mean, will we be reborn someday?"

The man looked sideways and whispered, "I heard that a few chosen ones have already been reborn. I don't know when or who they were. It's top secret. Anyway, a team here is taking care of the new rebirth process, and soon, they will have new chosen ones. All with a great purpose in life, like being a great and powerful politician. They trust me, and I have already applied. Imagine power, money, wealth, and women. This will be paradise, my friend."

"What does this process look like?"

"They select the families, cities, and countries for a secret future goal. The true astral conscience that would have been born is thrown out of the womb and one of us will enter instead. They can alter the DNA of the foetus, so we don't have to go through karma situations. They stop the cause-and-effect laws, like being born with health problems."

"And the original babies?"

"Who cares? The best thing is that when we are asleep, we will always be here, projected, no longer as zombies, fully conscious, and we will remember every detail when we wake up."

"Is this correct?" Vincent asked with a startled expression.

"Of course it is correct. It's just Darwin's law. It's the strongest who dominate the weakest. That's how the Earth and the universe work. Here in Aphasya, we are with the strongest team."

Vincent was displaying a frightened, reflective look – no more than I felt – because that place seemed like a high-tech hell, different from the allegories we'd heard on Earth…

Chapter 22

Dino's Escape

First life – Dino

Everyone at the front of the church awaited what was to come after Petrus returned with the sword.

Lyha raised her arms, uttering strange phrases. The image was of an expensive restaurant in London. At the table were Dino and Robert, the agent who had poisoned Petrus.

Robert handed over a briefcase. "There's what I borrowed with interest. I have plenty of money now."

Dino had begun to sweat.

The mysterious old man in the dark grey tunic, who had been sitting near the church, approached him, whispering in his ear, "You have only one chance of not suffering at the hands of these crazy people. Follow me. Count to five and run behind the church. I have a carriage with two horses ready for us to escape far away. I'll get you out of here, Dino." He ran behind the church and didn't give Dino time to ask anything.

Dino saw Petrus's countenance, exuding anger as he continued to watch the film, in which he was now one of the main actors.

"Thank you, Robert. I advise you to stop gambling. Gambling has always been an addiction for you. I have already recommended a help group."

"You are right, Dino. The urge to gamble and place bets is powerful in me. I am leaving London with my family in the next few days. I am going to Ireland, looking for a new life."

Petrus shouted to the witch, "That's enough! The revenge is going to start now." He looked back and heard the hoof sounds of two horses moving away. It was Dino in the carriage driven by the strange man.

Petrus smiled evilly. "This will be so much fun. I want a horse," he shouted. He received the enormous black horse belonging to the monster he had annihilated.

Bogat, with a voice of satisfaction, said, "This is how a true warrior speaks. You are the right choice to be the future leader of the dead men's army. Go ahead, we'll follow."

"Petrus, you said you didn't know how to ride," his friend Michael observed, ignored by the fighter.

"Now he knows..." the priest said sadly. "Unfortunately, he knows much more than we imagine. Lyha is cunning and powerful. She knew that by possessing the bewitched sword, he could access knowledge of bloody fights and battles from many of his previous lives. He is now living the sum of his dark past, which is dominated by power. Now, his mind has unimaginable cruelty. This was their plan all along."

After entering a portal that opened, I was in a carriage proceeding at high speed down a dirt road in the middle of a deserted plain. Dino was lying down and holding on to the back of it.

He screamed in desperation. "He's coming. I didn't know that the money was stolen from the fight. Maybe if I try to explain this to Petrus…"

"He will not listen to you, Dino. He is blinded by hatred and revenge. The damage that an astral sword can do to you will not be easy to heal for many years… I will take you beyond these lands; we must cross the bridge. There they cannot go because other beings of darkness control it."

"Other beings of darkness? This nightmare doesn't end."

"After the bridge, there is another town, where we will be safe. I have helped many men from that place, who have lent me this carriage…"

Petrus was approaching, getting closer and closer. The vehicle was climbing a narrow mountain road. A few metres below was a river with calm, dark waters on its left side. As we got higher, an intense mist obscured our vision.

"We are not far from the bridge. It connects the two mountains. After the other bank of the river, we'll be safe."

"He's coming! He's coming! We're not going to make it," Dino screamed.

The driver tried to make his horses run faster. Next to me, a portal opened, and I left the carriage, staying on the same road, about half a kilometre ahead, already imagining what would happen...

One of the carriage wheels hit a large stone on the side of the road. The two men fell onto the ground near where I was standing. The two horses ran on, abandoning the occupants and the wrecked carriage. The place was already many metres above the river. A loud clatter of hooves announced Petrus's approach. The man with the grey beard stood up, revealing his face for the first time. He took Dino's arm, looked into his eyes, and said with tears, "Get up, my little Dino. You must run away."

The older man had a wrinkled, skeletal face and no left eye. But only one eye was enough for Dino to recognise him. "Dad? But how can you..."

The image of this scene froze in front of me.

When I turned around, a big octagonal portal opened. I entered it, leaving the mountain behind. In this case, it didn't close; it remained open. I could see the frozen image of the men on the hill, but now I was in another place. I participated in two films simultaneously, but the first one was interrupted.

I was in a boy's room in a modest house. Dino was in his bed; he looked about twelve years old. He got up in his pyjamas and slowly walked down the stairs while listening to a couple arguing in the living room.

A thin woman in a dress argued with her drunken husband. “Dino and I are leaving this house now. That’s enough… I am tired of living with your addiction and violence. I want a divorce.”

The man took the woman’s arms, saying in a threatening tone, “You have nowhere to go. You are my wife and aren’t going anywhere with my son.”

“Don’t put your filthy paws on me any more, you monster,” the woman bawled, trying to get free.

The man struck her delicate face hard, causing her mouth to bleed, and she fell to the floor. Then she quickly stood up and reached inside her handbag for a small, thin knife.

She pointed the knife with trembling hands and arms towards her husband. “I won’t let you hit me any more. Get away from me. You coward.”

With a sarcastic and enraged laugh, he grasped his wife’s thin arm, and the knife fell far away, near the door. With an even more violent movement, the drunk man pushed his wife to the floor. Her head hit the edge of the fireplace.

A pool of blood formed from the woman’s fall. She had died an instantaneous death. The man approached her, running his hands over her head, now looking worried. He heard a cry and glanced at the entrance to the room. Dino was frozen, holding the knife that had fallen on the floor.

"Little… Little Dino…" the man stammered. "How long have you been there? You saw it. It was an accident. Your mother slipped."

The boy did not move; he only cried. The father raised his voice, trying to move slowly towards his son. "She was going to kill me with this knife you are holding. It was self-defence. This is what we will tell the police, OK? Give me the knife, and let's talk."

The boy said nothing, still crying, and shook his head. Dino ran up the stairs to his room, locked the door, and hid in the wardrobe, sitting in a corner behind some clothes and boxes.

His father, staggering from drunkenness, slowly climbed the stairs behind the boy. "Want to play hide and seek? I will not hurt you. We need to agree on what to tell the police. You are already a little man and must face life's problems. I am your father, and you must obey me. You will say exactly what I order." As the bedroom door was locked, he continued shouting while punching it. "Open it now. You're stubborn like your mum."

The man broke down the bedroom door with several kicks. He first checked under the bed and then opened the wardrobe. He found the boy shaking and crying in a corner. The father crouched down, pushed away some clothes and boxes, and brought his face close to the boy, who stabbed his left eye with the knife. Then he dropped the blade and ran down the stairs towards the front door.

He was followed by his father, who shouted in pain with his hands covering his eye. "Come back here, you little bastard. You blinded me. I'll kill you. I'll kill you."

Dino's little hands were shaking, which made it difficult to open the door while his father came down the stairs. Finally, he managed to leave the house and cross the street, but his father was right behind, shouting in rage.

He didn't notice the lights of a car travelling on the street. The man was hit by the vehicle and knocked to the ground. A couple got out of the car, and at the same time, neighbours came out of their houses. The young Dino approached the incident and looked at his father lying in the street, now just a dead body.

The scene froze. I looked back and went through the portal to the mountain. It closed instantly. Petrus calmly got off his horse and took his mighty sword from its scabbard.

With his one eye full of tears, the old man pleaded, "Please forgive me, little Dino. Forgive me." Dino was shocked. He looked at his father, not knowing what to say. "Now go. Jump!" ordered the man. "And swim to the other shore. But be careful not to swallow the dark water."

"Jump?" asked Dino, looking at the river many metres below.

Petrus was already one step away. The old man pushed Dino towards the river and grabbed a piece of wood from the wrecked carriage.

Petrus saw the older man with the piece of wood, gave a laugh, and ignored him. The fog was getting in the way. He was more interested in locating Dino, who was already in the river, trying to cross the murky water to the other bank.

Dino's father, surely knowing his total impotence, advanced with the piece of wood towards Petrus, who cut it with his sword as if it were a thin sheet of paper. Then the blade pierced his body, and he fell, sitting near the rocks. Clearly in pain, he smiled and cried simultaneously, repeating to himself until he was unconscious, "I asked for forgiveness, I saved Dino… I asked for forgiveness. I saved my son…" Several astral worms came out of his body where the sword had pierced him, entering the earth.

Petrus was like a beast trying to locate his prey in the river. Just then, Bogat, Lyha, and their group arrived.

"We can't go there, Petrus," Bogat warned. "It's a territory dominated by another group. We have an agreement."

An impressive scene happened as I looked at Dino's father, cadaverous and unconscious. An Asian man in white clothes stepped out of a portal that opened beside a rock. I realised that he was invisible to the eyes of everyone present there. Only Lyha could see him. The man, with a serene face, nodded to the witch, who reciprocated. They looked like two enemies on a battlefield who momentarily just looked at and respected each other. Perhaps because they both knew that far above them, a powerful force imposed certain limits in the fight between good and evil. The man pushed the unconscious man's astral body into the portal, and both disappeared.

Petrus kept looking in the distance, visibly unhappy that he couldn't pursue Dino, who could already be seen leaving the river, dirty with mud, towards the woods.

Lyha looked at Petrus and said, "Don't worry; he won't make it to the next town, where this chariot came from. The purple bounty hunters will catch him and bring him to us first."

"How are you so sure?" the fighter asked.

"Because I'm going to warn them," she replied with an evil smile.

The witch went to her horse and took out a bow and an arrow with a sphere of mirrored material at one end. She took two small vials from her pocket, one containing a blue powder and the other a red liquid. She inserted each of them into small holes on opposite sides of the sphere so that, by some internal division, they wouldn't mix. She shot the arrow towards the other bank of the river. A loud explosion came directly from the impact zone, followed by a cloud of purple smoke.

"Let's go, Petrus," Bogat said. "After your revenge with Robert, we will start recruitment for your army of dead humans. We need consciences like you, warriors who can access the Earth plane. The swords of Edinburgh Castle will be the next supply."

Everything seemed to disappear. At first, I felt suspended in total darkness. Then, I felt my body falling at high speed as if from a very high place…

Chapter 23

Dino's Crystal

I opened my eyes.

I was back in Yudh, lying on the table in the pyramid. After everything I had experienced, I felt powerless and exhausted. Adhya released me from the energetic rings holding my body. Jade offered me green, energised water to rebalance my energy centres.

Narquiamides talked to several people at a distant table, analysing holographic images and numbers. When he saw me awake in my astral body, he approached me. "Come on, Sandra, get your energy back quickly. Now is the third and last phase of the experiment. This time you will go personally with us. We must go immediately."

"Go where?" I asked in the voice of someone who had just run a marathon.

He removed the crystal from my forehead, opened the little black box, and said, "You see these three remaining crystals? They are not yours. We must put them on the three people who suffered the accident. We'll start with Dino."

"Put the crystals on them? But what—"

"We don't have time to explain it to you..." he said. "Soon you will understand. Let's go now."

I drank the water quickly, in large gulps. Through a holographic panel, Jade opened a portal in the golden part of the tube and said, "It was a pleasure to meet you, Sandra. May the Infinite Spirit enlighten you to complete your mission."

"I won't be coming back here any more?"

"You will follow the λ3 experiment personally in the astral plane. You will no longer shift around with your mental body," she answered with a kind smile.

Adhya grabbed my arm, as usual, and we went through the newly opened portal with Narquiamides.

We arrived near a river with a horrible smell. I quickly recognised the place; it was the riverbank where Dino had escaped. Bodies were slowly washed away by its murky waters.

We reached the area where the purple smoke remained. Narquiamides opened his palms towards it and uttered a few words in a strange language. It dissipated.

We found Dino lying down behind large rocks. Next to him, a black middle-aged woman came out of another hexagonal portal, which remained open. She wore a white dress adorned with three necklaces of precious stones of various colours. She had a scarf on her head, and near her eyebrows was a diamond-shaped crystal of a greenish tone.

"Sandra, this is Bha, an old friend." Narquiamides introduced her to me.

"Nice to meet you, Sandra. We were waiting for you on the astral plane." She smiled with the same look as a loving mother.

Inside the portal, I observed a modern lobby with several people in white walking all around. The woman approached Dino and placed her open palms about ten centimetres away from his face. At that exact moment, Narquiamides removed one of the three crystals from the black box and tried to make it adhere to the man's forehead.

"It does not adhere, Bha," Narquiamides said, concerned.

Adhya asked, "Why doesn't he go to the hospital, and then you can adhere the crystal inside? He needs to get out of here as soon as possible."

"He swallowed too much water from the river," the woman replied. "His vibration has become very heavy. In this state, he cannot pass through the portal, with or without the crystal." She looked carefully into Dino's eyes and continued, "We have to wait a few more minutes for him to expel the sludge gradually."

"I'm afraid we don't have a few minutes," Adhya said. "Lyha has given the smoke signal for the soul hunters to find him. They will withdraw some of his energy and sell him back to her."

We could already hear the shouts of the pursuers coming towards us.

"Can't we stop them?" I asked indignantly.

"Of course we can; it's easy… But we will not stop them," Narquiamides answered in an irritatingly calm voice. "Unfortunately, we cannot intervene. It is the law of the universe; it is above our wishes."

"Law of the universe? It's not fair!" I complained.

"If they find Dino, we have to let them take him without the crystal, and the λ3 experiment will be compromised."

Bha made a sign with her hands towards the portal, which was still open; out of it came a grey-haired gentleman and a young woman.

"What do we have here, Bha?" the man asked.

They both knelt near Dino with compassionate gazes. The young woman had a small light on the back of her neck.

"He has swallowed lots of water from the murky river. He needs to expel it as soon as possible. In this case, I need a load of ectoplasm from Clara." She pointed at the girl.

Adhya held Dino's head facing to the right. The man and the young woman, kneeling, pointed their palms, leaving a distance towards Dino's chest. I saw a bright white light emanate from their palms, especially Bha's, towards the patient's face.

Everyone was focused on that ritual, which seemed to continue with no end. I started to get quite nervous, listening to the different voices of the pursuers getting closer and closer.

"Let's head in this direction now."

"The smoke has gone. I think it was coming from the south. If the river's waters swept him away, we lost him."

"No, Bogat and Lyha wouldn't have warned us if this had happened. There must be an important person who wants to take revenge on this soul. Who knows, we can trade him for a lot of energy or a horse."

At this moment, Dino began to have some reactions and to expel sludge with a highly unpleasant odour from his mouth.

"His vibration is increasing quite a bit," Bha said. "We are almost there; we need a few more minutes."

Those few minutes she might not have. I couldn't just stand there and watch. I had to do something. I walked away from them, down the bank, and went back into the woods, purposely making lots of noise. I climbed, with difficulty, on top of a small tree. Sitting on its branches, I began to sing a song my mother used to sing when I was a child.

Five men appeared: two with white skin, one with ash-blond hair and the other black. Those two were incredibly good-looking, except for their orange eyes. They wore dark wine robes and carried silver swords. The remaining three had a cadaverous appearance.

They wore old and dirty clothes and carried improvised wooden spears.

"Look what we have here on top of this tree," the dark-haired man said.

I looked at them and said, "Do you guys know this song?" I started singing it again.

The blond man looked at me warily. "She's not dead. She is projected. Bogat sent us a sleeper?"

"Of course not. She is not the goal. Her vibration isn't from here. She's just trying to distract us."

The blond man pulled a cylindrical tube with a needle on the end out of his pocket. Then he threw it into the hands of the biggest of the three horrible-looking men.

"Here, a present for you three. Have fun. Take her energy and make sure she has the worst nightmare of her life." He gave an evil smile and approached the trunk of the tree where I was standing. Using his sword, he cut part of it like cutting a sheet of newspaper. I fell and was promptly pinned to the ground by two men, their dirty clothes in tatters.

I shouted for help, but the thunder's roar obscured my cry of despair.

"Remember, she is projected. Take her energy through her jugular," one of the bosses instructed. "Don't let her put her hand behind her head. Otherwise, she'll disappear and awake immediately. And we don't want her to wake up before her energy is drained." He gave a sarcastic laugh.

The largest of the men approached with the cylindrical tube. He put one of his grimy hands on my head, the only part of my body I could still move, exposing my neck. I could see details of his sickly expression on his pale face. His cruel smile revealed his few crooked and rotten teeth. His odour was no different from the murky river nearby.

My fear was diminishing, becoming uncontrollable hatred.

With great relief, I heard Narquiamides' voice. "Leave the girl! She's with me."

"Narquiamides, what a surprise that you are on our land. Where are you hiding our prey?" one of the robed men asked.

"First, leave the girl."

"You, more than anyone, know you cannot interfere with the lower astral."

"The projected girl is just a researcher. Her vibration is way above this region. In her specific case, I can interfere with freeing her. You know what I can do; don't make me interfere," Narquiamides said.

The blond man with orange eyes stood thoughtfully momentarily and then ordered, "Let the girl go."

"No. We are not going back empty-handed," the enormous man with the cylinder protested. "You promised us energy to enjoy ourselves for one night on Earth, and she has plenty for all of us."

Narquiamides was carefully watching the scene from afar. I was immobilised and could not move. I burned with hatred. I wanted to get rid of that filthy, white-faced, cadaverous-looking man with the needle just inches from my neck.

When he was very close to touching me, he completely lost control of his hand, his face and crooked teeth showing the enormous force he was using to get the needle near me. However, entirely against his will, his hand pointed the needle towards his forehead; his other hand, which he still controlled, tried desperately to stop the first one. The needle hit his forehead, neck, and chest dozens of times until he fell to the ground.

"It's all dark. I can't see any more. I can't see!" he shouted in despair.

His appearance had become even worse; his face had become very wrinkled, and his remaining hair turned completely white.

I was released by the two other men, and they ran away. Astral worms began to leave the ground and climb the wounded man's body, entering the various holes that had been made with the cylinder needle. He screamed. With great effort, he got up and ran towards the nearby river of mud. Unconscious, he was carried away by the slow current.

The two bosses looked at Narquiamides, astonished, and one said, "Narquiamides, I think you've crossed the line. He didn't need such a severe punishment."

Narquiamides was silent, with a calm expression.

The other man said, “It’s his problem with the Infinite Spirit. He will pay for that. Let’s go back.”

They turned and walked away.

We walked back to where we were before, and Narquiamides remained quiet and very thoughtful. There, we found Bha, Adhya, and the couple.

Dino already had the crystal adhered to his forehead. They placed him on an electronic stretcher that floated by itself. At the man’s voice command, the stretcher lifted and flowed into the portal, followed closely by the couple.

Bha said, “Narquiamides, everything is already prepared as we agreed. We’ll meet soon in the square where Stephanie is.”

He nodded. She entered through the portal and it closed. I didn’t understand what she meant and preferred not to ask. Narquiamides did not utter a sound.

“You were courageous, Sandra,” Adhya said. “Those were decisive minutes. We managed to put the crystal on Dino’s forehead in time.”

“Narquiamides freed me. I don’t know how, but he liquidated a man who would take my energy. What power… I confess it was frightening… He could intervene in my case. I understood that it was an exception, wasn’t it?”

The two looked at each other and remained in an awkward silence.

“What?” I looked at them, begging for explanations.

Narquiamides broke his silence. "We have the power to intervene, but we can't… Not the way you saw."

Adhya explained, "By the law of the universe, the only person allowed to intervene in the Earth's astral is an Initiate, as long as she is alive."

"Initiate? What are you getting at?"

"Do you remember the book written in Senzar that Kennis gave you to look at in Yudh's library?" Narquiamides asked. "That book is so sacred that only an Initiate can read it. You are an Initiate of Ancient Egypt. I did nothing; you alone managed to dominate that man."

"What? No way…"

"It is unconscious, deeply inside you. It would be best if you learned to dominate your mind. There is a thin line between love and hate. Both are powerful. You used the power of hatred. You also called the worms to attack him."

"Did I call the worms? How?"

Another enormous portal opened in front of us.

"As I said, it was unconscious… We don't have time to explain it to you now. We must put the crystal on Stephanie. Let's go!"

They never had time to explain to me… However, gradually, they began to reveal the occult truths.

I entered the portal thoughtfully, trying to process that new information.

Chapter 24

Stephanie's Crystal

We came out of the portal at the side of the square, where Stephanie was tied to the stake in its centre. She was babbling incomprehensible words. Her terrified face stared into the nearby black abyss, which exhaled a cold wind.

Her body was being hit by stones from her pursuers. The youths had eyes of vengeance; they were laughing, gesturing with their hands, and shouting at the thunder from a grey sky.

A little further away were Elisabeth, her one-armed brother, and the wizard Zorufh, wearing his black toga.

When the man saw us, he shouted, "Look who arrived: Narquiamides, the Indian witch, and a living woman. You're too late."

"Hello, Zorufh." Narquiamides greeted him calmly.

"Elisabeth, please stop this black magic." The shout came from a woman standing in a hexagonal portal that had opened next to us in the square.

"Mum?" the boy shouted, his eyes widening.

Everyone was now completely silent, seeing two women standing in the doorway of the new portal but not entering the square. They were Lydia, Elisabeth's mother, and her brother, accompanied by Bha, the lovely lady who had been with Dino minutes ago. Lydia wore a light beige dress with gold details and a veil covering her head. Her face was stunning, beautiful, and serene. She remained inside the portal while Bha came out and stood beside it. Bha's gaze was like that of a great mother, who seemed to see all those young people as her children.

In contrast to the present grey scenery, with lightning and thunder continuing to grow stronger and stronger, there was a beautiful landscape inside the newly opened portal. There was an extensive green lawn fed by the sun. In the background, several flowers and trees indicated the presence of a colourful garden.

"What are my children doing?" Lydia asked seriously.

"Punishing the murderer who killed all of us... including you, Mum," her son answered. Unlike him, Elisabeth still had orange eyes, staring at the scene without responding, seeming to be in an intense trance.

"Stephanie has already paid grievously for her mistakes, for centuries. Unfortunately, she has had her sufferings compounded with the help of all of you. Now we must leave her alone with the automatic laws of the Infinite Spirit without interfering."

"Your mother is right," Narquiamides agreed while everyone listened silently. "This wizard Zorufh is manipulating Elisabeth and everyone here to obtain a greater goal. Without knowing it, you are being used by the Golden Circle to fuel the world's hatred. The dark mental form of hatred you all helped generate is now going to London. See, that's absolutely nothing related to your revenge. When you discover the sick plan you are in on, it will be too late. You will be their slaves or severely punished by the laws of the universe."

"Don't listen to this old fool," Zorufh shouted, raising his arms. "Young people, please reflect. What is the universal law that allows a woman to kill children? She deserves to be eliminated for good. What is the universal law that allows little Elisabeth to rot for centuries in the depths of the Cave of Zugarramurdi? I found and saved her; I am her mentor now. Finally, what is the universal law that allows men to destroy themselves and the planet? Humanity is sick, not us... You all helped Elisabeth to send that gigantic mental form to destroy them faster. This proves that we are commanding the universal laws. Our Brotherhood protects Elisabeth today and will protect all of you who accompany us."

Elisabeth stood still, while the abyss was getting closer and closer to Stephanie. The dark mental cloud she had created was distant, slowly heading to its destination amid lightning and thunder.

"Look what the dark magic is doing to you, my little daughter," Lydia said from inside the portal. "Your appearance is monstrous. But it only reflects the vibration that dominates your inner self. The paths of good and evil are choices we make every second. Where is my beautiful little girl? She is there, presently, within you. I love you, my children; this powerful vibration of love is the true universal law. It vibrates in each of us, and no one can take it away. Let's vibrate. Love, my children."

Bha looked at the youths and said, "Come now, all of you. Go through this portal here. Your relatives are waiting for each of you with longing." Dozens of people appeared within the portal and stood far inside the beautiful landscape.

Her son, with eyes filled with tears, went to meet his mother, stepping onto the grass inside the portal. "Come, my sister; come, all of you. My mother is right; we need to stop this. Enough of this hatred."

The others stood in silence but were unmoving. That was when Bha cried out in a voice that vibrated with the authority of a matriarch. "Children. What are you waiting for, standing there like mummies? Hurry into that portal; you can't keep the people who love you waiting."

That was all the encouragement everyone needed to run, enter the gate, and cross the lawn to meet their loved ones who were waiting for them.

Elisabeth remained standing like a statue, just watching the scene. Tears began to well up in her eyes, which were no longer orange.

"Coward's youths, you'll regret running away," Zorufh said. "Elisabeth is here with me; this is what matters." He looked at Narquiamides and said, "That's enough, you idiot. Get out of here with your little Indian witch and this useless projected woman. My Elisabeth and I have much work to do."

"Not yet. We need to stop the evil dark cloud going to London." Narquiamides pointed towards it.

"It's too late. You know, the gigantic, created thought-form has a life of its own, and nobody can destroy it until it is absorbed by thousands of people in the city. With the energy of the black hole, it becomes so powerful that not even the one who created it can destroy it by magic."

Zorufh pointed to Stephanie and continued, "The only thing you could do is try to save the soul of this murderer who is about to disappear forever. But poor Narquiamides… you are a faithful follower of universal law; you can't interfere." He gave an evil smile. "Let's go, my powerful Elisabeth. Leave these idiots there. Our Brotherhood has great plans for you."

"You're right, Zorufh. I can't interfere." He looked severely at Elisabeth. "There is only one way to undo all this evil."

The young Initiate looked at Narquiamides. She ran into the open portal, towards her mother, with her wooden stick. Her appearance automatically altered as she stepped onto the lawn, returning to the looks of a beautiful girl from centuries ago.

"I'm sorry for everything, Mum. Please forgive me. I love you."

She emerged from the portal, returning to her old appearance, and looked back at her mother, brother, and friends with great emotion.

She ran towards us, looked at me intensely with her tearful greyish eyes, as if she had known me for thousands of years, and gave me a sisterly smile. She was about to hand me her wooden stick, but Adhya was quicker and grabbed it first, looking at the old girl, shaking her head, which she seemed to understand.

The crack was too broad, about to swallow Stephanie. The girl ran and threw herself into the abyss.

"No!" Zorufh screamed. It echoed around every corner.

He was furious. The portal of the black hole stopped and slowly began to recede. Stephanie, who was unconscious, her head hanging down, was saved. We then heard a distant explosion in the sky. It was the thought-form crumbling in the distance. The lightning, thunder, and wind ceased instantly, although the sky remained grey. All the buildings around the square collapsed, disappearing completely.

"Narquiamides, you have destroyed the conscience of a powerful Initiate. You certainly will pay dearly for this," the wizard said.

"No, Zorufh, I will not pay. I didn't do anything. It was her free will, her unconditional love, to save thousands. You were right when you said I couldn't interfere." He smiled.

"You think you are the great sage." Zorufh snickered. "But deep down, you know you won't be able to beat our Brotherhood. There are too many of us."

"The love of a few is more powerful than an entire army. It's a choice where you want to direct your conscience."

"Love? Choices? I made my choice centuries ago. I'm not going to go backwards and be like this idiot woman," he said, pointing to Stephanie, who was still unconscious, "and be reborn with a life of suffering and be persecuted by her enemies. Is this what you call Love of the Infinite Spirit?"

"It is the physical law of the Creator. No one escapes it. But the vibration of love can greatly accelerate this path."

Zorufh turned to the portal, which was still open, with Lydia inside, near the door, watching them.

"And you, stupid mother. Do you think you can go away quietly? You have destroyed my plans, you old German witch. That's why they burned all of you."

The wizard took a little bottle from his pocket and threw it at the portal door. Like curtains of fire, giant flames lit up on the ground about two metres away from where the woman was standing. Bha, who was near the door, jumped into the portal.

With his left hand, the man held the talisman on his chest, which lit up the red of the triangle. He positioned his gaze upwards, uttering words in a strange language. An incredible force propelled

Lydia out of the portal towards the flames. Bha was holding the woman with the help of her son, but they were losing the battle.

"We won't be able to hold out for long, Narquiamides," Bha shouted. "Neither can I close the portal. Lydia's astral cells are not prepared for this heavy astral place."

Narquiamides looked at Adhya and explained, "The talisman. It is achieving this magic with the strength of the Brotherhood."

Adhya left the wooden stick Elisabeth had given her on the ground and approached the sorcerer from behind.

Narquiamides shouted at the wizard, "You know the downfalls of races for greed and power. If you manage to be reborn, you will destroy each other. Because it's like an addiction, wanting more and more..."

Adhya, who was already very close, ran, pushing the man, who momentarily removed his hand from the talisman. Taking advantage of these seconds, Bha closed the portal, disappearing and saving Lydia.

Zorufh was furious. "You little Indian witch, you will now receive my revenge with the power of the Brotherhood." He concentrated again, with one hand on the talisman.

I realised that Narquiamides would do something to stop him, but I was quicker. By now, my uncontrolled hatred had flared up again. I felt my eyes burning. I was already holding the stick that Adhya had left on the ground. My only desire was to eliminate that man forever.

Intuitively, I hit the floor with the stick and heard a bang in the sky. Zorufh, who had been concentrating on Adhya, looked at me in amazement.

"You… you are a living Initiate. How is this possible? The Brotherhood must know this. We will kill you. You can't live on Earth."

After hearing that, my will and uncontrollable desire to annihilate him took on a gigantic proportion. I looked at the black hole that still hadn't closed completely. The wind that came out of it intensified. Now it was his turn to be dragged screaming along the ground as if pulled by a rope. He managed to hold his body with both hands while the black hole tried to suck him in.

"Sandra, calm down… That's enough," Adhya said, already close to me. I gave the wooden stick to her and nodded…

But I was bluffing. My eyes were still inflated with rage. I sprinted to him and crouched down. I saw his green eyes, once evil but now desperate, begging for an absurd clemency. He couldn't get hold of the talisman to save himself. Without indulgence, I removed the talisman from his neck, looked into his eyes for the last time, and pried away his hands. His soul vanished forever.

I sat on the floor, watching Stephanie, tied to the stake, her head hanging down, while the black hole was still closing slowly.

Narquiamides and Adhya sat next to me.

"I'd better put this away. Your eyes are still orange," Narquiamides advised, taking the talisman from my hand and putting it in his pocket.

"And I will also, for now, keep your gift," Adhya said, holding the wooden stick.

"Who am I anyway?" I asked them, looking at the grey sky, which was already much calmer.

"Part of the civilisation of Ancient Egypt never originated on this planet. They were born here with a mission to help future generations. Merit, whom you met in your visions of the witches of Bamberg, was one of them. At that time, she lived in Egypt and trained several elected young women in the art of the highest white magic. One of the conditions was to have reached the age of fifteen and to have great purity of heart. Several achieved the Initiation. However, only two girls got the highest degree of magic: you and Elisabeth."

Adhya helped to explain. "The conscience of a living Initiate has mighty forces. By the Law of the Cosmos, she is the only one who can intervene on these planes. You can connect with forces and beings of nature, to which we are all connected."

Narquiamides continued, "As I told you, there is a fine line between love and hate. In your current case, when you are overcome with anger, your conscience automatically connects to the Akashic field, where you get specific instructions on what to do. These instructions go directly to your subconscious, and your mind acts with cosmic forces without considering what is right or wrong."

"These attitudes also happen daily on the Earthly plane," Adhya added. "Many people commit serious mistakes, even causing the deaths of loved ones when they are incensed. Then, when they calm down, they realise what they have done."

"That's unfair. Why don't I remember these teachings and how to use them?"

"For your safety..." she replied. "We have temporarily erased access to your memories of that life. All discovered Initiates have been crucified, burned, murdered, or induced to work for evil forces. Initiates always possess birthmarks that identify them. The ancient Initiates of Egypt had a tiny image of a moon on their nape. It is a powerful centre for capturing cosmic energy, connected to the medulla oblongata."

At that moment, my eyes widened. I'd had a small mark on the back of my neck since I was born, but I had never noticed that it was a moon image...

"We have had to hide the truth until now. It should not be this way," Narquiamides added, "but a sickly thirst for power still dominates today's world. More than 2,000 years after Christ, people have not understood what it means to love one another. You will know the details of your past when the time is right. But for this to happen, love needs to dominate your mind."

"I don't understand..."

"Remember I commented that we have a secret weapon." He smiled. "Love is that weapon. When Elisabeth passed you, she recognised you, even with the grey eyes of an older woman. What did you see in her?"

"Regret, love…"

"Exactly. They are so strong that she sacrificed herself to protect thousands of people. But what would we see if we looked into Elisabeth's eyes a few minutes before her mother appeared?"

"Hate…" I answered.

"Within all of us is a Loving Light, even within Zorufh, only dimmed by his thirst for domination. This light is a vibrational state that connects us to a greater light within this vast universe." He looked at me and whispered, "The best thing is that it is free." He smiled. "It is available to everyone; you just have to light it."

Our attention turned to a hexagonal portal that opened next to Stephanie. The chasm had not yet closed; we had no way across, so we stood in the square, just watching. Just as it had happened to Dino, inside the portal was a modern lobby with several people in white walking all around.

Bha and the same couple I had seen before, a grey-haired gentleman and a young projected woman, came out of it. They released Stephanie from the restraints and laid her on the floor. Although unconscious, she was moving a little, and her expression was one of dread.

"What do we have here, Bha?" the man said.

"This woman had her physical body killed in a car accident and suffered much for centuries, aggravated by the persecutions of a large group who finally left minutes ago. In this last life, she was the victim of powerful black magic in her womb to keep her from having children."

She positioned the palms of her hands a few inches from Stephanie's face and continued, "I see that she is now suffering extreme nightmares. Her conscience had accessed the Akashic field, shedding strong images from her previous lives."

"How is she, Bha?" Narquiamides asked from afar.

"The trauma was severe. Her astral brain is having continuous nightmares… How long do you need her to be awake?"

"Just a few seconds will be enough. The important thing is that she sees the crystal when she opens her eyes." He withdrew the little box from his pocket and threw the small diamond-shaped crystal to Bha, who grabbed it and gave it to her companion.

Bha closed her eyes, continuing with her energisation procedure, now with the help of the lights from her palms. She babbled words that I couldn't understand. Stephanie began to exude a black mist from her head, and her eyes opened in fright. The man had enough time to stick the crystal on her forehead. Then Stephanie closed her eyes and became unconscious again.

"Thank you all. We couldn't make it without you," Narquiamides said, satisfied.

"We are a team." Bha smiled.

They placed Stephanie on the electronic stretcher that floated by itself. Then they walked back into the portal beside the stake.

"Well, only one crystal remains," Adhya said.

Narquiamides removed the box from his pocket and looked at the last crystal, and a new hexagonal portal suddenly opened beside us.

"Before we go, tell me the truth," I begged. "What are these crystals for?"

They looked at each other, keeping silent.

I said in advance, "Let me guess: you can't tell me now."

Narquiamides said, annoyingly calmly, "It is a little complex. We cannot reveal it now. I promise you will soon understand the usefulness of these crystals."

Adhya saw the look of disappointment on my face and quickly changed the subject. "This portal will take us to Aphasya, where Myrah took Vincent."

"Myrah was the woman in the red dress—"

"Exactly," she said. "She is a powerful witch; her extraordinary beauty hides an unhealthy conscience. She can easily go to the Earth's plane on the surface. There, she visits, as a ghost, the houses of important men who seek power at any price. In their moments of intimacy, she also participates, where she renews her energy. While they sleep, she takes them out of their bodies, takes them wherever she wants, and inspires them to do the dirtiest atrocities. When they wake, most of them remember her as if she were a virtual secret lover. They become hypnotised and blindly follow her foul suggestions."

"Men are fools even in their sleep…" I commented with a smile.

"She is brilliant," Narquiamides added. "She can exert an invisible dominance on men without them knowing…"

With a wistful expression, he paused and concluded, "Unfortunately, today, she works exclusively for Niskgar."

"Who is Niskgar?" I asked.

"Niskgarmides, my brother," he said.

"Your—" I tried to ask.

Giving no chance for further questions, Adhya grabbed me by the arm, and we entered the portal towards Aphasya.

Chapter 25

Vincent's Crystal

We walked out of the gate on a trail through the darkly vegetated forest. The sky was laden with greyish clouds and a fine mist, especially near the muddy river.

At the end of the trail, we spotted a massive black iron gate, and on its sides, walls several metres high protected a giant construction inside. Through its bars, we could already see an old castle. Its walls were dark-coloured, seeming to have been abandoned centuries ago. At the top of the central tower was a symbol made of stones. It was the symbol of the Brotherhood, with the inverted pentagram surrounded by a circle and the red triangle in its centre.

Narquiamides covered his head, forehead, and beard completely with his hood. As we approached the gate, an animal like a Rottweiler began to bark at our presence. It was gigantic, over a metre and a half from the start of its thick legs to its huge mouth and teeth. The beast's bark echoed loudly, warning of the presence of strangers.

Two sentry guards dressed in black, with the symbol of the Brotherhood, approached; one was tall and thin, the other quite fat and of medium height. Both removed their silver swords from their belts and asked us to stop and keep some distance from the gate.

Adhya, who was carrying the wooden stick Elisabeth had tried to give me, came forwards. “We come in peace. We have a meeting with Niskgarmides. Announce that three visitors from Yudh have arrived; he already knows about our visit.”

The tall man held his sword while the other guard ordered, “Stay put. Do not approach the gate until I check.” He pulled a tiny device from his pocket. A small holographic image appeared.

I whispered to Narquiamides, “Does Yudh also have swords to protect the city?”

“No. We don’t need swords. There, we have only love to protect us.” He laughed.

“You are free to enter,” the guard said, putting his sword in his scabbard and restraining the dog. “Stay away from this monstrous dog. He is already bound in chains, but I will not be responsible if you come any closer.”

When we entered, the gigantic beast showed its enormous, sharp teeth. It was trying to get free of the thick chains attached to the wall.

Narquiamides, remaining with his hood down, approached the beast.

"Hey, you! Don't come any closer; he might rip your head off," the guard advised.

Ignoring the warning, Narquiamides looked into the eyes of the beast. It instantly stopped barking. It began to wag its tail with its giant tongue out, as if it were a little dog wanting to play. Soon after, he made a small gesture with his hands and uttered a few words. The beast transformed into a beautiful, docile black Labrador, of the typical size. The iron ring that held his neck became so big that he managed to get out. Unexpectedly, he ran to the taller man, barking and licking him.

The man dropped his sword on the ground and hugged the dog happily. "Buddy? How could it be? Was that you, Buddy, there all this time?"

A hexagonal doorway of about two metres opened nearby, through which there was a beautiful sunny field, and the dog ran and headed inside it. He remained barking at its door, calling the tall man, who walked towards the portal, following him.

His friend warned, "This is witchcraft, Sam, don't go. We're safe here in Aphasya. They will imprison your soul forever with the demons."

Without listening to his colleague, the man entered the portal and happily hugged the dog lying on the grass. Before the portal closed, I could see his appearance becoming more beautiful.

We walked towards the castle's main entrance while the other guard remained perplexed, scratching his head, trying to understand what had happened.

Narquiamides uncovered his head and asked me, "Did you see how love works? We don't need weapons."

At a large old wooden door in the central tower, a man of medium height, with black hair, slightly dark skin, and orange eyes, was waiting for us. He was wearing trousers and a black shirt with long sleeves. On his left breast, the shirt bore the same symbols of the Brotherhood.

"Narquiamides and Adhya. You are welcome. It's been a long time since you've been here. I see you have brought a projected woman from Earth with you. Let's go up to the main room. Niskgar is in a meeting outside here and will be with you shortly."

He looked at Adhya and said, "Is it my astral eyes or do you look more beautiful..."

"Must be your astral myopia, Kek," she replied with a contemptuous frown.

"You have just arrived and have already eliminated one of our guards and a dog."

Adhya said, "You know it was past their time; this is why Narquiamides could intervene. They were trapped here."

"We don't imprison anyone; we help them," he said with a wry laugh. "It's an agreement. We get them out of the mud or away from their pursuers, offering energy and protection. In return, they work for us."

We climbed a wide staircase and came to a high-ceilinged room decorated with tapestries and antique furniture. Kek led us to the glass wall of the room. Below, we could see a modern and extensive laboratory. I recognised it immediately; it was precisely where I had been with my mental body.

"I'm impressed," Adhya exclaimed, looking at several people working on modern appliances, all wearing black clothes with the Brotherhood symbol. "Aphasya has grown quite a bit since the last time we were here."

"Everyone works here by free will; we do not imprison anyone. You and I would make a good pair, Adhya."

"By the law of the multiverses, Kek. Please leave me alone. Go and do your black magic, turning poor little dogs into monsters—"

"Kek," Narquiamides said. "Speaking of not imprisoning anyone. I have agreed with my brother that we will try to convince Dr Vincent Gitumed, a newcomer, to come with us."

"Yes, he told me, but there are three non-negotiable conditions for that." He snickered. "Number one: you are not allowed to talk to Vincent. I will go with Adhya, obviously without her new wooden stick. Number two: she can't use magic. Number three: she will have seven minutes to convince him. If she is successful, he will leave with you. We will not stop him; it is his free will. What do you think? Take it or leave it."

"Only seven minutes," Adhya complained, looking at Narquiamides.

"OK. We accept," Narquiamides agreed, "but let Miss Wonlecty go with Adhya. She is just a projected Earth scientist. People like her should know that Aphasya has advanced technology. It's an opportunity to show your power… I will wait here in the room for you to return."

Kek thoughtfully looked at me from head to toe with his orange eyes, checking to see if I offered any danger.

"OK. I agree; the girls will accompany me. Have a seat. We will be back soon."

We went downstairs and walked down a wide corridor beside a vast library. I was awestruck. Several people of different ethnicities projected, like me, reading books in holographic images like the ones I saw in Yudh. They wore a variety of outfits, from pyjamas to work clothes.

"Aphasya is a knowledge centre similar to Yudh, but the goals are the opposite," Adhya explained. "They bring in scientists from various nations. They learn, for example, to develop new nuclear, chemical, and biological weapons, laboratory viruses, and various advanced technologies, many of which are still unknown to humanity."

I was stunned when I saw Mr Williams, my project director at BA Physical Labs. He was in his elegant suit, reading a holographic image of a book on the table.

Adhya tried to stop me, but I ran to talk to him.

"Mr Williams!" I said.

"Hello, Sandra. Are you around here... How's the quantum computer project going?"

"Very well..." I answered awkwardly.

"That's great. Our international stock market investor is rushing..."

I was shocked. *It's not ethical to use this new technology on the stock market.* He turned his eyes back to his reading again, ignoring me. Adhya tried to pull me by the arm while Kek just watched.

"Sorry to interrupt you again, but do you know where you are now?"

He looked at me as if he had heard a ridiculous question.

"Of course I know. I'm in the new London public library. Mr Jordan is also around here... in there, in the next room. Why? Are you feeling well?"

"I'm fine. See you, Mr Williams..." I replied, already distant, being taken away by Adhya.

"What are you doing, Sandra?" she asked, furious.

"I've just found out that my director and the president frequent this hell lab. And I work on a project that could destroy companies, so—"

"They don't have to be here," she interrupted me. "It is a vibrational matter of their consciences, and changing them is not even that simple. Let's focus now exclusively on Vincent."

Kek seemed to be amused by my attitude.

"Let her delude herself, Adhya." He looked sideways at me and said, "We're not hiding anything. Make yourself at home. You can tell everyone when they wake up that they went here. Except for a few who come here conscious, the others will not believe you. They might put you in a mental hospital if you insist."

I felt powerless, to witness all this. As a scientist, I wondered how many colleagues in the world were involved, unwittingly or not, in these evil organisations.

We entered another hall. It was familiar. I immediately recognised the part of the lab where I had been with my mental body.

Kek pointed to one of the rooms. "You can enter. Vincent is in this room. You have exactly seven minutes. I will be waiting here."

In the room were Vincent and his friend Dr White, who was teaching him how to operate a device like the one used to remove his scars.

Adhya looked at Vincent and started talking. "Dr Gitumed, do you know which people have chosen to use these devices?"

Dr White widened his eyes and shouted, "Please leave this room. If you don't, I will call Kek."

"You can go; he is out this door," Adhya said in a firm voice. "Dr Gitumed, before you dive into this insane work, it is important to know what is behind it. When politicians, dictators, presidents, leaders, or anyone causing chaos in their countries fall ill, Dr White and his team bring them here while they sleep. Then, they can cure or relieve the symptoms of the disease. The goal is for them to regain physical health to continue their trajectories of madness on Earth. This is one of the reasons why some of these evil and powerful people live so long."

Vincent remained silent, just listening.

"Doctors don't choose their patients, young lady," Dr White said nervously.

"Listen, Dr Gitumed," Adhya continued, "I will try to be clearer. This is not a hospital that treats all kinds of patients. They exclusively treat people who commit humanitarian crimes, genocidal crimes, homophobic crimes, and all those who cause disorder and stimulate hatred in their nations or the world. If you stay here, you will be stuck with them, and the consequences will be severe for your conscience. Come with us while there is still time."

Vincent looked at her. "As he said, doctors don't choose their patients."

Adhya made the disappointed face of one who was being defeated in battle.

I was furious; my eyes burned again, and I couldn't keep quiet.

I shouted, "You know something, Dr Gitumed. You deserve to stay here and rot in your future lives because you are a big coward. I saw some failed trajectories of your conscience. Dr Walter had a chance to get justice, and he didn't. Daphne—"

"Get out now, idiot!" Dr White shouted.

My gaze went to him, and he could no longer utter a sound. He put his hands on his throat in despair.

"Sandra, take it easy," Adhya exclaimed.

I ignored her. I felt my eyes catch fire. Then I looked at Dr White again, raised my arms, and directed my palms towards him. He was thrown backwards, hitting his head on one of the devices in the room, and he fell unconscious. Vincent was terrified; he looked at the door to escape.

"Don't do this," I ordered. "I can crash your mind before you reach that door."

"What do you want?" he asked, frightened.

"I just want to finish what I was saying," I stated angrily.

Adhya stayed near the door, just watching. She knew it was impossible to get me to stop. Vincent stood in the middle of the room while I talked, pacing back and forth, looking into his eyes.

"Daphne was the only woman who loved you. She took her own life because of you… Why? You have exchanged her love for the temporary power of a laboratory, which is linked to this evil Brotherhood. Now she's in that disgusting cave, needing some help. But where are you? Here, with much energy, helping tyrants."

He would say something, but I shouted, "I have not finished, coward of hell... You met Ethan, the physicist from France who cured his brother. So why not dive in and understand these subjects in decent astral libraries? There are cities like Yudh, which I have known, where people study to improve the world and not destroy it. But your cowardice and egoism are so strong that they never allow you to go further."

Adhya broke the silence. "Vincent, there are many places to work on this plane. You know Thomas, who helps soldiers' consciences from wars. He needs your help."

I continued, "If you feel you must continue as a servant after all this, hiding behind these people, go ahead. If not, act to change the journey of your mediocre lives and fight."

"Time is up!" I heard Kek's voice as he opened the door.

Before I left the room, I whispered in Vincent's ear, "For the first time, be a man with a capital M."

Chapter 26

Meeting with Niskgar

We left Vincent motionless and thoughtful without saying anything. Adhya wisely stood in front of me, distracting Kek. She gave him a sensual smile, which only a woman knows how to do when she wants to distract a foolish man.

"Kek, you were right. I couldn't convince him." She put her arms around him. "Tell me more about what it's like living around here…"

I closed the door quickly so he wouldn't realise we had left Dr White unconscious. While Adhya got Kek's attention, I walked, looking down with my eyes barely open. I could feel that they were still orange. I took deep breaths to calm down gradually. Kek was so happy talking to Adhya; he seemed to have momentarily forgotten our failure.

Back in the main hall, it didn't take long for a portal to open near the wall, and Narquiamides' brother entered. To my surprise, they were identical twins. Their faces and white beards were the same. The only difference I could see was their clothing. His brother was wearing a black tunic, and hanging from his neck was the golden Brotherhood talisman.

"Niskgar," Narquiamides exclaimed, keeping some distance.

"Narquia, look at you. I think you're getting older than me in these millennia." He laughed.

"It must be the concern for my twin brother, who is lost in this astral underworld."

"Narquia, this astral underworld you refer to is growing fast. The vibration of the planet is decreasing. We will be reborn before the Virgo-Pisces Era ends." He raised his hands upwards.

"The inhabitants of the lower astral never stayed during the ascension to the next Era of Leo-Aquarius. You can no longer stay here if humanity goes out of illusion and the vibration rises. Few will be lucky enough to be automatically expelled to primitive planets. Others like you will have their consciences taken to levels of unimaginable suffering until they beg to be wiped out in some black hole."

"Nobody will be able to beat us, my wise brother Narquiamides. Let me tell you the latest news: for the first time in history, we will reach sixty-six leaders in six regions of the astral plane – I am one of them – each with a different magic power. United, we will be invincible. You know the prophecy."

Narquiamides made a worried expression when he heard those numbers and said, "Sure, 666, the magic triangular number… You can make it for a while, but the fate of this race will be the same as Atlantis. You all will use the magic power between you to cause an internal war and destroy yourselves."

Niskgar laughed. "It will not happen. They already know the mistakes of our Atlantis race. The sixty-six leaders are on the same page. We are many and now joined for the first time."

"I always say that the few connected to the Creator become the majority."

"Creator? We are using His law to our advantage. The history of the fallen races has shown us that we cannot act directly. In our case, it is different. We provide the fuel, but it's up to humanity to set it on fire and blow it up. Hatred, wars, and conflicts. They are fools, easy to manipulate."

His expression became thoughtful momentarily, and he continued, "I'll tell you a secret, my brother: even if we stopped influencing them now, the vibration of the Earth is already in a downward spiral. The energy generated by the chaos automatically feeds back hatred and revenge between people. This race is already in sharp decline because of themselves. That's why you can do nothing to save them... Finally, soon, all our Brotherhood members will be able to be reborn again."

"You will be reborn during the chaos..."

"We will be like kings. The kings control the army and the chaos. We will modify the DNA of the ignorant humanity to serve us without them realising it. Then, as gods, we will control the physical and psychic qualities and the level of intelligence of all those who will be reborn on Earth. It will be millennia of domination of the planet. I will finally be able to leave this ugly place and have all the pleasures of a new life on Earth: look at the sun without destroying my cells, enjoy good wine, feel the taste of good food, have a lot of sex… and all the pleasurable things we can't do here."

I looked in the doorway, and there was Vincent, listening to everything with wide eyes. He shouted, "You're all mad monsters."

Niskgar laughed. "Dr Gitumed, do you know why you are here? It is your vibration. You are exactly like us: you have an irresistible thirst for power in the depths of your primitive conscience. And you would be a powerful man on Earth if not for your death. Here is your assassin." He pointed to Narquiamides. "It was him, my brother, who caused the accident and sabotaged my plans. But by the universal law he follows to the letter, he will pay dearly for killing an innocent young driver. A source told me that he was not allowed to die."

He looked at Narquiamides and continued, "Only three were authorised, right? This mistake, my wise and poor brother, will change the whole future chain of a family tree. You will be lowered, who knows, in some astral hospital to clean up the mud vomit of these ignorant people."

"Unfortunately, there was a betrayal," Narquiamides said. "Julian from my team was responsible for looking after Dino's driver. He omitted that he had a heart condition and let him die. It was you who corrupted him; you are the real culprit."

"No, no, correction. Julian was the culprit. We are now like you, and we do not interfere either. We only provide suggestions." He snickered. "But the boy made the right choice, and now he is one of us. When he learned of these useless experiments, he came to us, and we helped him to choose the right side."

"What do you mean by right side?" I exclaimed. "You all incite hatred and cure psychopaths. You are behind the killers."

"We are not murderers, young lady," Niskgar replied, with his penetrating eyes on me. "What we do is only influence the living consciences on Earth, but we don't force anyone to do anything. They are the ones who kill themselves in wars, conflicts, and murders… It is humanity's free will. For example, look at the kings and dictators throughout human history. They love power above all else. I admire them. They are special and smart consciences. Their dream is to live a life dominating an entire nation. But, not content, they always want to dominate the entire world." He laughed. "We just help them fulfil their dreams. I love these guys. Many are with us, helping our Brotherhood, and deserve to be reborn in special positions."

"He is right, Sandra," Narquiamides said calmly. "They only influence, but it's up to humanity to decide which way to go. In the experiment, I modified a chain with the death of a person not authorised by the universal law. The young man should be alive and then have a family, relationships, children, and grandchildren in the future. We are talking here about disrupting a very complex chain. They will replace me soon. I will stay in Yudh without being able to use magic for a while. No one is exempt from the Law of Cosmos Ethics."

"The other two went to other regions of the lower astral. I'm sure my friends Bogat and Zorufh are caring for them."

I widened my eyes. He still didn't know that Zorufh was gone forever. And because of me.

"There will always be a place for you, my brother. Instead of sixty-six leaders in six regions, we could be sixty-seven." He smiled sarcastically.

"Thank you, but I don't want to spoil the prophecy numbers." He returned the smile. "Well, we need to go… Are you coming with us, Dr Gitumed?"

"Yes, I don't want to come back here any more," the doctor exclaimed.

"Dr Gitumed, 'here' is not a prison. You can go wherever you want, but you will soon return to the arms of the beautiful Myrah. The laws of the universe are cruel to consciences like yours. Narquiamides will not be able to keep you in a high vibrational state for long. You will come back to lower planes automatically because that is where the vibrations of your astral atoms are… Your body's energy will be drained; you will become deformed and old like how we found your friend Dr White. You will beg for us as much as someone who is drowning needs air. But don't worry, we are good souls and will help you. We always help those most in need."

Niskgar gestured with his hands, and an oval portal opened beside him. Inside it was a large hall. Through the tall windows was a view of a city I could not identify. "I must go to an important meeting. We will see you around, Narquia."

Suddenly, Dr White arrived at the door, flushed as if he had just returned from a marathon. "It… it was her," he stammered, pointing at me with a trembling hand. "She used the magic on me… She… She's a living witch. I saw her yellowish eyes." Unable to stand, without strength, he sat down on the floor, leaning his back on the wall.

"Narquiamides, the agreement was not to use magic," Kek stated.

"Correction, the agreement was that Adhya did not use magic, and you did not mention the projected woman. You know me, I always play fair."

Kek stood still and frowned.

Seconds before his portal closed, Niskgar raised his right arm, pointing his palm towards me, while the other held his talisman. "Don't come back to Aphasya any more, young witch."

I remember perfectly Adhya's scream when a dark orange light came out of his hands and hit me. I fell on the floor. I couldn't see anything; everything was completely dark. I unsuccessfully tried to open my eyes, but I could still hear Narquiamides talking to Adhya.

"She cannot awaken now on Earth," Adhya said. "Can we open a portal?"

"It's impossible to open here, inside. The strong energy of the inverted pyramid does not allow us to do it. We must get her out of here as quickly as possible."

"She's disappearing, Narquiamides. She will wake up in seconds. Lucius! Lucius, help!"

My physical eyes instinctively opened slightly in my flat in London. Like a short-sighted person without glasses, I could see a blurred image of the light fixture on the living room ceiling. I was in a state of catalepsy, unable to move my body.

In the few seconds before I woke up, minutes seemed to have passed. My mind inside the physical body was already starting to get confused, automatically playing logical information that I had just had a nightmare.

At that moment, I saw Lucius, the protector who had taken over the entrance to my apartment. He placed his big hands a few inches from my forehead. I felt a tremendous force that made my eyes close again, overcome by extreme drowsiness. Everything went dark. I was back inside my astral body.

"She is coming back." I heard Adhya's voice, relieved.

I felt Narquiamides' hands on my forehead, as he pronounced unknown words. Suddenly, I stood up and realised I was in my mental body. I could observe my astral body on the ground.

At last, my three bodies were separated but connected by the energetic cords. The mental body was much more translucent, composed of less dense atoms than the astral one. I felt like a ghost but in the astral plane.

Narquiamides looked to the side and saw me standing there, translucent and confused. He smiled, winked in my direction, and said, "We've bought some time."

I realised that he was the only one seeing me in the mental body. Kek kept a certain distance with his arms crossed, watching the scene with a sarcastic laugh. Dr White was also watching, sitting on the floor, leaning against the wall.

Vincent was standing motionless, not knowing what was happening. Adhya was kneeling, holding my hand, looking at my face and astral body that had returned after almost disappearing.

"Let's get her out of here quickly," Narquiamides said.

He lifted me with the help of Vincent and Adhya. They hurriedly removed my astral body, and Kek followed without helping. Outside the castle, they placed me on the floor. Narquiamides, with his hands and uttering strange words, opened two portals in the shape of hexagons. From the first of them came Thomas. Inside that portal, I saw the city in France that the doctor had fled to with Myrah.

"You took too long, Narquiamides. I was worried." He looked at Vincent and continued, "Come with me, Dr Walter. You have a soldier who was abandoned and needs our help. It's the beginning of your redemption process. I am here to guide you."

Narquiamides took the last crystal from his pocket and placed it in Thomas's hand.

"Put this crystal on as I told you... and change his Brotherhood clothes."

Thomas smiled, saluted, and disappeared with Vincent, who thanked us for getting him out.

Kek was at the door watching everything and said, "Adhya, come back here anytime you want. Just let me know. Or we can meet somewhere else..."

Adhya rolled her eyes. "Goodbye, Kek."

At this moment, we entered the second portal into a stunning garden. There were leafy trees, colourful flowers, butterflies, and birds singing. They put me down on the grass, and I instantly returned to my astral body.

"We almost lost you," Adhya admitted.

"Where are we? What is this beautiful place?"

"In the astral plane, there are not only murky rivers," Adhya noted with her girlish smile.

"Let's go for a walk in silence. The sound of nature helps to rebalance energies," Narquiamides said.

In silence? I have thousands of questions...

We walked on a stone path that ended in a bridge about fifty metres long by two metres wide. It was built of wood in the form of a curve. Underneath it ran a stream of crystal-clear water and many multicoloured fish. The timber was perfectly painted, white with red handrails. The bridge was decorated with inscriptions and symbols in black.

When we arrived at the beginning of the bridge, Narquiamides ordered, "Sandra, go ahead of us. Cross the bridge. The answers to your questions are after you cross it. Soon, we will meet you."

I crossed the bridge, amazed at the beauty of the place. At the end of it, a bright white light appeared. I could no longer see anything in front of me. When I looked back, the bridge, the river, and the garden had disappeared.

The brightness everywhere was so intense that I could no longer open my eyes.

Suddenly, I felt my body falling at high speed in spiral movements…

Chapter 27

The Reality of the Great Dream

I felt myself sitting somewhere in a comfortable place.

Finally, I managed to open my eyes.

A bright white light came from a giant spiral dome on the ceiling at a colossal height.

Beautiful music came from a white grand piano playing in front of me.

I was sitting in the large blue armchair in the centre of that immense round hall. The white light from the dome disappeared, allowing me to see stars and planets.

I tried to get up, but I had no strength. The beautiful woman I had already met was beside me, watching me. I remembered her name: Maya.

She removed the diamond-shaped crystal that had been stuck on my forehead and the chain that encircled my head. Then, the handsome young pianist finished the last notes of a beautiful song. I also remembered his name: Bhav.

"I know you are very sleepy," Maya said, holding a white bowl. "Take a few sips of this water; you'll feel better."

"Where… where I—" I tried to say some words.

She stopped me. "Please don't talk, take some of this water first…"

I couldn't move my body because I was so sleepy. Like a nurse helping a patient to eat, she had to help me position my head upright to drink the liquid.

"Don't worry, your astral energy will return quickly," the pianist said, approaching me and looking at me like a doctor. A holographic image appeared beside me.

He shouted to someone standing on the opposite side of the back room. "Silver cord vibration at ninety-five per cent, gold cord and mental body already fully stabilised, good prana level at ninety per cent, slow breathing at deep-sleep level, physical heart already upping the beats."

With a few sips, I already felt less sleepy.

I asked, "Who are you?"

"We have already introduced ourselves before. She is Maya, and I am Bhav. And who are you?" he asked, returning the same question to me.

"Me? In this life, my conscience is named Sandra Wonlecty. I have discovered that I am an Initiate, but I am not yet sure what it means…"

His teeth gleamed in a beautiful smile. "Do you know what day it is today, Sandra?"

"I'm not certain... It's been many days since I was here the first time..."

After my answers, he gave another smile, and I heard a round of applause. I was startled out of the armchair. Near the opposite wall of the immense hall were Narquiamides, Adhya, Bha, Priest José Archiolano, Jade, and Kennis, the mayor of Yudh. I also identified the Asian man who had helped Dino's father. There were several other people I did not know. From their clothing and appearance, they seemed to belong to different religions at different times in the world.

I went towards them, and they continued their applause. I did not understand at all why.

Narquiamides, standing next to a bearded man with a white tunic and vivid eyes, invited me to walk with him alone in a nearby garden.

When I left that place, I was impressed. I had just left an immense palace in a mountainous region. On the side, there was a waterfall that emitted a pleasant sound. The sky was clear, with various pastel colours, illuminating a vast garden in front of us. There were vibrant flowers, leafy trees, butterflies, and birds.

As we walked along a path, he pulled two small apples from his pocket, one for himself and the other he offered to me. "Eat it.

They're from the orchard around here; it'll energise you even more."

As he ate the apple, I noticed it was impossible to get dirty with its juice. He broke off a piece of his with his mouth and threw it on the ground. This disappeared, absorbed by the soil.

"At this astral plane level where we are, there are other laws for atomic transformation. But we are not going to go into these subjects now. Let's deal with your journey."

"Journey? What is this place? What was all that applause about?" I asked.

"Bhav asked you two questions, but your answer to the second one was incorrect… we expected this. What is time and space for physics, Sandra?"

"First, we need a referential. It depends on some variables. If we consider the speed of light as an absolute variable—"

"Time is an illusory variable," he said. "It's useful for particles that move with low velocity like those on Earth—"

"We have gravitation time dilation. Time passes more slowly near the Earth than at the top of a mountain." I interrupted him, trying to show some knowledge.

"Yes, that is true. However, let's go deeper. You know that the time of Earthly molecules is not the same for atomic levels. Imagine astral subatomic levels that we find ourselves in, where we can move through portals at immeasurable distances and speeds. If we take the Earth as a reference, its clocks' time will not be related to the astral and mental molecular levels. If we continue going far beyond the mental levels, in the seventh, we will reach the Creator, where for Him, time does not exist."

"I don't understand what you are getting at..."

"The accident hasn't happened yet, Sandra, but it will happen soon. You only sat in that armchair for a few minutes. It was only a piece of beautiful music played on the piano. Your physical body is still sleeping in your flat. Everything you experienced, from meeting Adhya in your flat to walking in that beautiful garden after leaving Aphasya, was only a future vision."

I was so surprised by the unexpected explanations that I couldn't say anything.

He continued, "Our consciences travel far beyond the speed of light. Our mental body can expand to reach the Akashic field, where the past, present, and future are recorded. In your journey, you have seen the future that has not happened yet."

"So, everything that happened was only a vision of the future. My mental body travelled to the Akashic field inside that room..."

"That's correct."

"I remember perfectly what you said when we talked about the prophecies. The past is recorded, and the future comprises multiple probabilities..."

"Exactly. The recorded future in the Akashic field has the highest probability of happening and can be modified. It would be like recording a new file over the old one in a computer's memory.

Humanity constantly reshapes its future through present actions intimately linked to its immutable past.

"Wow! It's amazing! Will I remember it all when I wake up?"

"Perfectly, but I suggest making your notes in the first twelve hours to avoid losing the details."

"It's strange that I will wake up and realise that I already know much about Dino, Stephanie, and Vincent, even though I've never met them."

"Now is the time to find out what the experiment λ3 is about. I will give you an example: imagine you won a beautiful and valuable porcelain vase and carelessly broke it when you bumped it with your arm. You were unfortunate and decided to glue the pieces back together. What will happen?"

"It will never be the same because now it has crack marks."

"Exactly. That's because you cannot return to the past. However, if you somehow had the foresight that it would break in an exact moment and place, you would likely have been more cautious and avoided damaging it… That is experiment λ3. We will give them precise information about everything that will happen to them during and after the accident, so, hopefully, they will avoid it and rewrite the future."

"How sure are you that they will avoid the accident?"

"There is no certainty, just a high probability… Their lives are much more valuable than porcelain vases." He smiled.

"How do they know their future?"

"To employ a term you know, the process will be like a quantum-level *download* into their consciences, three Earthly seconds before the accident happens."

"Only three seconds earlier?"

"What are three seconds for the quantum computer you are working on, compared to the best classical computer?"

"Thousands of times faster..."

"Three seconds is the maximum time allowed, but it is enough time for consciences to act. In the example I gave you, imagine that seconds before you bumped into the vase, you had already seen it breaking and you trying to glue the parts together... Similarly, they will have a strong intuition that an accident will occur and know everything that will happen to them if they don't avoid it. One of the reasons that three seconds is the maximum time is that if they receive the information before this, they may think they are delirious. Humanity has not yet mastered the mind; it is fast and distracted, causing mental confusion. One thought in seconds generates several others in an uninterrupted chain. That is the biggest challenge of a real meditation."

"How do they get the information?"

"Now, the three crystals will come in. Do you remember that we placed a diamond-shaped crystal on their foreheads in the future? These crystals contain all the information from the Akashic field about what they have lived and felt, from the accident until the moment we placed them. This morning, we placed another crystal on their foreheads. It was just before they woke up for activities, while their astral bodies were, as usual, slightly dislocated from the physical in their beds. The foreheads on these bodies we named as the third astral eyes—"

"They will make a quantum entanglement," I interrupted with enthusiasm.

"Yes! Each crystal will perform a perfect quantum entanglement with its counterpart, which was placed in the future. This will bring the experiences of the Akashic field directly into the consciences living in the present. In other words, all three will know everything about the accident, including their future events."

"That is amazing! And explainable by quantum physics," I said, impressed.

"It is time for scientists to start investigating some phenomena previously considered ghostly in more depth."

"Vincent will recognise me, then. He was the only one who saw me in the future," I said excitedly.

"He will recognise you perfectly. He and the others will be confused, and it will be up to you to explain it to everyone. This quantum entanglement is programmed to occur 3.01 seconds before the accident. So, they will have three seconds to avoid it, and then immediately change not only their future but also the future of many others involved in their lives and deaths."

"This is why you can't intervene – just provide the information and let them decide. Very clever strategy."

"We are all connected. Every decision we make has a powerful cascading effect on Earth and the astral plane. You will see it…"

"The planes are interconnected."

"Absolutely! Humanity doesn't know it…" He gave a smile that only a wise person can make. "Well, I must go now, and it's almost time for you to wake up. My accident team is already around the corner, finalising the details. They don't know I'm here or the next steps. Only the people you've just seen in the hall know."

"But what about Julian, the boy who betrayed you?"

"He's there. I won't be able to change his position. It's too risky to rewrite the future." He looked at me and winked. "But it would be vital to have an ambulance nearby, just in case."

Adhya had just arrived in the garden where we were standing, and he concluded, "I will leave you with Adhya, who will pass on the last instructions. Good luck, Sandra. Together, we will rewrite the future of three lives in just three seconds. And we will disrupt some of the Golden Circle's plans."

I walked with Adhya until we reached a solitary tree, different from the others. It was not very tall; from the beginning of its trunk to the first branches, it was about three metres. But it was very leafy, and its trunk had a vast diameter. Its thick and tall roots made tortuous paths along its sides that indicated its millenary age.

She looked at me and explained, "The day after tomorrow, you must meet the man who will write the book for you. For security reasons, I cannot tell you his name, only the coordinates for where he will be. Every year, he does a meditation ritual on the summer solstice. It is easy to remember the coordinates 36.7200 and -4.4040. He will be there at sunrise; it is a beach in southern Spain."

"Southern Spain?"

"Trust me. Even though you will only meet me in the future, we're already friends." She laughed. "Another important thing: he doesn't know he will write your book, but he will see after you introduce yourself and tell your story."

"Wow! It's the strangest encounter of my life." I paused. "Adhya, what is it to be an Initiate? What do I have to do? Which path should I follow?"

"Let's concentrate first on the book. After that, you will find the right way. I am your mentor, and I will help you..."

"Mentor? That means..."

"It means I've been protecting you and following your steps for many years..."

"So, you know everything about me."

"Almost everything. I know your family, boyfriends, tastes, favourite foods... Your little dog Luke can see me, and we play occasionally. Until now, I've just been watching you without intervening."

"This is an invasion of privacy," I joked.

"Narquiamides introduced me to you when you were still a baby. We were in your room, and your mother, asleep but out of her body, suddenly came in and saw us there. When she woke up, she said she had dreamed of angels."

"I knew about this dream…" I laughed. "Well, any advice, mentor?"

"Not now…" she replied awkwardly.

"Come on. I insist… we are close friends now."

"OK… just one thing. I want to talk about something important, woman to woman."

Why did I ask? Sometimes, it's better to keep our mouths shut. Now, I was highly insecure. I knew she would unload intimate matters we occasionally don't want to hear…

"I was not allowed to throw ideas into your stubborn mind, but now I can do it in person. The most beautiful consciences are not necessarily linked to stunning, perishable physical bodies or other superfluous factors that your current society values. A woman will only be happy in love if she can look further and follow powerful feminine intuition. It is the inner rational voice of conscience, and it never fails. You know who is suffering for you…"

The words were perfect for me at that moment. My conscience had already given me heavy internal explanations about my frustrated relationships. It opened a new perspective for me, which my unconscious had buried despite it being obvious.

"I get the message, Adhya. You are right… Thank you." I agreed and felt embarrassed…

She hugged me and said, "Now is the time. May the Infinite Spirit enlighten you. Soon, we will meet again. Good luck."

A portal opened on the trunk of the millenary tree in front of us, emanating a bright white light.

I followed through it to continue my mission...

Chapter 28

The Future in Three Seconds

London – twelve minutes before the accident

I woke up on the sofa in my living room. My rational mind wanted to convince me that everything I had experienced was just an absurd dream.

The wall clock showed that it was 8.45 p.m. I got up and approached the living room mirror. When I saw my image reflected in the mirror, I felt relieved.

However, Luke was behaving unusually; he started barking in my direction as if he wanted to tell me something I didn't understand. The doorbell rang, and it was my neighbour, Mrs Evans, with a plate in her hand holding her delicious apple pie. At this instant, my conscience told me those absurd events were not a dream.

"Mrs Evans, you are so lovely. I need to take care of an urgent matter. Please look after Luke for me." I grabbed my phone and handbag and hurried towards the accident scene.

As I ran, the rational side of my mind fought with my inner conscience, trying to convince me that this was all nonsense, but the conscience won the battle.

I called the emergency services, saying there had been an accident at the corner where I had been with Adhya. My memories intensified, with sensations of déjà vu everywhere I passed. I remembered various cars, buildings, and people. When I passed by Carl, my colleague in the lab, this time he greeted me with a look of astonishment at seeing me running.

At the corner by the Japanese restaurant Seikatsu, I could not see the older man with a suit and cane that I had bumped into. But he was around there, invisible to my physical eyes, like others I had seen around town.

Sometime later, I spotted the ambulance I had called parked on the corner with the siren lights flashing. The clock on the advertising light showed the time: 8.59 p.m. I approached its two occupants as quickly as possible, and one of them was talking on his phone. I stepped in front of the ambulance, not letting them go.

"Please move out of the way," the driver said. "We have a call to answer; this one was a false alarm."

"Please, you can't go. I called the emergency. There's going to be an accident here," I begged.

For the first time in my life, I felt how people with mental illnesses are treated.

The man next to the driver patiently got out of the ambulance. "Calm down, you don't look well. Let us—"

"It's going to happen. It's going to happen," I shouted.

The traffic lights for all pedestrians turned red, regardless of the direction. Then, all vehicle lights in all directions turned green. I positioned myself a few metres away from the pedestrian crossing and waved both hands like a traffic officer. Vincent recognised me, slowed down, and braked sharply. He was nudged by a car just behind. The vehicle driven by Stephanie, behind the truck, also stopped. The third vehicle, Dino's, managed to avoid the high-speed truck. The car mounted the pavement and hit a shop. Luckily, no pedestrians were injured. The impact was strong, breaking the shop windows. Some vehicles from both directions bumped into each other.

The traffic lights returned to normal.

The paramedics were looking at everything with wide eyes.

"We need a defibrillator," I shouted, pointing to Dino's crashed car.

Vincent and Stephanie got out of their vehicles and headed towards Dino's car; Dino was also alive.

The three looked at the young driver's body on the ground, as the paramedics tried to revive him. They glanced at each other and at the one thing they had in common: a slight diamond mark on their foreheads. The strong activation of the crystals in the astral body affected the physical. In a few seconds, Dino was in tears as the young man's heart beat again.

The three hugged emotionally, now knowing they had something in common besides the mark on their foreheads. They didn't know the three seconds would be a new chance for their destinies.

I stood beside them when Dino said, "The guys said you called the ambulance before the accident… Thank you. Who are you?"

"She was with me… there… you know…" Vincent answered awkwardly. "I can't explain it. When I saw her, I was certain there would be an accident, and I stopped the car."

"It's so strange," Stephanie said. "I also knew I was going to have an accident, with all the details. I was sure when I looked in the rear-view mirror and saw this mark on my forehead. Then I slowed down my car and stopped."

"I also knew," Dino said, "if I didn't warn my driver about the truck, the impact could have been fatal for both of us." He looked around and whispered, "I had a vision of after my death…"

"Me too…" Stephanie and Vincent said.

"What happened to us?" Stephanie asked.

Dino whispered, "I think it is a military experiment—"

"I can explain," I interrupted. "I am Sandra Wonlecty, just a physicist with a mission to write your stories. I know exactly what you three have been through, Dr Walter, Katharina, Petrus…" At that moment, they looked at me, frightened. "All of you know exactly what would happen if you were dead. But there is a complex physical explanation, which involves time and space."

They remained silent, looking at me, perplexed.

There was already a massive traffic jam, with people out of their cars, police, firefighters…

I suggested, "Now is not the time and place to talk about this. I must travel tomorrow but haven't booked the flight yet. I need to meet you all before my trip; we will keep in touch. Until then, please only share your story with someone who won't think you've gone mad. If you know what I mean…" They all nodded, and we swapped contact details.

"That's a good idea," Dino agreed. "The ambulance is waiting for me; I'm going with my driver, Joe, to the hospital. We'll all be exchanging messages."

Vincent gasped. "I also have something urgent to deal with." He was desperately trying to reach Daphne on his phone.

"Don't worry," Stephanie said. "You all can go. I will talk to the authorities here. The important thing is that there were no victims." After a sigh, she amended, "We are victims of ourselves…" Everyone nodded. "My secretary can make a reservation in a place for all of us. We will keep in touch…"

Another police car had just arrived. Vincent and I approached a police officer, talking about Daphne. He said that she would be close to suicide, probably by throwing herself off the balcony of the ninth floor of the flat where she lived. People needed to be sent there urgently to try to prevent it.

The policeman listened to the story and looked into Vincent's eyes, which were pleading for help. He called his station and asked a team to go immediately to Daphne's flat.

"What an evening..." the policeman exclaimed. "My friend will take you to the place you indicated. Good luck."

It was my first time in a police car. I felt the adrenaline activated with the sirens on, diverting the traffic jam that had been formed and proceeding at high speed. Vincent was sweating, with his eyes watering. He remained quiet. The silence was broken by several unsuccessful attempts to call Daphne. There were slow points in other streets that held us up. This made me think about time. How anxiety makes a few seconds seem like many minutes in our minds.

We arrived near a residential building. A crowd was watching from the street and neighbouring buildings: a woman was on the balcony, standing on the ledge, of the ninth floor. The police, firefighters, and an ambulance were already on the scene.

We went up, and when we reached the floor of Daphne's flat, a policeman, a fireman, and a couple of paramedics were at the door, which was already partially open. Inside, a calm, serene policewoman in the middle of the room was talking to the suicidal woman. She was slowly approaching Daphne, who was drunk, looking ahead at other buildings far away and sometimes at the crowd below.

On the table in the living room were a few bottles of alcoholic drinks, some of them open.

"I understand how you feel, Daphne. I'm a woman like you. I'll get a drink here too, OK? Wow! Gin with fruit," she exclaimed. "This is my favourite drink... I see we have a lot in common. Please tell me more about Vincent."

"Vincent is a sexist pig... I think all men are... we women don't deserve this... what's the point of living in this male world?" she mumbled, crying, and looked up at the sky. "Where is God to protect us?"

The policeman in the corridor warned his colleague inside, who was wearing a wire, of Vincent's presence. He wanted to help. He provided a microphone for Vincent to talk to the policewoman, who listened to him through an earpiece.

The policewoman was getting closer and closer and continued, "What would happen if Vincent came here and apologised—"

"That is impossible... he can't even say sorry... I will make him feel sorry for cheating me. He'll never get his hands on me again." She looked at the crowd below, who were emanating desperate sounds.

"Look at the sky; what do you see now? Up there are powerful forces." Daphne looked up; the policewoman was already quite close. "What if a miracle happened right now? Vincent came here, saying that he was deeply sorry with all his heart and wanted to marry you. And even more, he would say that this powerful and inexplicable force, which many know as God, made him reflect that love for you was the most important thing in his life."

"Impossible…"

"Nothing is impossible for the Lord, Daphne. We are not perfect; we all make mistakes in life… If Vincent came here and told you that one of the most exciting moments of his life was the first kiss you had at the door of this building when he brought you home after dinner, that he wanted to repeat this emotion every day until the end of your lives…"

"But… how do you know?" Daphne turned and saw Vincent standing in the middle of the room in silence, tears streaming down his face.

At this moment of distraction, the policewoman slipped her arms around Daphne's waist, pulling her to the floor of the balcony. Daphne fell on top of her, the policewoman cushioning her fall.

The crowd who had watched the rescue applauded. Vincent ran to embrace her; he said he would give up all dreams of power for a true love dormant in his conscience. Then he knelt before her and asked her to marry him right there. Vincent thanked the policewoman for doing an exceptional job.

Before I left, she commented in private to me, "Thanks for the warning you gave us. We arrived in time to save another life. We managed to open the door just after she had climbed onto the balcony, where we started talking. Thank God we managed to avoid another suicide in this city. Unfortunately, when we arrive, it is often too late…"

I called a taxi and went to the hospital where Dino and his driver were. On the way, I found the city of my destination with the GPS coordinates that Adhya had given me: Malaga, Spain. Immediately, I bought a ticket for the following day in the late afternoon from Luton airport and booked a hotel nearby. I sent the information to the group, suggesting we have lunch. It certainly would be a long night for everyone.

In the hospital, Joe was sleeping, monitored by some machines. Dino was talking to a black lady sitting near the patient's bed. When I entered the room, he introduced me to Mrs Lindsey, the boy's mother. She had a beautiful smile that conveyed an indescribable peace.

"I want you to know that I have great admiration for your son," Dino said. "I experienced trauma with cars and have never wanted to drive. He is the best driver I ever had, as well as his talent for making sweets." He paused, sighed, and continued, "I've done a lot of wrong in this life, but I've never involved this boy in my dirty dealings. He's always been a—"

"You don't need to explain the details of your business, Dino," the woman said. "I know this world and the underworld very well. I've taught my son since he was a little boy, when he lost his father, to follow the path of Christ. It was through Him that Joe always drove your car. Jesus is also present in the underworld, Dino, but hidden. You must take the right path to find him."

At this moment, Dino collapsed in tears, and the woman got up and hugged him like a mother hugging her son. I also could not hold back my tears.

We were interrupted by a man in a suit, who gave Dino a briefcase. "Dino, I'll wait for you outside. We need to go; I've already made an appointment with Inspector Hunter at the police station."

Dino handed the briefcase to the woman and said, "I'm going to fix some wrong things I've done over the years. We probably won't ever meet again. Here's enough for Little Joe to follow his dream of opening a confectionery shop—"

"We can't accept your money. I'm sorry," she said.

"I left this money aside with my trusted lawyer for emergencies, if something happened to me, and today it happened. I can't explain it now. Please accept this money as a demonstration of one who has found a light in the underworld and will try to take the right path."

Without giving the woman time to refuse her gift again, he kissed Little Joe on the forehead and hurriedly left, wiping away a few tears. I walked with him to the hospital door.

"Sandra, I'm going to see the inspector, Hunter, reveal all I know, and try to negotiate some benefits… but first, I have another delivery to make. I think it would be interesting if you came with us."

I got into his lawyer's car, in the back seat with Dino. He had another black briefcase, similar to the one he had left with Mrs Lindsey.

We arrived in a residential neighbourhood, where the lawyer stopped the car and pointed to one of the houses. I got out with Dino and his briefcase, and we walked towards the residence.

A woman opened the door, wearing the uniform of a fast-food brand. She started talking. "Look, if it's about money, I'll let you know that Petrus has passed away. We have been separated for over two years, and I am busy now…"

"No… I knew Petrus… well, how can I say it?" Dino said, embarrassed.

I interrupted to help him. "Your ex-husband won a big fight. His dream was to have a new life and stop fighting. He deeply loved his son and loved you very much, too. He was going to try a new job with the money he won and save another part for the boy's future."

"Deep down, he was a good soul," Dino commented. "Something powerful that was born with him drove him to fight. It wasn't entirely his fault…"

Dino paused momentarily and handed over the briefcase. "This is his. Petrus would like his son to have a better future than him."

The woman opened a small gap in the briefcase; there was a lot of money inside.

She looked, startled, at Dino, who continued, "He was murdered. Here is the money that he earned. I am sure this will make him happy, wherever he is now."

"Murdered? But by whom? Who are you?" she asked with tear-filled eyes.

"Never mind. Leave this job to the police; they will find out and do justice, I guarantee it," he assured her. "Follow up in the newspapers in the coming days. I wish you and your son the best."

"Before I forget," I said, looking into her eyes. "Promise me that you will go to a church with your son tomorrow and light a candle for Petrus. He will feel the energy. Please promise."

"Yes… I promise," the woman exclaimed, still in shock.

Before getting into the car, Dino asked me, "Tell me something, Sandra. Does this whole candle thing work?"

"You can't imagine how…" I smiled.

"We are now going to the police. Will you come with us?"

"No. I'll call a taxi. I must do something personal that I should have done long ago." I checked my phone and said, "Stephanie just sent us a message for lunch tomorrow with everyone."

"If I'm not locked up in a cell, I'll go. I want to hear your explanations of what happened to us."

~*~

I called Alex, my best friend and colleague, and asked him to help me with something urgent and personal. I invited him to my flat and told him to bring his notebook, without further explanation.

When I opened the door, he had a worried expression. He knew something was wrong because we'd already said goodbye. The following day, I was going to visit my mother and sister in Italy.

He looked at me, with his blue eyes behind his black-framed glasses. I removed his glasses and started kissing him madly, without saying a word. We jumped on the couch, but my little dog wanted to play, so we went straight to my room. For the first time, I loved and felt truly loved. It was a pleasurable exchange of indescribable purity that only emanates from kindred souls.

For several hours, throughout the night, Alex helped me in my mission. I did not know anyone better than him for this Herculean task. I told him in detail everything that had happened to me. As I recounted my experience, he made many small recordings and numbered them in his notebook, dividing them by subject and chronology. It was amazing how I remembered every detail.

Alex also drew a chronological diagram on various sheets of paper that he placed on the wall in my living room. We could visualise what was being recorded, and, at the same time, he meticulously edited my voice for text. When I remembered the details of passages already registered, he put them in the previous recordings and rearranged the text.

It was already dawn. Everything was clear and organised, without missing one single detail.

Exhausted, we slept...

Chapter 29

The Day After

"Get up, Sandra!" a familiar female voice called to me.

I felt an intense burning between my eyebrows, like a flame close to my face.

When I opened my eyes, I saw Adhya looking at me. Then I got up from the sofa. When I looked back, my physical body was on the couch, sleeping with Alex. His astral body floated about twenty centimetres above his physical body, connected by the silver cord.

It was past eight o'clock in the morning.

Looking at Alex thoughtfully, she said, "Sometimes what we seek is right before us. We must look with our consciences to find a beautiful soul and not with our physical eyes, which are perishable and blind to this kind of light."

She was correct; Alex was not the stereotypical male beauty society makes us look for. But after having given myself to him, I understood the immense love that was latent. The handsome prince women seek is far beyond the physiques exalted by the media.

Luke, who was awake, stood next to us, wagging his little tail.

"I've already told you dogs have clairvoyance, and Luke is one of the best… Come on, Sandra, we can't be late," Adhya said, always rushing.

"Again? Another accident?" I asked.

"No," she giggled. "We must go to a few places here in London. You will love the experience. We are going through portals. Let's do your first lesson as an Initiate. Hold my hand and learn how to open one. Clear your mind and concentrate only on Dino. The portal will open and take us to where he is now."

After a few seconds, she shouted, "More intensity – you can do it. Awaken the Initiate within you."

"OK. I'm trying…"

"No, you aren't."

"What do I have to do?"

"You must concentrate. Think of Dino with strength; breathe, breathe, and think… Wow! You did it! It is opening."

I saw a portal opening, and we entered a room in a flat.

A man was sitting on the sofa smoking and looking at messages on his phone. I recognised him immediately: it was Robert, Petrus's manager. He was interrupted by the sound of the doorbell announcing Dino's arrival.

"What is so urgent that you need to talk to me, Dino?" Robert asked nervously. "I have already paid my debt to you. I am going to hand over this flat and leave London later today." He pointed to a bag in the corner of the room. "My wife and son are already at my brother-in-law's house in Ireland; you know I will be starting a new life there."

"Robert, be honest, how did you get the money to pay me?"

"I told you, Dino, Petrus won the big fight," he replied anxiously.

"You are a great liar. I have many contacts, you know this. We are orphanage friends. Let's be frank with each other. I heard you bet all your money on Thunder, the opponent." Robert looked at Dino with astonishment.

Dino continued, "I imagine this is what happened: you found Petrus, a good street fighter. He asked you for a big fight. You were sure Petrus would lose, a novice versus the undefeated Thunder, but decided to send him to his death."

Dino took out his phone and showed some website pages. "You sold the false image that he was an Eastern European champion. You created fake profiles and convinced the fight house that it would be one of the year's biggest fights. Instead of trusting your man, you bet everything on your opponent, and what happened? Petrus won. But I know you always have a plan B. You faked Petrus's death and stole all his money. I don't understand how you did it."

"Don't give me moral lessons, Dino. You are dirtier in this world than me. The difference is that you were lucky enough to be adopted by a wealthy family involved in shady deals… you already got your money back. Yes, I found Petrus lost in street fights. He earned a few pounds, barely enough to pay for his dressings. I felt he had potential and booked a few fights. He earned some money and soon insisted he wanted to fight the invincible Thunder."

He paused and lit another cigarette. "What did you want me to do? I told the fight house a few lies about his past and potential and booked the fight. I was sure it would be a quick fight, and with luck, he would come out alive. He started by getting beaten. But soon after, I don't know where he got this tremendous strength I had never seen before. He transformed himself into a fighting machine and defeated his adversary. Nobody expected it. There was absolute silence when Thunder fell unconscious."

"Then you decided to kill him and keep all the money."

"He was a nobody. He would die sooner or later. His brain had only muscles. I had no way out. I never imagined I would have to use my plan B. I already had a copy of the key to his flat, and I poisoned him with a drug that slowly led to cardiac arrest. Then I left the flat locked, everything intact without any sign of a break-in. I destroyed his phone so no one could access his contacts, and it was as simple as that."

"You know he had a little son and an ex-wife."

"Who cares? I had to protect my family."

"We already have a confession, don't we?" Dino asked, looking at the door.

"What?"

"I am not talking to you, Robert."

The door opened, and Inspector Hunter entered with the police. He handcuffed Robert. Dino removed the wiretaps on his body.

"You traitor, Dino. Why? Why?"

"I know you will not understand, but I'm helping you. Petrus will be less angry when he comes after you. Pray he spares you when he finds you in jail, paying for what you have done."

"He is dead. Dead! Idiot!" he shouted as the policemen took him away.

"No, Robert. We don't die the way you imagine. This is the problem..." Dino shouted.

~*~

"Sandra, open a portal now to go to where Stephanie is."

I managed to open a new portal.

We entered a lift. There were Stephanie and her husband in a wheelchair. She was looking younger and different. Her hair was loose, light make-up highlighted her blue eyes, and she wore a blue-and-white-flowered summer dress. Her husband was wearing a suit and tie.

The secretary was waiting for her with a look of surprise. "Good morning, Mr and Mrs Puizhant."

The woman reciprocated by smiling at the young woman, who offered to help push her husband; however, Stephanie did not allow it, saying that she wanted to take him herself.

"Everyone is already in the room waiting, and as per your message, I have scheduled a press conference for later this afternoon. I have not prepared anything for this meeting because you have not yet informed me of the agenda—"

"Don't worry," Stephanie said. "I'd like to tell you something I've never mentioned before." Her secretary looked at her weirdly. "You are an excellent professional; your work is precise and perfect. Whenever you need anything, count on me. I appreciate your patience with me over our years together."

The woman thanked her, visibly taken aback. The other employees were also astonished. As Stephanie walked down the office corridor, taking her husband to the meeting room, she said good morning to her employees; she even called some of them by name.

When Stephanie entered the meeting room, the board of directors were awaiting her. She looked at them and said, "Firstly, I want to thank everyone for being here. I had to schedule this meeting at the last minute because it is crucial. That's why my husband, Edgard, is also here, for his participation as a partner in the company."

They all left the room, and Stephanie stood next to them. Her secretary called all the employees, including those on the other floor, to approach.

"I want to see everyone's face," the chairwoman shouted. "You can bring your chairs and stand; whoever wants to can sit on the tables or on the carpet nearby. However you feel best."

A few dozen employees quickly approached, positioning themselves in a U-shape. Their facial expressions were varied. Some showed great concern, perhaps expecting a devastating announcement about their jobs. Others showed curiosity because it was an unprecedented attitude from the president. Invisible to human eyes, a black lady in a white dress and a scarf wrapped around her head entered. I immediately recognised Bha, with her mother's smile. Her astral body emanated a bright white light when she passed by us. I could feel the powerful vibrational energy directly hitting my astral cells, bringing a sense of calm and peace.

I accompanied Adhya by making a bow sign with both palms together, and she reciprocated by saying, "Girls, may the powerful energy of God pour a drop of His infinite love into the hardened hearts at this meeting."

She went right next to Stephanie, who was unaware of her unseen presence, and immediately benefited from that loving energy.

Suddenly, an impressive communication between planes took place. Invisible to human eyes, just above the U formed by the employees, many youths were sitting on various stone steps that extended far beyond the office walls. The physical office was now in an astral arena. Elisabeth was on the lowest part, with her long white hair and old face, holding the wooden stick. Next to her was Narquiamides, her brother, and her mother, Lydia. At that moment, everyone in the arena silently watched the physical plane as Stephanie began her speech.

"It was an intense night. I talked to many people: my husband Edgard, lawyers, investors, and my right-hand friend, John. I want to inform everyone that I am stepping down from the company's presidency, and John will take over in my place."

She looked lovingly at her husband and continued, "Edgard and I have enough resources to live quietly. But this does not mean that we will stop. Since I was a little girl, I've always loved baby clothes. When I started Steph Baby, it was initially geared towards babies, and then we added a children's line at the mothers' requests. I had no idea that our company would grow so much. I didn't do it alone; you all made the company grow."

She paused momentarily. "But I discovered that I need to contribute a lot more to the world, not only by creating jobs, and that is why my husband and I are going to open the Steph Child Foundation: a company dedicated to helping orphaned children of all ages to have a more dignified future. We want to ensure quality housing, food, and education, fulfilling their true potential."

There was a round of applause. "I will dedicate every minute until the end of my life to this project, which is being born today... And you know what happens when I work hard..." she joked, and everyone laughed. "I dream the Steph Child Foundation can reach other countries, just as our shops have. We don't intend to solve the world problem, but aim to reach as many orphaned children as possible within our resources."

After another brief pause, she continued, but now with a saddened look and tears. "I am always asked what the biggest secret of my success as an entrepreneur is, and I always reply that it is my passion for children. When we are in love with something, sometimes we aren't able to reflect the true reasons behind such a strong feeling. Passion without maturity can lead us to destruction. Success and power blinded me, and I didn't realise how many children suffer around us."

Her tears were flowing. "I consulted the best doctors in the world for years, hoping for some possible treatment. But all were always unanimous in stating that I would never achieve the greatest dream of my life, which was to be a mother. Several times, I watched children playing in the parks and cried, hating God for why He did this to me. Then, I decided not to believe in Him any more. Edgard tried to convince me we should adopt children several times, but my selfishness was superior, and I never listened to him."

She looked at Edgard and said, “Besides taking care of all these children, I will take care of you too, my husband. That is what we do for the people we love.”

She wiped away the tears. “This situation caused me a massive inner turmoil, and I became a sceptical, bitter, and envious person – envious of mothers who had precious jewels, which I could never have. I owe you, Alison, a special apology for my recent stupidity.”

With her eyes filled with tears, Alison made a small gesture with her head and hands, showing that there was nothing to apologise for.

“Today, I fully understand what God has prepared as a mission in this life for me. Instead of being selfishly the mother of my biological children in a closed bubble, He allowed me to be the mother of many orphaned children. Now I can see this great gift. Today is when I turn the most important page of my life to write my story following another path. From the depths of my soul, I thank God. Nothing, absolutely nothing, happens in our lives by chance. Being barren was, in fact, a great blessing; it is the great opportunity I have in this life that passes so quickly to help children with total love. A latent love, and that I finally found…”

She took a deep breath. “I want to end by thanking you all for your work and dedication. Finally, to humbly ask forgiveness, not only of everyone here but others, wherever they are, who lived toxic moments with my inner monster that I have finally buried…” She lowered her face, putting her hands on it, flooded by tears.

The silence was broken by several employees, who wiped their tears after hearing these unexpected confessions from their president.

"Whatever you need help with at the Steph Child Foundation, count on me," Alison exclaimed.

"And me…"

"And me…" All the employees stood up and repeated Alison's gesture.

"The whole team is with you, Stephanie," John said emotionally, hugging her and the other board members.

Bha raised her arms and opened a hexagonal portal in the room's ceiling, invisible to human eyes. It emanated rays of pastel-coloured light that bathed both planes simultaneously. It was impressive to see the powerful energy of love emanating from the room, which was shared with that astral arena where the invisible spectators were.

Bha gave a signal to Narquiamides. He opened a new portal next to the arena in the astral. Elisabeth was crying and was the first to enter, beside her mother. Her appearance transformed again into a beautiful girl. Her brother and all the other youths followed.

Narquiamides looked at me, smiled like only a wise man can do, and closed the communication between planes.

I felt that the power of love is as contagious as hate, yet at the opposite extreme; it can make all weapons, wherever they are, be put down.

~*~

Adhya pulled me by the arm. "Come on, Sandra. We must go now. I have already opened another portal for us," she said. I was so excited that it was difficult for me to concentrate.

She led me towards a nearby room. When we opened the door and entered a church, this time, as it was projected, I could observe that some people were also out of body but visibly unconscious of where they were. Some wandered the aisles babbling nonsense words, and others sat with distant looks.

We got close to Dino, who was lighting a candle and then knelt. Inspector Hunter stood beside him, perhaps making sure he wouldn't try to escape.

"God, it's been a long time since I went into a church to talk to you… I don't know how to pray or what to say to the Lord…"

At that very instant, at the top above the candles, a portal opened, and inside it was his old father in the grey hooded tunic and the Asian man in white clothes that I saw in the experiment, who had carried him into the portal when Petrus had knocked him down.

"I have never killed anyone," Dino continued. "But I know many people have been harmed, and maybe even killed, because of my business… I never imagined there would be an afterlife. I hope I have time to fix a few things around here before I leave Earth. So,

I regret what I did, and I can only ask for forgiveness from you. However, I have learned that words alone are not enough..."

He stopped momentarily, his eyes full of tears. "I lit this candle for my father. A friend told me it works. I've never forgiven him for what he did to my mother. I confess it is still difficult because I loved her very much. My conclusion is that asking for forgiveness is much easier than forgiving. But I feel deep pity after seeing where he is and his appearance. I believe he is sorry and paying dearly for what he did. I do not hate him any more, and I want to talk to him one day on the other side and understand his moments of madness. So, I can also talk about my mistakes. My friendships have always been exclusively for mutual interests; I have been surrounded by many people, but today, I realise I am a great loner."

Tears flowed not only from Dino and his father but also from Inspector Hunter, who secretly heard the words of his prisoner.

"Forgive me, Lord, I seem to have woken up today after decades of a meaningless dream. I have possessions and money that have completely lost their value. I am no longer interested in power, parties, false friends... I hope that, from now on, I can somehow recover my lost time and do something meaningful for my soul. Thank you for the new chance. I will not let you down this time. Amen."

The energy of the candle with its prayer was intense. His crying father disappeared with the man in white clothes. At that moment,

I remembered when I had also lit a candle for my father. I missed him so much…

Adhya looked at me and said, "The power of love has no boundaries… Well, it's time to wake up. You know how to do it. I'll see you soon."

She was right. I put my hand on my neck.

Chapter 30

Sandra – The Fugitive

I immediately returned to my physical body. The sensation was like falling from a great height into a perfectly fitting box.

Alex woke up, and I precisely recorded my experience for fear of missing important details. I was hurriedly packing a suitcase for the trip. But first, I had to go to the restaurant to meet everyone.

"I've told the lab I'm ill," Alex said. "I will stay here to finish editing these last audios, turning them into text and putting them in the cloud in my home directory with the others. I'll download them onto your laptop so you can take them to Spain. Speaking about the company we work for and their links to Aphasya…"

At that moment, I remembered my meeting in Mr Jordan's office. "It's worse than that."

"What?"

"I've just remembered something important. Yesterday, when I entered Mr Jordan's office, a painting with geometric symbols caught my eye: a golden circle with an inverted pentagram symbol and an inverted red triangle in its centre."

"So, Mr Jordan is a member of the Brotherhood of the Golden Circle..."

"That's right. And I think he is related to the new nuclear weapon that Vincent would be involved with..."

"Maybe you are right... the basement of the lab has restricted access. They work on equipment that emitted radiation for medical use."

"We need to give up our jobs. Now that I know who I am, there's no way I can work there..."

"Sure! I'll stay with you wherever you go. I've always loved you, Sandra. It was a spiritual love. I never thought I had a chance."

"I was a fool. I never realised that my conscience had always loved you, but now I know," I admitted, and felt tears welling up in my eyes. "When I return from Spain, we'll go to Italy together. We need a few days away from London to plan our next steps. These investigations from the astral plane can't stop, Alex..."

"You're right. I'm in... I'll pick you up at the restaurant after lunch, and we'll go to the airport together. Leave your suitcase here, and I'll take it with your laptop."

"OK." I said goodbye after a kiss, a woman truly in love.

On the way, I talked to my sister by video call. She had tried to contact me several times after I sent a message that I had already cancelled my flight to Italy. I told her that a critical appointment had come up.

"Sandra, finally! What's more important than your beloved family?"

"I'm going to Spain. I'm going to meet a man, and it's important—"

"Wow," she said. "Look at you. I know you... You look like you're happily in love. Don't you? Tell your sister."

"Am I showing that much?" I asked, surprised.

"Who is this lucky Spaniard? Tell me everything: where you met him, what he's like, what he does—"

"No. In Spain, it's another man. I don't know him yet." I realised I was making a mess of my sister's head, so I decided to summarise. "In Spain, it's a mission... or a work commitment that's come up, and I return tomorrow evening. It's Alex; I'm involved with him."

"Alex? The boy who works with you?"

"He's a man. He looks like a boy."

"Mum is here beside me and says he is a good boy. She likes to talk to him when she visits you in London."

"See, mums know everything. Tell her to keep the vegetarian lasagna in the fridge."

"But... How did you know? It was a surprise," she asked.

"Ah... Sorry, I must go," I interrupted. "I love you; I'll talk to you tomorrow."

I left Hyde Park Corner Tube Station in Knightsbridge and arrived at an elegant restaurant. They immediately directed me to a private room. Everyone was chatting, very cheerfully sharing their experiences: Dino, Stephanie, Edgard, Vincent, and Daphne.

The diamond marks on their foreheads had disappeared completely. I sat down at the table and told them, in general, what had happened to me and that I had seen a little of each person's life, past and future.

I even told them that I had been present at the events that had taken place in the morning. That was full proof of my leaving the physical body. It would have been logistically impossible for me to go to the three places quickly if I hadn't gone through portals.

They asked me dozens of questions, some of which I didn't know how to answer; I needed Narquiamides or Adhya. Without going into the details of when, how, and where, I commented that I would publish a book about everything we had been through. Even if I chose to change a few names, their lives would certainly be exposed. They all agreed and were happy to tell the world what they had been through.

"I already know about Stephanie. And you, Vincent and Dino, what will your lives be like from now on?" I asked.

Vincent looked at Daphne and answered, "Well, we're getting married, and we're going to spend our honeymoon in Paris."

"Excellent choice. I love Paris, a beautiful and romantic city," Stephanie commented.

"Paris has always been Daphne's dream. There, I will try to meet a physics student called Ethan. I treated his brother, and I think I owe him an apology. I want to understand more about unconventional sciences and how to apply them to my patients."

After a pause, he continued, "The hospital director where I work holds meetings with a team. They take in lost people who don't know they've died. If it hadn't been for this experience, I would never have believed that something like that existed, even if someone had sworn it was real. I will ask him if Daphne and I can do something. We're truly interested."

Daphne added, "I want to help. I've been interested in spiritual matters since I was a child, but I never had the chance to study them. Now I wish to understand them better, especially suicide, which I came close to…"

"Another thing I'm going to do," Vincent said, "is to look for more information about my life as Dr Walter. I've seen some information online, but I will dig deep."

Daphne took out her phone and showed a black-and-white photo of a man wearing round glasses and an old suit. "Look at the photo we found on the internet."

Everyone stared in amazement at the resemblance, especially the eyes, to Vincent.

"And I also want to find out about Katharina's life," Stephanie exclaimed. "As soon as possible, I intend to visit Bamberg,

Würzburg, and neighbouring towns in Germany to learn more about my past life."

"In my case, I slept in a cell at the police station," Dino said. "Inspector Hunter is outside waiting for me. I made a big deal with the authorities. Coming to this lunch is part of my negotiation. He knows I'm not going anywhere; I'm being monitored." He raised his right leg a little, where there was an electronic tag. "I've handed over many documents and evidence involving important people. When the bomb explodes, I'll be sentenced to death."

After a pause, he made a funny face and whispered, "They don't know that we don't die. Please don't tell them… I'll return to haunt them." Everyone laughed.

"They're going to take me to a safe place near London for witness protection. I'll leave the country with a new name and passport soon. That's the deal. In any prison around here, they'd kill me in a few days."

"Do you know where you're going?" I asked.

"I was thinking of the Caribbean or the Bahamas." He laughed. "Seriously, it's so top secret that even I don't know. It's a country in Africa. That's the only clue they gave me. I said that I want to work from now on in international humanitarian movements, helping people. I'm leaving everything I have to the UK government. My lawyer is dealing with everything. I no longer have any value to them."

Inspector Hunter approached the door worriedly and called me in for a private chat.

"Miss Wonlecty, I've just had a call from the station, and two investigators specialising in terrorism want to talk to you urgently."

"With me? Sorry, but I can't. I'm going to the airport soon; I've got an international trip. In two days—"

"Unfortunately, it must be today," he said. "They suspect you might be behind some terrorist organisation."

"Terrorist? This is insane," I exclaimed.

"We have your phone records and the paramedics' testimonies. You requested an ambulance minutes before the accident with Dino's car. In addition, we have reports from several people at the scene that the traffic lights mysteriously failed, and so far, the technicians can't explain it. You're a scientist, and you work with very advanced technology... They won't let you leave the country until they understand better."

"Look, Inspector Hunter, I know some things may be strange, but this terrorism story is absurd," I protested nervously.

"Calm down, don't worry. I've been dealing with criminals all my life, and I'm sure you're not one of them," he commented, and I felt relieved. "I know Dino better than anyone else in this city. I've tried to arrest him many times. Suddenly, everything changed. He went to my office with his lawyer. He was so happy handing over all his connections, documents, and proof. We thought he was drunk or on drugs, but no! He said he was sorry and apologised to me. This is strange…"

He took a breath and said, "I'll call my colleagues now and tell them you're here in the restaurant, and I'll take you to the police station when you've finished lunch. Don't worry; they'll only ask you a few questions, and that's it. But they will probably hold your passport."

I returned to the table and told them what I had just heard. They looked at me worriedly.

"Sandra, listen to me. I have experience with these people," Dino advised. "If you must leave the country today, go out the back of the restaurant now. Before you do, switch off your phone and don't take it. When they find out you escaped, they will search for you everywhere. I hope you can buy enough time to reach your destination."

"Our driver is waiting for us nearby, and he'll take you wherever you want," Stephanie said, picking up her phone. "He's been working with me for over ten years. He's extremely reliable. I'm calling him now to pick you up at the back."

"Take my phone," Daphne said, writing the unlock password on a scrap of paper. "Send the contacts you need to speak to before you switch yours off. Let me keep it for when you get back."

"I just need the contact of my boyfriend, Alex, who's in my flat."

"Your flat?" Dino exclaimed. "Call him to get out of there immediately if he doesn't want to be interrogated. Another thing:

don't use the conventional line; always talk through voice apps and, if possible, through a VPN. And then erase all of them."

I called Alex on Daphne's phone. He should leave my flat immediately, with my briefcase and laptop. He needed to destroy all the experiment evidence and notes and remove the papers we stuck up from the wall. I wrote down the passwords to extract the files from the cloud.

I was already in the car on the way to Luton airport when Alex sent me a voice message on Daphne's phone:

"*Sandra, I'm here with your neighbour, Mrs Evans, and Luke. Two strange men have just entered your flat. I think it's easy to trace your journey to Malaga from Luton using your credit card details. I've got another idea; see the document I'm sending you now.*"

An image of a London–Madrid ticket arrived in my name. The problem was that not only was the destination not Malaga, but I was also boarding at another airport: Heathrow. I was travelling in the opposite direction.

"*I bought a ticket at the last minute. I've already checked in electronically with your details. Take a picture of this boarding pass. Then delete the messages, switch off the connection to your phone operator, internet, Bluetooth, and hurry straight to the boarding gate at Heathrow. When you arrive in Madrid, take a taxi to Malaga. Pay for everything in cash; don't use your credit or debit cards. I have the name of the hotel you booked. I'll ask Mrs Evans to call them and cancel the reservation. They must know that you won't be there. Please don't call me again. Only contact me once you've done your mission. Then I can buy your return ticket. Love you."*

I asked the driver to change direction and speed up as much as possible. On the way, I realised why Narquiamides had planned for an unknown person living in another country to write my story. After my experience, I didn't know how far the Brotherhood of the Golden Circle's tentacles reached, who they were, or who they manipulated.

I only had my handbag, so I didn't need to check luggage in.

I rushed through Heathrow Airport, which, in my tense state, seemed to be even larger than usual.

There was a massive queue at security control. I asked to go ahead, explaining that I was late for my flight. I was agitated, nervous, sweating, and couldn't disguise it. How do criminals learn to be calm? It was like a light flashed above my head: she's here, everyone. You can arrest her…

I put my handbag on the luggage belt, and when I went through the metal detectors, a female security guard asked me to go back and remove the metal objects. She was correct; I had forgotten to take Daphne's phone out of my pocket. When I returned and successfully passed through again, she called out to me from the side. *They've found me. I will not make the plane…*

No, she wanted to inspect my bag. I don't know if I was randomly selected or if she just saw my guilty expression. When we're rushing, everything seems to slow us down.

I was already running out of time. I ran as fast as I could. At crucial moments, when we need it most, flights are never late… When I arrived at the boarding gate, there was only one airline employee.

"We've just finished boarding, I'm sorry," she stated calmly.

"No! I need to get on board. I have an important meeting. The flight can't go without me." My voice was a plea for the life of someone drowning.

At this point, she received information on the radio that the aircraft door had something wrong with it. Although it was closed, the pilot said the panel showed it was open. They had to open it again and examine it.

"OK, you're lucky. It seems we have a technical problem with the door. I'll let you in. But next time you board, please arrive early."

They closed the door again just after I got on the plane, and the issue seemed solved. The adrenaline only subsided when the aircraft took off.

All the money I took with me, converted into euros, was a little lower than the pre-fixed taxi fare. But the driver, a very kind man, accepted the money I had available for the night journey of more than 500 kilometres.

He was surprised when he asked me for the destination address to put into his GPS. It was the first time a passenger had given him the coordinates rather than a conventional address. Throughout the journey, we exchanged a few words; he spoke little English, and I didn't know Spanish. To be on the safe side, I did not mention my real name.

When we arrived at our destination, an avenue with several buildings overlooking the sea, it had gone 1 a.m. local time.

I walked along the pavement and saw many restaurants and bars under the buildings, and tables and chairs outside. Despite the time of day, a few people still enjoyed the pleasant warmth of the early morning.

With no money and unable to use my cards, I had to make do with half of the last cereal bar in my handbag. I'd eaten the other half when the taxi had stopped briefly on the road. I sat on a wall, enjoying the beach, whose darkness hid the beauty of the Mediterranean Sea. Luckily, there was a public toilet and drinking fountain nearby.

I found a discreet bench to sleep on. I set the alarm on my wristwatch for 6.50 a.m. There were only a few hours left before dawn for my strange meeting with the man who would finalise my mission. I lay on the bench, using my handbag as a pillow. I admired the star-studded sky, listening to the small waves on the sea, remembering my father…

I fell asleep.

Then I felt my forehead burn and heard a familiar female voice.

"Hello, Sandra. Get up. Leave your physical body asleep on the bench. We need to go now."

Adhya stood looking at me, pulled me by the arms, and my astral body immediately detached from my physical one. Next to her was a three-metre hexagonal portal. Inside it, I saw an illuminated glass pyramid.

"Go where? I'm already here, near the coordinates—"

"To France. We need your help to stop Petrus."

Chapter 31

Disarming Petrus

We came out of the portal.

I immediately recognised the place. It was night in Paris. I was near the glass pyramid that gives access to the Louvre Museum, where Petrus got his astral sword.

As during the λ3 experiment, I could see many people, with diverse appearances. Some of them were out of their bodies, others deceased and wearing ancient clothes from other times. They were scattered everywhere, crowding around the main entrance or walking along the pavements.

Near the door were the two protectors I had seen before. Both were very tall and wore white clothing.

A young sleeper in pyjamas and glasses passed us, holding a briefcase. When he saw me, he asked, "Do you know what is happening in the museum? These two guards won't let us in. Why is it closed today? I need to go to the Denon Wing. I must finish my work on Ancient Greece."

I did not know what to say… I looked at him and said, "Yes… It is under renovation, but it will certainly be open tomorrow. Don't worry. You better go back to your home."

"Tomorrow? No! No! It will be too late… too late… I will wait a little longer by the door. Who knows, maybe they will open." He turned away from us, grumbling, towards the crowd in front of the main door. I was curious to know what kind of dream that boy would think he had when he woke up. Our brain likes to fool us every night about the truth of our astral projections.

"You know exactly what will happen," Adhya commented. "Petrus will come here for the sword, and we need to stop him. Well, you are the one who must stop him. You know I can't intervene," she said with an irritating calmness.

"Let me guess," I said jokingly, "only a living Initiate can intervene."

"That is right, it's the law of multiverses," she replied with a mischievous grin.

"How can I stop a professional fighter carrying a bewitched sword?"

"Well, first, let's get the help of a friend of yours from other lives."

We were close to a crowd, so I had not noticed that next to us was Elisabeth, holding her wooden stick. Her appearance was that of a beautiful girl, no longer showing signs of old age.

"How long have you been here?" I asked.

"You need to pay more attention to your surroundings…" the girl advised. "Adhya commented that you still do not have access to the memories of our Initiation."

"Unfortunately, not yet…"

"So, this is why… But it doesn't matter," she said in a gentle voice. "This is a gift." She held out her hands, offering me her wooden stick.

"Thanks, but I don't know how to use this."

Adhya was about to comment on something, but we were interrupted by the image of a tall man who passed further ahead – shaved head, muscled, and tattooed. As predicted, there was Petrus, blending in with the crowd. In the distance, we spotted the old wizard projected out of his body, wearing a black hooded cloak. He would help the fighter enter the museum.

"We can't let him enter the museum and get the sword. What is the plan?" I asked, distressed.

"This is not the time to change what is scheduled to happen," Adhya explained. "We need to disarm him just before he goes through the portal in the Arc de Triomphe du Carrousel."

"But why?"

"Look at this crowd. If we act ahead, we risk innocent people getting hurt, and we will change their future. We are not allowed to do this. It is against the law of the Creator. Remember, he will take a girl as a hostage. We can't change her future, either. That will be an important dream for the present moment of her psychic life. Nothing, including dreams, happens by chance…"

After a short pause, she continued, "So, he needs to be disarmed before crossing the arch, where his portal for return is. This must happen only after the hostage is released. Be very discreet. Do not underestimate the intelligence of Lyha, the witch with Bogat in the lower astral. She guides Petrus's mind and can see everything through his eyes. Petrus will go to another place if she suspects anything, and we will lose him."

Petrus had already entered the museum. The old wizard headed towards the arch to open the portal.

Adhya withdrew two tiny light blue crystals from her pocket and explained, "Lyha is guiding Petrus, and you, Sandra, will be guided by Elisabeth through these crystals to use the wooden stick."

She pointed to the arch. "You can go. I will stay here in the middle of these people. I can't show up. Lyha knows me. I will accompany you from afar. Place the crystals on your foreheads, between your eyebrows, but only after the wizard opens the portal and leaves. He is wise; if he sees these crystals on your foreheads, he will know something is wrong and quickly change his plans. Beware, the talisman has the strength of the Brotherhood of the Golden Circle."

I was a neophyte Initiate, taking commands from a girl against a strong fighter and a wizard with the Brotherhood superpower… *is there anything worse than this?*

"Ah, I nearly forgot." Adhya advised, "The astral sword is bewitched. If he manages to injure one of you, it could affect your astral cells severely..."

Now, yes, I knew it could get worse.

Elisabeth and I strolled towards the arch. We could already see the old wizard concentrating beside it, holding his talisman in one hand and leaning on the arc wall with the other.

However, an unexpected problem occurred: when he finished the ritual, instead of moving away, he continued leaning against the portal wall, waiting for Petrus to arrive. We were already very close to him; he was looking at us sideways, and we were trying to disguise ourselves as if we were lost. I held the wooden stick in one hand and Elisabeth's hand in the other as if we were aunt and niece.

We heard shouting in the crowd near the pyramid. Petrus was already running with his sword and he reached the hostage, aiming his sword at the middle of her forehead.

The old wizard was not moving. Elisabeth moved away from me and made a sign to place the crystals on our foreheads. When we took the crystals, I managed to attach mine, but hers fell to the ground. The wizard saw it, grabbed her from behind, and pointed a small knife at her head.

"This wooden stick," he shouted. "Do you think you can fool me? Throw it away. Now! You don't know what this dagger's blade might do to this little girl's astral cells here."

"No, Sandra, don't worry about me."

I was in a state of panic. Petrus was coming. I saw Elisabeth's little eyes on that disgusting wizard man and me with the stick in my hands. That was when I felt my eyes burning. I hit the ground with the wooden stick and heard a thunderous noise in the sky.

The old wizard looked at me, astonished. "It is not possible. We have a living Initiate in the world. The Brotherhood must know that."

I controlled his hands now; I released Elisabeth and caused his blade to strike him several times in his face. He fell to the ground and disappeared.

"He is coming; we need to close the portal," Elisabeth shouted, pointing at the fighter approaching like a raging bull.

My feelings were rather strange. Instinctively, I knew how to act but I did not understand where this knowledge came from.

I marked the entrance to the famous arch with a yellowish powder from the tip of the stick. When I finished scratching it, I hit it on its extremity, generating huge flames. Petrus stopped just before the portal door; his passage was impeded.

The protectors stopped nearby and tried to fend off a crowd of curious onlookers who wanted a closer look at what was happening. The fighter looked at me momentarily, his face exuding pure hatred, intensified by Lyha, who guided him. He went towards me like a hungry lion.

With agility – I didn't know where it came from – I managed to evade his sword twice. His silver blade glowed with the flames that prevented his escape.

A strange word came into my mind: *bhuukamp*. I slammed the wooden stick on the ground, and a loud bang made the earth move, in a radius of only three metres from where we were standing. It shook so hard that we both fell. He dropped his sword, and I dropped my stick. With much experience in wars and fights, coming from the power of his sword, he rolled his body to the side on the ground with impressive speed and managed to grab the weapon again. Just as he was coming to annihilate me, the flames ceased. Indeed, following the instructions from Lyha, he changed his route and entered the portal, disappearing.

Elisabeth, who was nearby, shouted, "Let's go after him."

Enraged, I picked up the wooden stick and ran through the portal.

On the other side, to my surprise, I was not in Llyn Din, where Bogat, Lyha, and those monsters were supposed to be. It was a room of a house in England. Petrus's wife and his little son, and Bha and Narquiamides, were projected out of their bodies.

"What is going on here?" I asked. Narquiamides looked at me, gave a mischievous little smile, and winked.

Petrus was in a state of shock, still and silent. He was exactly like me. He didn't know what it was all about. His wife looked at him with a loving gaze. Astral tears of longing flooded her eyes. His little son ran to hug his giant tattooed body, followed by his wife.

His wife looked into his eyes and said, "They arrested Robert. The police discovered that he had killed you. I received a visit from a man who handed me a lot of money. He said it was from your fight that you won. The money will be used exclusively to raise our son with dignity. He is the fruit of our love, Petrus. I do not deserve a penny; I could not see the great man you have always been… I love you very much, and I am sorry… I am sorry for everything…"

In silence, Bha, Narquiamides, and I saw that exciting encounter. My eyes had returned to normal. Petrus remained silent; his eyes filled with tears. He didn't even look like the cruel warrior fighting with me just now.

"Bogat and Lyha have omitted many facts, Petrus," Narquiamides said. "Your son has the money from the fight, and Robert will be imprisoned for many years. Revenge was already taken here on Earth… Let me hold this." He carefully removed the sword from Petrus's hands.

"Dad. You are the greatest fighter in the world. He, Grandpa Narquiamides, showed me a film in which you defeated three monsters and saved my little friends."

Petrus crouched down to listen better to his son.

"Is that so? Tell me what you saw?"

"Two of them were in the mountains. There was fire. And another was in an ugly town. You fought them off and freed my little friends and two horses. An evil witch bewitched them."

"Little friends?" Petrus asked.

"Yes, Grandpa Narquiamides took me to visit them. They are everywhere in nature, in the forests and rivers." The boy moved closer to his father's ear and whispered, "They are also in Hyde Park here in London. But it is a secret."

Petrus emotionally said, "OK, I'll keep this secret."

"They are looking for a true leader, a warrior, to free more of their friends," Narquiamides commented.

Petrus stood up, looked at him, and exclaimed, "So, tell them that I, Petrus the Great, will be their leader."

Bha, in her white dress and colourful necklaces, spoke for the first time. "But first, Mother Bha will treat you in a hospital, give you energy and instructions." A portal opened to an immense hall with many people in white walking around.

"But I'm fine…" he said.

"You have pain in your stomach and chest, don't you?"

"Yes… That is true, but—"

"It is the poison you have taken," she said. "It still reflects around here in the astral. A warrior leader must have good health. Obey Mother Bha. Come on. We also need a more decent outfit…"

Narquiamides took the scabbard and the sword. We went through the portal back to the arch near the Louvre Museum.

Waiting for us were Adhya, Elisabeth, and the shaven-headed protector. They all looked at us calmly, as if they knew what had happened.

"As agreed, put it back where it should never have left." Narquiamides handed the sword and its beautiful scabbard to the guardian, who nodded and returned to the museum.

"What do you mean by 'as agreed'?" I asked.

I was utterly baffled. I looked at Adhya, who was wearing that naughty-little-girl smile.

"Someone, please explain to me what happened around here. You two knew about it, didn't you? About the portal? And of Grandpa Narquiamides?" I asked while Adhya and Elisabeth laughed.

"While you distracted Petrus," Narquiamides explained, "Adhya over here helped me open another parallel portal behind the flames, a few millimetres ahead of the original, and she was hidden behind the column. Lyha could see only through Petrus's eyes; she didn't see her. Her connection with the fighter was automatically cut off when he stepped through our portal."

"To be able to open a new portal in another place," Adhya continued, "Lyha could only succeed with the help of the living wizard. But her friend was knocked out. By the way, he must have woken up in serious trouble. You have been very cruel, Sandra. You have damaged his astral cells too much, and they will affect his physical—"

"But who is he anyway?"

"He is a powerful wizard living in Scotland," Narquiamides answered. "He met Lyha and Bogat on an astral journey. His powers increased greatly when he joined the Brotherhood."

I removed the small blue crystal from my forehead. "We ended up not using the crystal, and—"

"It is not a crystal." Narquiamides took it from me and threw it into a nearby garden. "It is fake; it was made of elements of astral nature. It serves only for decoration. It is not for communication, as we said. It will decompose."

I looked at Elisabeth. She had the little smile of a girl keeping secrets.

Then I shouted, "Wait a minute. Elisabeth also knew it was fake—"

"I purposely dropped the crystal," she said, "and let myself be threatened by the wizard. We needed to put him out of action. Otherwise, he could easily open another portal anywhere else..."

"I know you are confused, Sandra," Adhya said, seeing my irritation.

"Me, confused? No, I feel betrayed. Even those museum protectors knew about the whole plan, except me... It was all a big act, and I was the clown."

"We have a reason," Narquiamides explained. "You are not yet prepared to remember your Initiation. However, exclusively in situations of extreme stress, your astral brain can search the

Akashic field for teachings to get rid of a specific danger. In your future vision, this is precisely what happened when you sent Zorufh to the portal of the black hole. This happens instantaneously."

Adhya added, "If we had told you the truth, your mental state could not have been so intense, and we would have had a serious risk of failure."

The sage took the stick from my hands and said, "I'd better put your present away. It will be in a safe place. The day you can master your mind and learn to use it with more love and less cruelty, I will give it back to you. There will be no risk of failure with love because it is linked with the Creator. I know you will succeed."

"How can I not feel anger at these bloodthirsty people? I feel like opening that black hole like Elisabeth did and wiping them out... Love seems to be a difficult task," I said thoughtfully.

"That's why we need an Initiate. You've never heard of Jesus, Buddha, or Krishna killing people and little children. They had spectacular powers to do whatever they wanted on Earth. But, during their meditations, they accessed the Akashic field and knew what could happen to them and all its consequences for the next millennia... Jesus, for example, was so powerful that he could easily kill his persecutors, become a king, and lead his followers into bloody wars. But at every moment, every second, he chose the magic of love."

He took a deep breath and continued, "With this experiment, we could rewrite the future of three lives in three seconds. But not just for them. With λ3, we helped thousands of others with the love path… we don't need swords."

"I know. Love: the secret weapon."

"We are all connected to the Infinite Spirit… Now, you must go and finish this mission. This is not a final goodbye; we still need you. Let's keep in touch. Adhya will return with you."

Trying to process all that information, I said goodbye to Elisabeth and Narquiamides. He opened a portal with his hands, pronouncing some strange words.

Through it, I could see the beach in Malaga, Spain, where my physical body was sleeping.

Chapter 32

From the End to a Beginning

After the portal, Adhya and I sat near my sleeping physical body. This astral vision of the beach was incredible. Dozens of people were projected onto it, including several in white clothes.

Seeing the look of curiosity in my eyes, my friend explained, "Many people, when they sleep, unknowingly, are brought in from distant cities and receive energy to alleviate illness or their mental states. Others wander the beach unconscious. The energy of the sea alone has great restorative power. It is not by chance that it is salty."

"It is wonderful to see all this," I commented. "We come from the astral plane, and when we sleep, we spend about one-third of our lives in it. After death, we return to it. Now that I understand the vastness and complexity of the astral plane, our brief time in the physical world seems like a short illusion."

"In a sense, it is."

"When I saw you for the first time in my flat, you said that my life was mediocre... now I see that you were right. In a short time,

I have become another woman, with other values and another vision of the world. I know how much I have learned, and how much I still must learn…"

"We all can transform ourselves into better consciences whenever we wish. Occasionally, it only takes three seconds… By the way, I am so happy that I finally saw Alex. There is so much love that the boy overflows with it for you."

"And you? I've noticed Kek's glances…"

She looked for a moment at the starry sky. She said, with a certain nostalgia, "His name was Nadim. Kek is the nickname Niskgar gave him. I met him in the region of India in my last life. It's a long story of an impossible passion…" She paused and changed to a firm, decisive tone. "We have no time to waste on it now…"

"But when will we have time?"

"I don't know. It will depend more on you. Surely, when you die, we will have more time to talk. We can visit beautiful astral cities together on different planets." She laughed. "I still need to pass on some important information to you that Narquiamides has requested of me before you wake up for your meeting."

"I'm listening…"

"When we met for the first time in your flat, I told you that we always had a plan B and would look for someone else if you refused to go ahead. I had to lie to convince you. You're already plan B."

"Wow. And what was the plan A?"

"Plan A was a similar experiment that should have taken place with you and your father on last year's summer solstice. He had researched and studied the astral world in advance. After much practice, he could walk with his astral body while he slept or meditated. The priest José Archiolano, whom you met, inspired him to go deeper and deeper. His biggest mistake was not involving you, but we couldn't force him to—"

"When can I meet him?"

"When you master your emotions better," she answered. "So, unfortunately, he passed away, and we had to cancel the experiment and wait for the summer solstice this year. We decided to do it only with you, but without training you in advance as we did with him. It would be safer for everyone."

"Safer? There is something related to his death... tell me... you accessed the Akashic field, something went wrong—"

"I am sorry. I can't tell you now... I can only say that many things would have been easier for us with you two together in the astral plane..."

She looked at my eyes that begged for answers and said, "Read his research, and I promise you'll understand."

"Which research? He left nothing; the fire destroyed everything."

She paused and looked at me deeply. "Now it's time to look harder. Follow in your father's footsteps. We will inspire and help you."

"I definitely will."

"Always remember the extraordinary evolution of our consciences: we are what we were and will be what we are..."

"Three seconds' choice..."

"I must go now. You will briefly meet the person who will write your book."

She smiled and embraced me. Tears welled up in our eyes. I had never imagined that we could have friends in the astral plane.

"Please answer me one thing before you go," I asked curiously. "That strange problem at the plane door in London. You delayed the departure, right?"

She looked at me with a big sister's eyes. "No, you did it. You are a powerful Initiate and need to trust the powers of your mind... Step by step, we will open your conscience, and you will remember your Initiation. And soon you will be ready."

"Ready for what?"

She gave again her girlish smile and said, "To save the world."

Without giving me time to ask further questions, she ran her hands over my neck. I woke up immediately, feeling like I was being pulled back into my body.

I sat on the bench for a few minutes, admiring the beach. It was dark and seemed deserted now, but it wasn't. My physical eyes tricked me into believing that. At that moment, I felt like the beginning of my true purpose in life had arrived.

Printed in Great Britain
by Amazon

45956824R00199